The Lasko Tangent

Richard North Patterson has been a San Francisco trial lawyer and a partner in the firm of McCutchen, Doyle, Brown & Emerson. He is now a full-time writer. His first novel, *The Lasko Tangent*, won an Edgar Allan Poe award and his last four books, *Degree of Guilt*, *Eyes of a Child*, *The Final Judgement* and *Silent Witness* have been top five *New York Times* bestsellers.

Also by Richard North Patterson

THE LASKO
TANGENT

Richard North Patterson

ARROW

For Aileen Taylor

This edition published by Arrow Books in 1998

3 5 7 9 10 8 6 4 2

© Richard North Patterson 1979

First published by Arrow Books in 1994
Arrow Books Limited
Random House UK Ltd
20 Vauxhall Bridge Road, London SW1V 2SA

Random House Australia (Pty) Limited
20 Alfred Street, Milsons Point, Sydney,
New South Wales 2061, Australia

Random House New Zealand Limited
18 Poland Road, Glenfield
Auckland 10, New Zealand

Random House South Africa (Pty) Limited
Endulini, 5a Jubilee Road, Parktown 2193, South Africa

Random House UK Limited Reg. No. 954009

A CIP catalogue record for this book
is available from the British Library

Papers used by Random House UK Limited
are natural, recyclable products made from wood grown in
sustainable forests. The manufacturing processes conform to
the environmental regulations of the country of origin

ISBN 0 09 955011 3

Printed and bound in Great Britain by
Cox & Wyman Ltd, Reading, Berkshire

Introduction

Eighteen years ago, at the age of twenty-nine, I set out to write a novel before I turned thirty. I don't know what made thirty seem so important or, more fundamentally, what made me think I could write a book. But I found that I took great delight in creating a character, Christopher Paget, and the milieu that I had experienced during an affiliation with the Watergate Special Prosecutor.

The result was THE LASKO TANGENT, which, to my deep pleasure and surprise, won the Edgar Allan Poe Award for Best First Novel of 1979. What I did not know then was that, fourteen years later in my own life and that of Christopher Paget's, I would revisit him in DEGREE OF GUILT—a book that became an international bestseller and, to put it somewhat grandly, the second book in a Christopher Paget trilogy which will conclude with a final novel to be published in January 1995.

During those fourteen years, Christopher Paget matured quite a bit, and my narrative strategies changed. But on rereading, I found THE LASKO

TANGENT not only fun for its own sake, but that Christopher Paget seemed very true to himself—a twenty-nine-year-old version of the mid-fortyish trial lawyer and father found in DEGREE OF GUILT. And the edgy relationship between Paget and Mary Carelli prefigures the heart of DEGREE OF GUILT, where Paget—albeit filled with doubt—defends Mary against a charge of murder.

For me, rereading LASKO was interesting for another reason. Without meaning to back then, I realized that I had set Christopher Paget on a journey through many of the experiences that have defined our times, from government corruption to political compromise; broken marriages to second families; the problem of rape to the abuse of wives and children; even the media-fed self-consciousness that pervades our society—true-life murders into movies, felons into celebrities, etc. In the end—at least for me—the three novels seem to cover quite a bit of ground, yet form a satisfying whole.

All that aside, I think THE LASKO TANGENT remains timely and exciting on its own. I hope that readers will agree, and am very grateful to all of them for helping me share my imaginings of the life and times of Christopher Paget.

R.N.P.

October 1993

ONE

It was the Monday morning before they killed him. I didn't know then that he existed. Or that I would help change that. I dealt with swindlers, not killers.

I was crossing Capitol Hill, the part that looks down Pennsylvania Avenue toward the White House. It was only ten minutes since I'd left my apartment, but already the morning clung to my shirt. The air felt like steam in a closed bathroom after a hot shower. A torpid sun seeped through a haze of humidity and fetid exhaust fumes. Washington August, thermal inversion time.

Three years had programmed me for the walk. It took me across Constitution Avenue toward D Street, past the fountain and the reflecting pool. The cherry trees which lined the walk had long since lost their blossoms and had a tired disappointed look. On the other side of D Street sat the square opulence of the white marble Teamsters of-

1

fice, built for deserving officers by grateful members.

I turned down D Street and walked toward a huge cement building of New Deal vintage with hundreds of glass windows. A blue and white sign in front read "United States Economic Crimes Commission." Pushing through the glass doors, I flipped my ID card to the black, uniformed officer who guarded the agency from the public and other subversives. Cerberus at the gate. His obsidian eyes regarded me impassively. Daily, I tried to imagine what he thought. Daily, I failed. He pushed back the card.

"Thank you, Officer Davis."

"Thank you, Mr. Paget."

I cut through the artificial wood lobby and took the elevator to the third floor, marked "Prosecutions Bureau" by a smaller blue and white sign. The bureau handled the big stock frauds, consumer swindles, and political corruption cases, choice stuff for the dedicated public servant. But the three years had made a difference. I straggled toward my office, in no hurry.

On this floor, the paneling had been swapped for grey cinder blocks which lined corridors as crabbed as a rat's maze. I walked through the grey catacombs and past the door marked "Special Investigations Section." Inside was a large open room jammed with metal desks and secretaries and bordered by offices.

The section was packed; two happy faces peered out of each office. I glanced over my shoulder at the schoolroom-type clock. 9:15. I was late again. I went to the office marked "Christopher Kenyon Paget, Trial Attorney," walked across my grey tile government rug to my armchair of specially molded indestructible grey plastic, and sat at my antique grey metal desk.

My secretary peered in gingerly, as if testing the atmosphere with her forehead.

"Good morning, Chris."

"Good morning, yourself." But I smiled. I liked Debbie—and she could type. Among the ECC secretaries, that was a rare combination. She smiled back and stood in the doorway.

"How have you been?"

"Peachy. As a matter of fact, I was just surveying my kingdom. How's the coffee this morning?"

"What's this thing you have about the coffee?"

"If I'd ever tasted Woolite stirred with a cow chip, I imagine I'd know." The corners of her mouth cracked upwards, then broke into a smile. She was dark and pretty and had a prettier smile. I liked to see it.

"You're in a good mood."

"I spent last night thinking about what McGuire did to the Hartex case. I shouldn't let myself do that."

She shook her head in exaggerated disapproval.

"Misplaced idealism. Have you ever thought about chucking it all and joining the Reverend Moon?"

"That fat little maharishi is more my type. Anyhow, I'm probably too large a spiritual problem for any one religion." She smiled again. "Speaking of which," I added, "if you have to perform an exorcism on that coffee, do it."

"You can try the coffee at McGuire's office. He called for you ten minutes ago."

I wasn't in the mood. "What's it about?"

"He didn't consult me," she said dryly. "Just sounded annoyed that you were late."

I got up and headed reluctantly out the door.

McGuire's office was located off another central area. These offices had wooden desks, upholstered chairs, and, as further marks of federal status, featured single occupancy and an unobstructed view of Capitol Hill. The blue sign near McGuire's door read "Joseph P. McGuire, Chief, Prosecutions Bureau." Next to the sign was Joseph P. McGuire himself, staring fiercely out of a framed *Newsweek* cover entitled "The ECC's Tough Enforcer." Grouped around this were several pictures of McGuire in conference with other great men, such as Lyndon B. Johnson. The bare spot in the middle of the collection represented Richard Nixon, now an unperson.

Directly below sat the curator of this cult of personality, McGuire's secretary, blonde, chubby, and fortyish. As always, she looked like a complacent munchkin. She swiveled her round little body in my direction. "Mr. McGuire is waiting for you, with Mr. Feiner," she said in her round little voice. In this case, it carried a tinge of disapproval.

"Am I late?" I asked innocently.

Her round little eyes narrowed, and her tone flattened out. "You can go right in."

I complied.

McGuire's office was standard federal executive: plastic wood paneling, a money green rug, wooden desk and conference table, and Venetian blinds. Save for an inscribed pen set—a gift from his staff—the desk was bare of personalizing touches, and the walls were as stark. The total effect was that of a room rented by the month.

The only fixture in the place was McGuire. He sat at the end of the conference table, fidgeting with an air of impatient expectancy. McGuire was the only man I knew who could pace sitting down. But for this and piercing blue eyes, he could have passed for a struggling encyclopedia salesman. He had red-brown hair and a middle-aging potbelly hung on an average frame. His clothes were a baggy afterthought. But McGuire somehow invested these plain materials with an arresting vitality. Even his paunch seemed aggressive.

My immediate boss was there to provide an audience. Feiner had black curly hair and the rapt ascetic look of a man seized by some compelling inner vision. It had taken me about two months' acquaintance to perceive that the inner vision involved McGuire's job. McGuire was either too self-obsessed to notice or too secure to care; he let Feiner dog him like a skinny shadow. I suspected that McGuire was fonder of pets than people.

"We've got something big here." McGuire spoke in bursts, as if complex sentences required too much patience. "Where the hell were you?"

"Conferring with my secretary." I sat facing McGuire and tried for an expression of polite interest. "What have you got?"

McGuire stared at me a moment longer, as if I'd insulted him. Then he leaned back from the table and eyed the ceiling, as if gathering his thoughts. Feiner assumed an expression of grave attention. "This is a very sensitive thing," McGuire began.

I was surprised. "Sensitive" was not in McGuire's standard lexicon, in any context. "Why?"

"Do you know William Lasko?" McGuire asked.

"Sure. The President's favorite industrialist."

McGuire nodded. "We got a tip while you were gone that someone was playing some games with the price of his company's stock."

"Who's 'we'?"

"Me. Someone called me last week."

I was interested in spite of myself. "And that's all he told you?"

"Yes."

I glanced at Feiner. "What about Ike's market watch people? They spot any pattern in the stock?"

"No."

"Any idea who called?"

"No. He wouldn't say."

"Did he tell you enough to let you guess?"

"No." McGuire looked edgy, like a man being forced to play Twenty Questions with his twelve-year-old son. "He disguised his voice. I've told you all I know."

"It's not much."

It was intended as a statement of fact. But McGuire took it as criticism. His eyes bored in. "We can't let this go. Lasko's controversial. If I don't check this out and then get caught with my pants down, I'll have to answer over on the Hill." McGuire was using his usual institutional "I." The motive had a tired familiarity. "This thing has to be done carefully. No wild charges and no one pissed off. And I want a report on every new development."

I nodded. McGuire leaned back, hands folded on his belly, taking in Feiner with a tight smile. The smile looked like an invisible hand was stretching his mouth sideways at both ends. "Now," McGuire was holding school, "what are you going to do?"

My three years made the question insulting. McGuire knew it; he was reminding Feiner that he could make me do tricks. I wondered if I should roll over and beg or stick my paw out to shake hands. "What are you going to do?" he demanded again.

"I'm going to call up Lasko and ask him to confess."

McGuire's reaction was surprisingly mild. "Seriously."

I selected a civil answer. "Seriously, I'll get trading data from the major brokerage houses in New York to see who's been buying and selling Lasko Devices stock and when. I'll have our local office— Lasko's in Boston, I think—lay a subpoena on the company for trading data. If any stock trades look strange, I'll haul in the trader for questioning. And I'll check the stock's price history in the *Journal*."

McGuire's rubber smile restretched, this time for me. "While you were out of town, I had Ike"—he gestured at Feiner with his thumb—"get out a subpoena to Lasko Devices. They are in Boston. Jim Robinson has checked the *Journal* and gotten the trading records. And I've asked Central Records to send you the Lasko file."

I smiled back, half at McGuire's one-upmanship and half to admit that he knew his job. "Assuming those idiots in Records haven't lost the Lasko file," I said, to remind him that nothing was perfect. His smile strained wider. It was a good time to leave.

"Is that it?" I asked.

"No." McGuire looked at his watch. "I've got Mary Carelli at ten o'clock."

It didn't ring any bells. "Who's she?"

"Mary Carelli is special assistant to Chairman Woods."

"And?"

McGuire surprised me by sounding defensive. "Look. All our cases have to be approved by a vote of the commissioners who run this place. They stop approving, we stop prosecuting. The Chairman runs the other commissioners, and Woods is just over from the White House staff. Lasko's the President's friend. If we hurt Lasko, it hurts the White House, and that hurts us. So I tell Chairman Woods what we're on to. We have to get along or my program goes down the drain. So," he concluded, "don't fuck up."

I considered that. "Maybe you'd better clue me in, Joe. Who's running this case—us, Woods, or the White House staff?"

McGuire looked stung. "There's nothing wrong with talking to our own Chairman," he snapped. Technically, he was right about that. But the repetition of the words "White House" seemed to diminish him. The restless body slumped. For the first time I wondered whether McGuire wanted to be a commissioner.

McGuire snapped out of his reverie. "You're to

get along with Ms. Carelli. I've put you on this because you're good. Don't screw it up."

He had said that before. "I haven't yet," I answered quietly.

He knew that was true. Some other people knew it too. It was the main fact that kept me sitting in McGuire's office instead of cleaning out my own. But the problem was bigger than Hartex or I. Something had gone sour in McGuire's psyche. The drive to achieve had turned into an addiction to praise. His staff aped him and outsiders plied him with obsequies. It was as if McGuire were presiding over his own memorial service. *Newsweek* had done him in.

TWO

McGuire's munchkin opened the door, breaking the uncomfortable silence. "Miss Carelli's here," she bubbled.

She was eclipsed by a striking young woman. Tall and slender, her long hair was as black as her eyes, which took us in with a quick, opaque stare. The eyes were her startling feature; they were wide set on high Indian cheekbones. I figured her for my age, twenty-nine, but she threw off a primal force.

The impact was softened a bit by her delayed smile; the flash of white teeth gave her an amused adventurous look. "Gentlemen," she nodded. The word was faintly sardonic. I watched her as the gentlemen said their hellos. It struck me that she thought she was slumming.

Feiner whisked out a chair with the expertise of a butler. She sat, long legs flashing as they crossed under her simple white dress. The dress set off a dark tan which had been acquired with some trouble. The little vanity was curious; it made her seem less remote. I filed the thought away and sat back.

"I appreciate your time, Mr. McGuire." Her voice was low and carefully modulated. The effect was almost consciously well bred.

McGuire was unusually formal. "Of course. The Lasko case is a complicated matter."

She nodded. "Chairman Woods has asked me to monitor the case. I'd like someone here to keep me up to date." The language and tone mixed command with request. But the eyes didn't miss anything. I revised my opinion. She wasn't slumming; she was an anthropologist.

McGuire's interest in Carelli was strictly derivative; he spoke through her as if she were a microphone wired to the Chairman's ear. "We'll be happy to do that. I've assigned Chris here"—his thumb jabbed at me—"to keep your office informed."

She had forgotten my name. She looked at me now with the cool appraising air of a scientist touring a dog pound, searching for experimental subjects. I hoped she would pass me up.

"Now you're who?"

"I'm Christopher Paget."

She nodded briskly. "OK, I'd appreciate it if you would come by my office this afternoon." It was not a request. The Chairman was becoming a palpable presence.

"I'll be sure and do that," I said dryly.

McGuire shifted uncomfortably and looked through the ceiling at the Chairman's office, four stories up. Ms. Carelli made a quick mental calculation and decided to overlook it. "I'll call you to set up a time."

I nodded. She looked at me a split-second more, then turned back to McGuire. She spoke with more assurance, as if knowing that my annoyance signaled McGuire's compliance. "Anything surrounding Lasko is very delicate. The Chairman wants to clear investigative steps before they happen. He's concerned that this case not hurt the agency." Her eyes flashed to me. "We have to keep out of trouble." I figured she intended to keep me well out of trouble. I kept silent, and made a mental reservation about the frequency of my reports.

McGuire was nodding for me. "Chris will keep in touch. Is there anything else we can do?" His solicitous voice still seemed to waft upwards.

"Not now." Ms. Carelli knew when to get off stage. She rose quickly. "Thank you for your time." She swept us with a quick, obligatory smile, and let herself out. The closing door cut off the last probe of the black eyes, looking at me.

"Terrific," I said, to no one in particular.

McGuire turned. "Just what's your problem?"

"Other than Typhoid Mary?" It might as well be now, I thought. "The Hartex case. This one is starting like Hartex ended up."

McGuire's eyes showed both defensiveness and anger. "Go on," he challenged.

"Look, I worked on Hartex for a year. I talked to people who had lost their shirts. There wasn't a week I didn't have some ruined life haunting my office like Hamlet's father. I told them we would help. Then I go on vacation for a week. I call in last Thursday and discover you've settled the case. While I'm gone, the Hartex people send down a Wall Street type, the one who used to be Deputy Secretary of State. He tells you how much he respects you, and how a lot of trouble can be saved. In return for no jail, he agrees to an injunction promising that his clients will never swindle anyone again. They don't need to, because they've just waltzed into affluent retirement. And we issue a press release that makes this out as the biggest coup since Tricky Dick turned back into a pumpkin. I tell you, Joe, the way we play the game is really amazing."

McGuire's eyes were stupid with surprise. He slowly turned to look out at the Capitol, as if calling upon it for support. Apparently, he got it. He pivoted with an expression of righteous contempt. "Look, I don't run this place just to please you. Every year I have to justify my budget to the commission and Congress—show them I close my cases. How do you think I've gotten here?" Now McGuire was shouting; each word thrust him out over the table toward me. Somehow I thought of an earth-mover. "I can't let you get tied up on a frigging cru-sade. Your job is to question witnesses and get me the facts, not make policy. So if I don't have time to consult with you that's tough shit."

McGuire's face was attractive red. Feiner had the bleak satisfied look of a Jesuit who had rooted out a heresy. But disillusion pushed me on. "The Hartex people should have been indicted, prose-cuted, and jailed. And we could have helped get some money back. Instead, our settlement shafted the stockholders. The only places it will ever look good are in our press releases and reports to Con-gress. Both of which are unadulterated bullshit."

McGuire smashed his palm on the table like a murderer squashing a fly. Feiner winced as if he were the next fly. He was all caged tension with no-where to go. McGuire stared at the dead invisible fly, then at me. "I don't get this crap from the other guys." Feiner nodded on behalf of the other guys.

I shrugged. "They're not my problem, Joe."

"So what makes you so courageous?" This was half inquiry, half sarcasm.

"Because I have to live with myself."

This last echoed back to me with an unhappily pompous ring. Suddenly I was tired of McGuire, tired of the argument, and tired of myself. Most of all I was tired of feeling cynical, and wishing I didn't.

McGuire was just tired of me. "Maybe people like you don't have to pay your dues," he said in a flat oblique voice. McGuire had never had money; he'd had a lifetime to consider his attitude toward people like me. It wasn't hard to see how the former Deputy Secretary had cut his deal. He was a fine old WASP who treated McGuire with deference. The deference was McGuire's reward; it made punishment negotiable.

The insight didn't help me. I felt superior and disliked myself for it. The fight had taken on a whining undertone of buried resentments older than Hartex and bigger than the ECC. I tried to end it. "OK, I've said what I wanted to say."

McGuire hesitated, as if distracted by his failure to have the last word. The thought got the best of him. "You think because you're a hotshot, I have to put up with this. I don't."

"That's true. You don't." One day, I thought, I would push it too far. But I had Feiner to remind me of what I didn't want to be. His face was a frozen mask of attention, turned to McGuire. I figured he must spend his nights chiseling McGuire's every word in marble.

McGuire was looking me over, as if sizing me for a firing. "You'd better get with it," he finally said.

There was nothing more to say. I left, his sourness trailing after me.

I walked back to my office. I wasn't happy. The

Lasko case came complete with White House interest, a meddling Chairman, and the supercilious Ms. Carelli. I was on a very short leash, and didn't know who was holding the other end. So I decided to call Jim Robinson.

"Hello?" he answered.

"What's Mary Carelli?"

"I don't know, Chris. Maybe if you take penicillin it will go away."

I laughed. "I'm especially interested in political connections, how she got her job—stuff like that."

"You a lawyer or a reporter today?"

"I just want to know what I'm dealing with."

He paused. "I'll see."

"Thanks. Catch you this afternoon."

I depressed the receiver and called Lane Greenfeld at the Washington *Post*. After that I got the Lasko file. I riffled it for an hour or so. Then I checked my watch and left the building.

THREE

Greenfeld and I had agreed to lunch near the Hill.

I beat him to the restaurant and secured a table which was jammed to the side of a darkish room. The decor was instant men's club: brick walls, stained brown beams, and heavy furniture. I ordered a light rum and tonic and looked over the clientele. The faces moved through intense talk, explosive laughter, and professionally amiable smiles. In one corner a squat man with a lobbyist's beefy confidence was jabbing a stubby finger at an obscure and worried-looking junior senator. I resolved out of boredom to watch whether the senator's attention broke. He was still hanging on when Greenfeld cut off my line of sight.

He grinned. "Is this déjà vu, malaise, or ennui?"

I considered my answer with mock gravity. "Fin de siècle," I concluded. I inspected his Cardin suit. "Are you bucking for Paris correspondent?"

He sat down. "Just fashion editor." Greenfeld

was a taut testament to good metabolism. He had black hair, large, perceptive eyes, and a faintly amused look. The eyes suggested that he was amused because he understood more than the rest of us. "Now, you"—he stretched out the words— "look the very figure of entrenched capitalist privilege."

I smiled. The banter was typical. Greenfeld's reporting was spartanly self-edited; the excess found refuge in his speech. He liked wordplay, sonorous phrases, and verbal sparring. His conversation was a pleasure which sometimes required strict attention. I had the pleasure fairly often; we were what passed for close friends among people too busy to achieve intimacy. The knowledge reminded me unhappily of how little time I'd had since school.

Greenfeld ordered an old-fashioned. "How are things at the commission?"

"Kafka lives." I tried to contain my problems with the place. "And the *Post*?"

He turned his palms upward in a little shrugging gesture. "They keep the pressure on." He didn't seem terribly impressed. It was one of the things I liked about him.

I hadn't seen him for a couple of weeks and had to stretch for his roommate's name. I retrieved it. "How's Lynette?"

The boyish face became guarded and he stared at his cuffs. They seemed to interest him. Finally he spoke to his old-fashioned. "She hasn't been around lately." The words were uninflected, as if someone had unplugged his personality.

It seemed less awkward to finish than to switch subjects. I stumbled on. "What happened?"

He shifted slightly in his chair. "It wasn't working." Greenfeld was an observer, not a revealer; he discussed the personal only by indirection. I guessed that he had called it off. But his friendship required recognition of limits I probably understood better than most. I tried to slide out on a light note.

"You're a hard man, Lane."

Greenfeld gave me a wry, sour smile. "I guess it's just part of 'being cool in the seventies.'" He used the phrase to mock his own detachment. But he could already identify a time when he had liked himself better. I wondered if that were the problem.

Greenfeld snapped to the realization that his second persona was warring with his first. "I can give you a pretty good rundown on Lasko. He's a splendid fellow." Quickly Greenfeld was back on balance, his voice animated, as if his own working competence had given him a foothold.

"One of America's heroes," I smiled. "Give me what you've got."

"Tell me what you know and I'll fill in the rest."

"OK. Lasko's about forty-five. Very smart. Son of

a steel worker from Youngstown, Ohio. Nice place. Ran with a pretty tough crowd when he was growing up. Apparently he's kept some for friends. Got drafted and became a Korean War hero of sorts based on a not-too-surprising talent for killing people. He went to college on the GI Bill and then got an M.B.A. So far, a heartwarming but typical story of upward mobility. Then he somehow managed to get himself involved in Florida real estate, which is where he made his first money. Also did some land deals in Arizona. Supposedly, these were pretty sleazy—a lot of it involved selling undeveloped land to Mom and Pop pensioner types, although presumably he had no inherent objection to ripping off widows and orphans either. Things got sticky for him after a while, so he sold out his interests and bought a chain of nursing centers. Apparently he'd decided to make a specialty of the aged. From what I hear the nursing centers were better than Bergen-Belsen, but worse than Fort Benning. He sold them at a profit just before the state legal authorities decided to investigate. Which left him wealthy, but underemployed." Greenfeld had reassumed the amused look. Occasionally, his eyes would focus on a fact, as if indexing it in proper order with his own information. I paused. He nodded me on.

"The next part is more directly relevant. Lasko decided to become a captain of industry. In the early sixties, he bought a small outfit in Boston called Technical Instruments, which was into computer and electronic equipment. Lasko renamed it Lasko Devices, and built it up. Among his supposed techniques were strong-arming and blackmailing competitors, as well as industrial espionage. None of that has ever been proven. When the company got larger in the mid-sixties, he came out with a public stock offering. It's traded on the New York Exchange. He also joined the conglomerate movement, and was sued for looting one of his acquisitions. He settled that one out of court.

"Lasko Devices is still his main interest, though. He's landed some good contracts with the Department of Defense and the company has increasingly taken over certain parts of the electronics industry. He's also gotten more respectable. His success was helped along by mere garden-variety violations of the antitrust laws, like price-cutting. About four years ago, the Department of Justice sued to force Lasko to give up certain holdings of Lasko Devices so that he couldn't monopolize parts of the electronics market. That would really hurt him and he's fighting it in court. Other than that, Lasko has cleaned up his act. He's traded in his white shoes for pin-striped suits. Lectures at business schools. Visits the White House. Has audiences with the Pope. Holds seminars on world poverty. He's fa-

mous. He's a prince. I love him." Greenfeld smiled.
I was out of material. "Does that do it?"

"Well, it's a decent start." This was said with the
cheerful condescension of the bright boy upon
whom the teacher would call when no one else
knew the answer. I didn't mind. Greenfeld's arrogance had an engaging ingenuousness about it.

"Your facts are OK," he went on, "but they don't
make total sense until you appreciate the context.
I've had the advantage of seeing the man from time
to time. He's an impressive-looking fellow, large
and domineering, with a very deep voice. He projects a great deal of confidence. It always amazes
me how much size can do for some people."
Greenfeld was short himself. "Of course, I'm always impressed in meeting prominent people how
ordinary most of them are. It's just that they
wanted it more—whatever 'it' happens to be. Back
to Lasko, I'm told that he also has some social
charm. It would be interesting to see what a good
psychoanalyst would make of him." The thought
stopped him for a moment, as if he were pondering
what a good psychoanalyst would make of the rest
of us. A waiter wearing a precariously placed black
wig arrived to take our order. We made a quick
choice, and the waiter retreated to the kitchen.
Greenfeld's eyes followed him. "Nice rug. Looks
like something died on top of his head."

"What else?"

"The second thing you need to think about is politics. He was in shady land deals in Florida, but was never prosecuted. He sold out his nursing centers at a profit just before an investigation started. His good luck isn't the whim of the gods. He clearly had some Florida politicians in his pocket. These days he's got large defense contracts, takes movie starlets to White House parties, and dines with the Pope. They aren't just products of his boyish charm. He's a powerful man, tough and ruthless. He's given off a whiff of corruption for years, but no one ever catches him." He paused for emphasis. "No one at all. And now he's friends with the President. I'm not implying anything corrupt. As far as I can make out, the President just likes him. It doesn't matter that Lasko's not a very nice man. The President's not a very nice man, either. And he admires Lasko because he's richer than shit. Just like the President always wanted to be, but gave up for politics. And Lasko knows the value of good friendship. So," he finished wryly, "I wouldn't count on this one to make your career."

"Then why is Justice trying to break up Lasko Devices? It doesn't fit."

"The lawsuit is why I know all this about Lasko. It was filed during the last administration, before the President came in. He inherited the lawsuit, or it probably would have never been filed. Part of my job these days is to watch that case to see if it's pushed or dropped. I'm on the lookout for White House pressure, trade-offs between Lasko and the President—stuff like that. The paper's pretty hot about it."

"Find anything?"

He shook his head. "Just PR. Lasko very much wants Lasko Devices kept together. A breakup would really hurt him. The philanthropic ventures are Lasko's effort to be the modern Andrew Carnegie—a benevolent image might help ease his legal problems. He's hired a New York PR firm to work on it. They schedule his speeches, suggest his seminars, and give other helpful hints. This firm could probably market Charles Manson to the mothers of America, and they've done a lot for Lasko. He's started his own philanthropic group, the Lasko Foundation, and made mental health his special interest. Contributes generously to mental health institutions. So if he ever wants that psychoanalysis, he's got experts on tap." Greenfeld had psychiatrists on the brain today. He flashed into instant mockery, his voice acquiring a spurious German accent. "And so you see, my students, how every fact," he raised his finger in the air, "must be viewed in its context to reveal its true depth and meaning. Otherwise, we are just as ignorant and benighted as when we came and have learned nothing." He banged a fist on the table in satiric emphasis, stared at it in a parody of thought, then snapped his head up smiling. "So there it is, Chris," he said in his own voice.

Lunch arrived and surprised us by being good. We ate in grateful concentration, spaced around a discussion of foreign films. We both liked Bertolucci and Truffaut. I thought Fellini was over-rated. He thought Buñuel was too bizarre. We ended by agreeing to get dates for the new Wertmuller film. All through it, Lane looked as if he were chewing on a thought with his lunch. The thought popped out over coffee. "Why didn't you just talk over Lasko with your boys at the commission?" Greenfeld was still on the job; he had a working reporter's instinct for conflict.

There was no point in explaining Hartex. "I still have newspaper habits, I guess."

Lane didn't buy it, but decided to pass for the moment. "You mentioned an investigation over the phone. What's it about?"

"Off the record, we have an anonymous tip that someone was trying to maneuver the market price of Lasko stock. We don't know whether it happened, or if Lasko's involved if it did."

Greenfeld fell unconsciously into his press con-ference rhythm. "So why all this interest?"

"Just background," I said. I looked uncomforta-bly back at Greenfeld. But his eyes were fixed over my left shoulder. They stayed there long enough to make me curious. "What did you see, Lane? The Vice-President in drag?"

"Nothing that interesting. But someone you might run into. Robert Catlow."

"Who's he?"

Greenfeld kept on looking. "One of the unofficial White House talent scouts. Very influential. He helps clear appointments to top federal jobs, like to your commission. Has a private law practice here in town. Also represents your friend Lasko. I wonder which hat he's wearing today." He squinted slightly. "You know the guy with him?"

I half-turned. Greenfeld pointed me to a fiftyish man in a dark-blue pinstripe. He was talking easily across a corner table. I felt a small start of surprise at his listener. Apparently, Greenfeld didn't know Joe McGuire on sight.

I felt the silence and turned back to my coffee. "Fairly mediocre-looking fellow," I said casually. It was an effort; I felt as though I had just opened a closet full of dead rats. McGuire and Lasko's lawyer. It wasn't a new twist. I'd seen months of work go down the tubes in two hours at the Sans Souci, while the poor sucker who had done the work bolted a bologna sandwich at the agency cafeteria, fighting the flies for possession of the table. Sometimes the sucker had been me.

Greenfeld looked a moment longer before our waiter reappeared with our tab. I took the check by way of penance for pretending I didn't know McGuire. In turn, Greenfeld overtipped the waiter. "That was for a hair transplant," he explained on the way out. McGuire was still hunched in conversation as we passed. The other man was talking intently now. Neither looked up.

We stopped outside the door.

"Good luck," Greenfeld said. "I hear that your what's-his-name—McGuire—keeps pretty close tabs on you guys."

It was droll, in an unfunny way. "I think it's safe to say that he's involved." Greenfeld missed it, as I intended. Still, I felt a little rotten. I was more of a bureaucrat than I realized. Or perhaps I just wanted this one to myself. It was already too crowded, and the McGuire part was pretty thin.

Greenfeld was looking reflective, as if he were combing through the file drawer he kept in his head. "You know," he finally said, "back when Lasko was building up, one of his competitors refused to sell his business. One night the guy was stabbed to death coming out of a warehouse. The cops fooled with it and finally wrote it off as an attempted robbery. But the deceased still had his wallet. And Lasko bought the business. Cheap."

That stopped me. "Is that for real?"

"As always."

I smiled. "In a couple of weeks, you'll probably find me at the bottom of a lime pit, rooming with

Jimmy Hoffa." It wasn't my brightest remark. But right then it was just another chat with Greenfeld.

Greenfeld's wry look had returned. "Anyhow, let me know how this one goes." Either Greenfeld was curious, or Lasko was a safe subject.

I nodded. "What I can. And I'll call you about the film."

He eyed me for a moment. "Good enough." He smiled. "Well, back to the Hill. I haven't bagged my daily quota of lies, evasions, cretinism, and horse-shit."

I wasn't so sure about the lies and evasions. But he was off, walking with the tensile alertness of the inquiring reporter. I watched him for a while. He was all self-possession. No one would think to ask him about Lynette.

FOUR

I was back at my office before I remembered to check my mail. It was consistent with the rest of the day.

The first two letters were from Hartex stockholders reminding me that I had sold them down the river. The less enthusiastic one was from an ex-stockbroker taking exception to my police state methods, with a copy to the American Civil Liberties Union. The return address on its envelope read "Danbury Federal Penitentiary." I filed it in my wastebasket. Then I scrawled "Attention: Joseph P. McGuire" on the Hartex letters and put them in the interoffice mail. It seemed the least I could do.

The telephone message was better. Jim Robinson had something for me, it said. I cut through hallways left, then right, and knocked on the door marked "James H. Robinson, Senior Investigator."

"Come in."

Robinson sat in a rabbit warren of an office,

wearing glasses and his habitual look of quizzical bemusement. It changed to a grin when he saw me through the stacks of paper on his desk. "Christopher Kenyon Paget," he intoned. "Last of the independent men."

"More like 'eunuch to the King.' See the Hartex settlement?"

He nodded, still smiling. "Sit down, Chris. This one may be better."

I sat, glad to see him. Robinson was late thirty-ish, round faced, and his short brown hair was dashed with early grey. The quizzical look gave an impression of ineffectual kindness. It hid a retentive memory and an encyclopedic knowledge of stock swindles. These traits served an indispensable talent: a feeling for the logic of events. Robinson could do with three or four facts what prehistorians achieved with stray dinosaur bones: project a complex structure revealing the hidden whole. I had tried this analogy on him once at the end of a tough case. He had grinned then, too, and told me that I had much the same talent. It was one of the finer compliments I'd ever had.

Robinson was waiting. It struck me that he seemed pretty pleased with himself.

"Get a break on the Lasko case, Jim?"

"Maybe. Remember Sam Green?"

"Sleazy Sam? Sure. The kind of guy who would hang around playgrounds with candy bars if he didn't have stock fraud to keep him busy. What does he have to do with this?"

Robinson donned a magisterial expression. "I'll take it in order. First, the price of Lasko stock rose sharply between July 13 and 15. Six points in two days, from ten to sixteen. But there weren't any big developments, good news, or any other reason why the price should go up like that. The price went up because the volume of stock transactions on the Exchange nearly doubled. There was a hell of a lot of demand for the stock. Again, no reason. But all that artificial demand drives the price up. So, I checked the records from McGuire. It turns out that three brokerage firms had big buy orders for Lasko stock on the fourteenth and fifteenth. Between them, they account for the doubled volume. So I called friends at the firms. Guess who placed each order?"

"Green?"

"Uh-huh."

"Any notion why?"

"There are several possibilities. I'll give you one. I got to thinking about the dates—why the fourteenth and fifteenth. I remembered them from somewhere else. So I checked our files on Lasko Devices. On July 16 Lasko Devices offered 300,000 new shares to the public. Because the price of new shares is based on the market price of the stock the day before the offering, each share sold at $16 instead of $10, which was the market price two days earlier. Six more bucks multiplied by 300,000 shares means that Lasko Devices made an extra $1,800,000 on the offering. All because of Sam Green."

"So your thought is maybe someone at the company put him up to it."

"It's possible."

I leaned back. "Let's see how that works. Green could have waited for the offering and bought it cheaper. So the timing stinks. What bothers me is Lasko. Lasko Devices doesn't need another $1,800,000. They're making money. And with his antitrust problems over at Justice, he doesn't need more problems with us. Besides, it's pretty crude."

Robinson took off his glasses and inspected them for smudges. He found one and rubbed absently. "I never would have found it except that McGuire got that tip."

"Still, I wonder why my genius boss, Feiner, didn't catch it. He has market watch people monitoring the stocks for things like this."

Robinson shrugged. "I never speak ill of the dead. It's my theory that Feiner suffered brain death years ago."

I smiled. "OK. A few questions. Why would the company go to Sam? And what's in it for him? As I recall, he had one foot in jail the last go-around, before he wangled immunity by trading in his friends." I paused. "How many shares did Sam buy?"

"About 20,000."

I multiplied. "Even accounting for the rise in price, that's about $300,000. Where did he get all that money?"

Robinson looked curious himself. "Which is why you should run Sam in here for some questioning, under oath."

"I'll do that."

Robinson was looking at me askance, waiting. I went ahead, anyhow. "Did you check out Mary Carelli?"

He thought for a second, then faced me with bright, candid eyes. "Anyone else, Chris, and I'd figure this for bureaucratic dirt gathering. But you neglect your self-interest to the point of irresponsibility. You're investigating Mary Carelli like you're investigating Lasko. Look, you're the brightest lawyer I've seen here. Don't screw yourself up. You've got to learn to let things go that can't be helped."

I tried to find a way to ask for help. And to tell him that I appreciated the concern. But I couldn't seem to combine them. He saw my confusion. "Chris, what do you want to be doing five years from now? Private practice? You could make a lot of money. You could do well here, too, if you wanted. You've got a great record."

Hearing the alternatives out loud gave me a bleak, wasted feeling. "So where am I?"

He answered me indirectly. "I hear you had another hassle with McGuire this morning."

"News travels fast."

"You gave Ike Feiner fifteen minutes alone to chortle."

"I didn't know he was capable of chortling."

Robinson gave a smile which didn't connect with his eyes. "Look, McGuire and Feiner are already pissed at you. If you start rattling the wrong cages, they could really screw you. On the outside too. Don't think the firms in this town don't ask around before they hire a government lawyer. If McGuire lets the word out you're not welcome here, you'll be as popular as the clap."

That was right, I knew. But the rewards of good behavior seemed weightless. I didn't know what I wanted and didn't want what I could have. Perhaps McGuire was right about people like me. "I appreciate what you've said, Jim. But I just got it tucked to me on the Hartex case. The next time I go down kicking and screaming."

He looked disturbed. "That may happen."

"I'm running out of time here, anyhow."

"It's the only career you've got. I wouldn't take it so lightly."

"Believe me, I don't."

Robinson stared at me thoughtfully. "OK," he finally said. "I called a friend of mine at Civil Service. Carelli got out of law school when you did. University of Chicago, top 10 per cent. Scholarship student. The records show that she went to work as a staffer on the Senate Commerce Committee, the bunch that keeps tabs on us. So I called a guy I know over at the committee. Turns out he knew her, but not as well as you might think. She keeps her private life to herself. He did say that she is very tough and very partisan. She didn't have any rank on him, but he crossed her up on something and nearly lost his job. Turned out she had some senator's ear. So my buddy's not her biggest booster. But he admits that she is very smart. So that's it," he concluded in an unimpressed tone. "A typical Washington biography. If you hanged people in this town for being political, you wouldn't have anyone left to answer the phone."

He was still eyeing me. "All right," I smiled, "I'll put her on the back burner."

Robinson looked relieved. I rose, then remembered McGuire's lunch. "I heard a rumor," I fabricated, "that one of the commissioners was leaving." If one really was, it was news to me. "But I forgot who. Heard anything?"

"Yeah. I had lunch with Ludlow's assistant the other day. He says Ludlow's going back into private practice. But keep that down. He hasn't announced it yet, and the White House hasn't come up with a replacement."

Joe McGuire would do nicely. "That's too bad. I liked Ludlow. Well, I'd better get to work on a subpoena for Sam Green. Next Monday OK with you?"

"Fine." He leaned back. "You know, this kind of case only makes careers in reverse. So stick to Lasko and leave the other alone."

I knew what he meant. Robinson liked thinking about Green and Lasko much better than thinking about Mary Carelli. He had organized his world long ago. Carelli, he, and I were all "shirts"; Green and Lasko were "skins." I couldn't really blame him. It made keeping score a lot easier.

I took some files back to my office to work on Green's subpoena. Debbie had a phone message from Mary Carelli. The first tug on my leash. I thought about ignoring it. Then I headed out to see what she wanted.

FIVE

The trip to the Chairman's office was upward, both literally and esthetically. The top floor suite was a soothing collection of rust shag rugs, white walls, padded leather, and impressionist paintings. What struck me, though, was the quiet, as if good taste swallowed noise. I was used to the third floor catacombs—sounds of typing, telephones, shouts, and footsteps ping-ponging between tile and cinder blocks. It was as though I had stepped from a rush hour subway directly into a library. The sensation was pleasant. I found myself wondering how it felt to McGuire.

The receptionist fit the room. She was a thin, birdlike woman who could have been the custodian of rare books. I stifled the urge to request the *Summa Theologica* and asked instead for Mary Carelli. I had barely sunk into one of the leather chairs when Chairman Woods surprised me.

"You're Chris Paget, aren't you? I'm Jack

Woods." He was tall—about six feet two—and broad shouldered, with short brown hair. He offered me a large, strong hand, and gestured toward his office with the other. "Come on in and chat for a second. Mary's running a little late." He had a deep, rich voice and a youthful lopsided smile which knocked several years off an age I gauged at late thirties. It was all very democratic. I trailed him into his office.

Woods waved me in and sat behind a simple cherry desk. I chose another padded chair and looked around. The office had the same look of shag and cool white. The walls were improved by two bright Chagall prints, from which effect I subtracted the stolid cheerlessness of one formal picture of the President. His books ranged from financial tomes to the *Meditations of Marcus Aurelius*, several Faulkner novels, and a volume of poetry by Dylan Thomas. I searched his face for clues as to whether he had read any of them. The dark blue eyes, strong jaw, and broad, open face were pleasant, but uninformative. Of more interest was his nose; it had once been aquiline but now featured a couple of detours to the right. I remembered that he had played football; someone's elbow had lent his face some character. It gave a faintly jarring hint of subcutaneous tension to the niceboy look. But it told me nothing about the books.

He had followed my eyes. "I don't have much

time for reading these days. Breaking into this job has been a real experience." The engaging smile reappeared. "I hope I can keep up."

I wasn't used to commissioners seeking my encouragement. "I'm sure you'll be fine."

He looked thoughtfully at the Chagalls, as if they had some connection to his work. "Still, I'm concerned. A lot of commissioners come into agencies like this for PR value. They punch their tickets and leave. But they never really learn their jobs. Never really have an impact. I don't want to be another one." I agreed with him about ticket-punching. But if this was just for my benefit, he was an awfully quick study. I half-believed in his sincerity.

Woods waved up at the law school diploma which hung behind his desk. "You went there, too, didn't you, Chris?"

I wondered whether he knew as much about McGuire's other ninety-nine lawyers. "Yes, I did. I got out three years ago."

Woods smiled slightly at the diploma, as if satisfied that we were peers. Then he turned his candid eyes to me. "I'm very concerned about the Lasko case." He spoke seriously, leaning forward as if he wished to share the full weight of his concern.

I chose a neutral tone. "So I understand."

The eyes seemed to at once accord trust and demand attention. He was very, very good. "I'm concerned for several reasons. To be honest, I know

I'm young for this job. I want to do well here. And I don't want this agency to act indiscreetly. That means both that I don't want us to go out on a limb and that I don't want inaccurate charges against Lasko to rub off on the President. Is that understandable?"

I said that it was. He continued. "But most of all, I want this investigation to be good. I don't want anyone to say we dropped the ball, or pulled punches. It's how an agency handles cases like this that sets the tone for whether it's got basic integrity or is just another hack outfit. I'm political, sure, and I've existed in a political world. But I came over here to do a job." His eyes locked in an intent, determined look. "And I believe the best politics, in the long run, is to do that job as fairly and honestly as I can."

If that were true, I was all for him. "I'll do what I can to help."

"Just keep in touch with Mary," he said easily. "I want to know what's happening in this thing." His voice dropped, and his words took on a slow rhythmic emphasis. "But if you need anything, any help at all, don't hesitate to come to me direct. I'll do anything reasonable to help you out."

"Thanks. I'll keep that in mind."

"Good." He rose. "You'll be wanting to talk to Mary." I wasn't so sure, but my time was clearly up. We walked together to his door.

"Thanks, Chris." He shook my hand again. "I hear you're very good at this. I'll look forward to seeing you." The smile that went with the handshake said that he meant it. "And I'll need your help on other things as I go along." The warm voice bespoke pleasant hours of purposeful escape from my catacombs, amidst the impressionist serenity. He instructed the receptionist to get Mary Carelli, then backed into his office and closed the door. He left behind a bracing warmth, like a shot of good whiskey. I returned to the subject of the books. My best guess was that Woods read them, then recorded choice quotes on index cards to be fit into future speeches. Substance and surface rubbing together. It was a measure of his skill that I didn't mind.

I was enjoying the padded chair when I noticed that it was 5:15. Mary Carelli emerged from her office and wordlessly waved me in. The experimental subject had been sealed and delivered. I liked her less than ever. When I got to the door, she was already behind her desk looking at a notepad and waiting for me to sit. So I leaned against the door frame until she looked up. Her eyes were watchful and didn't change with her smile, which seemed to measure itself to the nearest millimeter. She nodded toward a chair. "Come on in and sit down."

I looked at my watch with studied deliberation.

"Does whatever we're going to do have to be done today?"

She sat up in her chair and squared her shoulders. Set against the white walls and the hanging plants in her window, she looked mint cool. "Don't be bureaucratic. I'd just as soon talk to you now." The voice was cool too—a touch of scorn amidst a lot of indifference.

I didn't move. "I'm not bureaucratic. Just thirsty. I've talked more today than I care to and listened to more than I like to hear. A good deal of it nonsense. So I'm thirsty—and bored."

She sat holding her pad, still except for her left hand, which idly rubbed the pad between forefingers and thumb. It was as if all but her fingertips was under military occupation. She spoke with measured impatience. "So what do you suggest?"

"I've suggested to myself that I have a gin and tonic on the deck of the Hotel Washington, and marvel at our nation's capitol. I'd be happy to buy you a drink and talk business there." Once I'd asked, I wasn't so sure. But it beat sitting at attention in her office by a comfortable margin.

Her body was a stiff parody of resistance. Finally, she willed it away. "All right. But I don't intend to make a habit of this."

I knew what she meant, but played dense. "Why?" I asked innocently. "You married?"

She looked at me askance. "No. Divorced."

I believed it. We left, more or less in tandem.

The deck of the Hotel Washington overlooked the Potomac, the White House, and the Washington, Jefferson, and Lincoln memorials, surrounded by grass and trees. From this distance, the squalid brown of the Potomac was blue, and carried a toy armada of trim pleasure crafts. Arlington Cemetery sat in soft green hills, an optimist's glimpse of eternity. The vivid view had an odd unreality, like a mural of the tourists' imagined Washington. It was possible here to drink oneself into a dazed belief in the dramatic Washington of political fiction: statesmen launching soliloquies at moonlit marble, musing over the fate of Western civilization. The real Washington sat around me: knit-suited bureaucrats, drinking gin with tight mouths, nibbling on salted peanuts and calculations of small chances for petty gains. I looked out again and decided that I had a mild case of overcynicism. On its merits, the view was lovely.

Mary and I sat in awkward silence staring out at the view. She was as remote as the marble. I would have preferred having a drink with the Washington Monument; it wasn't so embarrassing when it didn't talk to you. Instead I ordered two gin and tonics and waited for something to happen. Nothing did. Finally, I asked her what it was that she wanted. She told me. So I gave her the rundown she requested—what I had found and what I intended, including the subpoena to Sam Green. The last part caught her interest.

"Have you already sent the subpoena?"

"Yes," I lied.

She looked angry and unsettled, for reasons I couldn't fathom. She sat erect and marshalled her shoulders again. I was beginning to read her better. She seemed to expend a lot of energy just keeping herself under control. And the rest of it controlling others. "I thought it was understood that you would clear investigative steps with our office before you took them."

"It was?"

She looked annoyed, like a teacher with an over-aged discipline problem. "You don't seem to understand the implications of this thing."

"You know, I didn't get the impression from your boss that you and I were going to be Siamese twins."

She wasn't sure what Woods and I had talked about. She shifted ground slightly. "You're making this Sam Green come all the way to Washington on pretty weak evidence. It's like a form of harassment."

I thought of my pen pal, the jailbird stockbroker. I grinned. "Tell it to the American Civil Liberties Union. They've got a file on me. You can find it under 'N,' for 'Nazi.' "

Her eyes seemed to look clear through me, as if

I wasn't there. Which was clearly her wish. She bunched her hands in a determined little gesture. "We're going to have to get this situation straightened out. I don't have time to sit here feeding you straight lines and watching you stuff your ego. Which is already overfed."

I remembered Robinson's friend at the committee, and his brush with unemployment. I suddenly realized that the day hadn't been all bad; I didn't want to lose this case before it began. "Look, please understand some things. I'm not used to this kind of supervision. I like to follow the facts where they take me. Anyhow, hauling in Sammy Green is routine, like bringing in a lifetime deviate after a sex crime. He's our version of a jailhouse character, and all the facts point to him. Would you prefer that I subpoenaed Lasko?"

The last suggestion startled her for a second. Then she tagged it as an idle threat, and dismissed it. She started to look for my new pigeonhole. "Well, then, what's your understanding of your role?"

"I'll keep you posted, as I have. If something major comes up, I'll let you know before I do anything." I didn't like this; I clung to the loophole word "major." "But I can't loiter around your office like a truant with his parole officer, seeking advice. I'd never get anything done."

She wasn't mollified. "Christopher Kenyon Paget

is a pretty name." Her careful voice lingered on "Kenyon," as if reading an indictment of false pride. What it told me was that she had read my personnel file. "It doesn't go with taking direction. But you're going to have to learn."

That got me. "The nice thing about being Christopher Kenyon Paget"—I mocked her diction—"is that I can make these decisions for myself."

She reached her own decision, put down her half-finished drink and snatched at her purse, ready to leave. "This has been fairly disagreeable."

"Yes," I said agreeably, "and it's been so easy."

We stood and left, single file. Then we grabbed the elevator and walked to her car. She broke the uneasy silence only to ask if I wanted a ride home. We set a new world's record for non-communication, all the way to my apartment.

I opened the door as soon as we had stopped. "You forgot to thank me for a lovely evening," I said. I meant it as self-mockery, but it came out wrong, like everything else. She gave me a cold look back to tell me that she wasn't wasting more time, and leaned over to shut my door.

I was thrilled with myself. Paget the wit. Paget the charming. Paget the amateur psychologist. I had screwed up with Mary, and I had to learn to handle her better were I to keep the case. If it wasn't too late. And there was an ephemeral personal regret. At least she wasn't boring. Of course,

I told myself, someone had probably once said that about Lucrezia Borgia.

My apartment was on the first floor of a seventy-year-old red brick former townhouse, on the six hundred block of East Capitol. My landlord had largely gutted it in the process of preparing to charge $500 a month. The neighborhood had a healthy crime rate, and I didn't walk around at night. But the place suited me. The fireplace and the fine old wood floors were still there. The living room was large, with a chandelier and shuttered windows which looked out on a garden. And there were two bedrooms and plenty of room for my paintings and books.

I opened the door and knocked over my tennis racket. I had forgotten to play this evening. I plodded to the kitchen nook, poured myself a careless martini, and stuck a frozen pizza into the oven. I bolted the first martini and, in a reckless mood, poured a second. Then I pulled the pizza from the oven. I ate hungrily, my good-taste buds desensitized by gin, then contemplated an empty evening. I was rereading *War and Peace*, but wasn't in the mood, and was dating a couple of women, who somehow didn't seem to fit. In desperation, I flicked on my seldom-used television. It carried a special treat, a press conference starring Lasko's friend, the President. I felt neither antipathy nor admiration. I looked over the image for something

I had missed. If he lived anywhere other than deep within himself, it was in the eyes. He was poised enough, but on the occasional question, the eyes blinked for a moment, as if in doubt of their owner's adequacy. I wondered what accounted for that. His well-ventilated early poverty, perhaps. That could twist some people into admiring a Lasko and doubting themselves.

I decided to listen to the words. "And so, in response to the justified concern of our citizens, I am proposing to the Congress the Safe Streets and Neighborhoods Act. My study of history persuades me that at the heart of every fallen civilization which has preceded us was the lack of will to resist crime and disorder. Our administration is already moving to eliminate the root causes of crime— racism, poverty, and deprivation." The head shook disapprovingly at the words. I found myself wondering where he stood on the Four Horsemen of the Apocalypse. "Now with the pledge of five billion dollars to assist and augment local law enforcement, we promise to all Americans safety, security, and freedom from fear in their streets and neighborhoods."

I turned him off. Then I advanced to my window to see if the neighborhood looked safer. I couldn't see any difference. A police siren whined in the distance. I went to bed disappointed.

SIX

The day before he died was clear and bright.

I went to the office early, closed my door, and finished Sam Green's subpoena. I was just signing it when Marty Gubner telephoned.

"Christopher, how are you?" Gubner's strong New York voice carried friendly irony. He was one of those lawyers who made his living representing the people we investigated. In a way, we were his personal Works Projects Administration. Gubner and I liked each other well enough; we took our work seriously, but related in an offhand way. After all, we had to get along.

"Fine, Marty. Are you calling because you miss the sound of my voice? I didn't know we were doing business at the moment."

"I didn't know until this morning. I hear you're investigating Lasko Devices."

I didn't bother denying it. "Where did you hear that?"

"Ike Feiner sent a subpoena to Lasko Devices asking for trading records. The subpoena showed you as investigating officer."

"All right," I said. Gubner's voice carried a strange undertone, more tentative than usual. I waited to find out what it was.

"I'm calling on behalf of someone who wants to talk about Lasko Devices. He's asked me to set up a meeting."

"Sure. Who is he?"

Gubner remained silent. "Marty?"

"I can't tell you right now."

It was a first. "This is fun," I said. "Let me guess. Is it Judge Crater?" The silence was deafening. "How about Martin Bormann?"

"I'm serious."

"Hang on. Does his name start with a consonant?"

"Look, Chris, I called up to give you some information, not solicit your little funnies."

I hesitated. The anger was real and seemed to include himself. "OK, let's take it from the top."

"My guy is close to Lasko Devices. When the subpoena hit, it got him thinking that he should talk to you. Apparently, there's something going on up there, although he won't tell me what it is over the phone. I'm going to Boston today to see him."

"Why all the secrecy?"

"I'm not sure. It's clear he's pretty scared. One

reason he doesn't want to give his name is so you can't go after him with a subpoena."

It made a cockeyed kind of sense, except for one thing. "So why are you calling me now, if he isn't sure he wants to see me?"

"He wants to set it up in a hurry, if he decides to do it. He's under some kind of time pressure; I don't know what. It's sort of half-baked."

I was half-exasperated. "All this is pretty vague."

Gubner sounded a little exasperated himself. "I didn't write this scenario. He wrote it. All I could do was decide whether to represent him or to tell him to take his business elsewhere. But I didn't, for reasons personal to me. Are you going to meet him or not?"

I was getting very curious. "Just exactly what does our mystery guest have in mind?"

"You're to meet us at 2:30 tomorrow afternoon by the Boston Common, unless you hear from me otherwise."

My own willingness surprised me. "Can I spot you by your trench coat and sunglasses?"

"Meet us in the area by Commonwealth Avenue. The Public Garden. As I recall, you know Boston."

"I know Boston."

The question hung in the air. Finally, he asked, "So will you meet him?"

"I'll meet him."

I heard a faint exhaling sound as if Gubner had

been holding his breath. "Thanks much, Chris. I appreciate it. See you tomorrow, hopefully." He sounded relieved; I wondered what his relationship was to the nameless client. But I said good-bye and hung up.

I sat and thought about it. I had the feeling that the case was falling into my lap, for no good reason. It was disconcerting. I went to see Robinson, and told him about Gubner. He was pensive.

"Have you told McGuire?" he asked.

"Not yet. I've been waiting to figure out how to put it to him."

"He's going to think you're crazy."

"Probably. What would you do?"

He thought for a moment. "I'd go. It's pretty screwy but you've got nothing to lose."

Something hit me, for no particular reason. "Our subpoena to Lasko only covers documents relating to stock transactions. It doesn't ask for financial stuff—like books and records or the records of their outside accountant from their yearly audit. Do you think you could draft a subpoena to get me that?"

Robinson gave his fingernails a doubtful look. "Sure. But you really don't have any grounds for fishing in the company's financial records. McGuire may not let you do it—let alone Woods."

Woods' name reminded me of Mary Carelli. "I'll try to figure something out."

Robinson smiled at me skeptically. "OK. I'd rather have my job than yours. I'll get the subpoena out this afternoon. Incidentally, you might pay a courtesy call on Ike Feiner, at least for the sake of the case. You may be the only thing which makes him look good," he added dryly, "but Feiner tends to forget how grateful he should be. You may have felt those little knives in your back."

I shrugged. "This should be invaluable." Robinson's semi-smile followed me out the door.

Feiner was sitting in his book-lined office. He looked up with the trapped, wary look of a cop drafted to bring in a rabid dog. I was clearly something beyond his life experience, and he'd already been burnt on the Lasko case. I sat down across from a bust of Martin Luther King, which Feiner had acquired at a safe distance from the sixties. "I need to go to Boston."

Feiner considered this. "Why?"

I told him. He grimaced. "You better ask Joe. I'm keeping out of this one."

"I can see how you'd feel that way," I said, with a voice too full of understanding.

Feiner looked annoyed, as I had intended. His tone was didactic. "Cases like this should be handled at the top."

Maybe I should write that down, I thought. Instead, I left.

McGuire was alone when I cracked open his

door. He looked up with narrow eyes, as if surprised to see me. Then he remembered that he
wanted to know what I was doing. So I told him
about Sam Green, skipping my clash with Mary.
McGuire cleared Green's subpoena. Then I explained Gubner's call. He propped his feet on the
desk and folded his hands, listening.

"That's ridiculous," he said, when I'd finished.

I felt defensive. "That's what I told Marty. But I
either go or I don't go. I want to push this thing to
see what I get."

McGuire screwed his mouth to one side. "This
business of sneaking around the Boston Common—"
he waved his arm in dismissal, letting the phrase
speak for itself.

I felt the chance slipping away. "Gubner's not an
idiot. And if this is a waterhaul, all we've lost is one
day of my time."

"And the taxpayer's money," he retorted.

McGuire was reaching. "I didn't know you were
an advocate of thrift in government," I said.

"We can't be wasting the public's money on
things like this."

"Jesus Christ, Joe, if you really cared about that,
you'd pass out cyanide tablets to half the civil servants in town. How do you seriously justify not
doing this?" My suspicions of McGuire shadowed
the words.

"It's not your ass if we look like fools."

At least that was closer to home, I thought. "If it were my ass, Joe, I'd do it."

McGuire clasped his hands again, then stared at them as if in prayer. He looked up. "OK. Let me know what you find."

I waited for more, astonished at the concession. There wasn't any more. I felt as if I had just won Wimbledon by default. It was as though McGuire had been playing along, having already decided that if I pushed hard enough, I won. As he had known I would. I couldn't figure it out.

So I tried selling McGuire on a subpoena for Lasko's financial records. The idea seemed to revive him. "That subpoena absolutely will not go out. There's no justification for it."

McGuire gave me his determined *Newsweek* look, from which there was no appeal. I was both frustrated and relieved. The refusal at least fit with my suspicions. I told myself I had a compulsion to impose order on events. So I dismissed it, and fished for a way around McGuire. The plan hit me on the way out the door.

I went back to the office and called Mary Carelli. She answered on the third ring.

"Mary," I said, "this is Chris Paget. What kind of apology would you like?"

SEVEN

Mary Carelli lived in Georgetown. So I walked home about a quarter to six, showered, and put on corduroy slacks and a faded blue work shirt. Then I got in my car and drove too fast through the Ellipse toward the Kennedy Center, mashing the buttons on my radio until I hit an FM station playing a Pink Floyd album. Then I reached under the seat to check the small cellophane bag of grass. Still there.

The little ritual amused me; I was grasping at corners of my college identity like an old woman fondling a scrapbook. I wondered which of my friends were doing it too—leaving jobs at places they had scorned in college to put on blue jeans and blow some great Colombian dope they had cadged from the guy next door. Knowing that this shallow alchemy trivialized all the differences they had felt, the things they would do or never be, but seizing it to avoid the unpleasant truth: they were just like Mom and Dad. So I drove Mom and Dad up Waterside Drive and onto Massachusetts past the embassies. I turned up the radio and listened very hard to Pink Floyd all the way down Wisconsin. By the time I hit Georgetown, I was alone.

Mary rented the basement of an old white brick three-story on R Street. It was a good part of Georgetown, where you could still park, away from M Street's weekend circus. The house itself was at least one hundred years old and sat amid quiet oaks a good bit older, giving off the subtle aroma of money and good taste. A lot of the money probably belonged to someone else. When people said that they were dying to live in Georgetown, they usually meant financially.

Mary was wearing white slacks, a green silk blouse, and a real smile. "I'm taking a chance—seeing you. You're nicer on the telephone."

"I know. It's terminal smart-ass. Someday I'll probably die from it."

She looked amused. "I wouldn't doubt it. Anyhow, dinner's a good enough apology. I was a little officious myself."

"Then let's call it even and start over."

We got in the car and headed for the deck at the Washington again. The city had few outdoor bars, and the night was cooled by a pleasant breeze. We ordered the same two gin and tonics and looked out at the city.

Mary smiled. "Here we are again," she said, picking up her drink. But she was leaning back easily in the wicker chair. Her body had declared amnesty. She looked across at me. "You're rather quiet tonight. Is this what happens when you run out of smart things to say?"

I grinned. "I spend my life concealing that I'm duller than hell. You're sharp to catch it so soon."

She gave me a glancing smile. "The commission seems to be filled with people who don't know anything more about you than what they see."

Her voice had a dash of challenge. I seemed to spend a lot of time explaining why I didn't talk about the things that felt personal to me. I didn't enjoy it. So I threw back the ball. "Have you been checking up on me?" I tried to register genteel shock at the notion.

"A little. Between college and law school you were a reporter for two years, supposedly a good one. Why did you quit?"

"It was just a holding action. Anyhow, I did crime stuff—started out with muggings and ended up with murders. Pretty soon everyone I met was a corpse. I began to feel like a pathologist, and I wasn't doing anyone any good."

"Is that why you're such a cynic?"

"Look around you," I shrugged. "So what else did you learn?"

"That a lot of people think you're the best lawyer

McGuire has. That you've put some people in jail, though not enough to suit you. And that you go your own way. Nobody seems to know a lot about you—personally, that is."

I had been listening to her talk. Her voice had a buried Mediterranean intensity, as if she had once lived with people who talked with feeling and then had trained her voice into upper-class politeness. The thought was interesting. So was she.

"What was your husband like?" I asked.

"Frank?"

"Your husband's name was Frank?"

She sipped again, nodding with her drink. She looked up to see my eyes. "What's so funny?"

"I'm sorry, Mary. I have this thing about names. I can't see you married to someone named Frank."

She gave a small smile. "It looks as if I couldn't either."

"What happened?"

She pulled the black hair from her face, then tossed it around her shoulders. "Don't subjects like this just get us into trouble?"

I grinned again. "We've been in trouble from the time you forgot my name."

"You're an arrogant bastard, aren't you?" The flat voice was matter of fact, as if she were committed to finding out.

"A little. Sometimes a lot." I tried to head her off. "But I'm not my own favorite subject."

"Why not?"

How many reasons would you like, I thought. "Because self-analysis is a bore. Because most of what people tell you about themselves is bullshit, intentionally or otherwise. And because if someone really interests you, you'll learn about them yourself." I softened my voice. "So what was Frank like?"

Her forehead furrowed as if she were organizing a summary. "Frank was a good Catholic boy. We were classmates in law school. He was very smart and very serious. I thought we would do well together. But when we got married, he reverted to type. I was going to stay home and have children." Her tone turned dry around the edges. "He told me that I could 'use my education in the home.' I guess he thought I was going to sit around with beet stains on my blouse and pablum in my hair, lecturing infants on Constitutional law. I told him that idea had gone out with hula hoops. And that's where it started."

"I take it you never got around to mothering Frank, Jr.?"

She shook her head. "I never even got around to mothering Frank."

"Where did it finish?"

"When we started to hassle, everything else seemed to go bad. I couldn't talk to him about my career, so I stopped talking to him about a lot of things. I developed a very rich interior life," her voice was ironic, "which didn't include Frank. And every time he wanted me, I could hear imaginary children scampering under the bed." She paused. "You know that you're a sort of voyeur, only the listening kind. Is that why you like your job?"

"Who said I like my job?"

"You did. By hassling with me about it."

We ordered a second round and looked out at the fading light. I turned back to Mary. "Let's put it this way. I like some parts of my job."

She shot me an amused look. "You and McGuire seem to have a nice relationship."

"Yes, it's very warm. He thinks of me as the son he never had." I saw my chance. "Which reminds me. I was talking to Joe this afternoon about sending out a subpoena for Lasko Devices' financial records. I thought it should be cleared by Chairman Woods first." More like revived. I didn't bother to mention that McGuire would sooner have me keel-hauled than send the subpoena.

"Why don't you talk with him about it tomorrow?"

It was a subject I'd hoped to avoid. "I can't. I'll be in Boston tomorrow."

"On this case?"

I tried to throw my brain into overdrive. "Yes, I'm meeting a lawyer there tomorrow who says he has information about the case. A man named Gubner."

"Why didn't you tell me?" Her voice suddenly cooled.

"I just did. Gubner only called today. I don't know what he knows, but I'll tell you when I do." Maybe.

"Where are you going to meet him?"

"Our Boston office seems like the logical place." I decided to keep the conversation moving. "I'm really a little mystified by the whole thing."

"Why do you want to subpoena Lasko's books?"

"It's a hunch, really. I think we should clear up all these areas at once and move on, if there's nothing there."

She nodded. "I'll talk to Jack Woods in the morning."

We finished the drinks and left for dinner. On the way to the car, I felt a light touch on my elbow—Mary's fingertips. She turned to me as we got into the car.

"You've asked me about Frank. Were you ever married?"

"No." It was true, as far as it went.

"Ever close?"

"I suppose everyone's been close."

"Do you conceal your height and weight, too?"

I smiled. "I should just send you my resume. Actually, the Army told me that I'm about six feet, one-seventy." I pulled the car out into Pennsylvania.

"You were in the Army?" She sounded surprised.

"Yeah. I was an infantry lieutenant. I had a low lottery number and had to hop into ROTC in law school to beat the draft. Fortunately, when I got out I was a trained killer with no one to kill. So they kept me at Fort Benning three months and let me go."

"What was it like?"

"I've repressed most of it. My only clear memory is of one poor bastard dying of heatstroke in the chow line at noon, waiting for some stew that looked like strained dog-shit. I always wanted to see the letter they sent his parents."

"Are you serious?"

"About the heatstroke? Absolutely."

"I've never been able to cope with death." Her voice had an odd, cold tenor, as if she coped by not thinking about it.

"I imagine everyone has trouble." What I was having trouble with was integrating her personality. The self-control had eased into ironic candor. The cutting edge of perception was the only constant.

We stopped at a carry-out on Connecticut and grabbed an eight-pack of beer, which I said was to impress her. Then we drove to the restaurant. The Bangkok Room was stark and brightly lit, with a few booths and a couple of Formica tables in the corners. The food ranged from good to great. And it was spicy and cheap. I explained that to Mary while I ceremoniously yanked the flip-tops off two beer cans, adding that the Bangkok Room didn't have a liquor license. She took the can and tilted it to her lips.

"You're laughing," she said.

"If you must know, I'm laughing because very few people could look so stylish drinking out of a beer can. You know, you never told me what you were doing before you worked for Woods." Which was true; Robinson had told me. "Were you living in wedded bliss with Frank, ironing his shirts?"

She gave me a mildly hostile look. "You know, you find Frank a little funnier than I do. I was on the staff of the Senate Commerce Committee, mostly drafting legislation." And collecting scalps, I remembered. "That was my first job. I came straight from there."

"Did you go to school in town?" I didn't really like this part. I told myself that I was a secret agent for the Civil Service Commission, checking the accuracy of their records.

"No. Chicago."

"How did you get here?"

She hunched her shoulders. "I was interested in politics. Why did you come here?"

I considered what level of truth to give her and

selected medium. "I thought I could do some good. Fight white collar crime and all that."

"Were you ever interested in politics?"

"I was. I stopped."

"When?" It was her eyes which told me that the question was important; they were back on the job, probing.

"About 1968. Do you still think it's important?"

"Do I think what's important?"

"Politics."

"Yes, very."

"Why?"

Her answer was impatient. "Because government matters more and more. And who controls the government determines how people are going to live their lives. You need the right people directing it. And a lot of other people pushing to make sure they get there and stay there."

Her eyes snapped; the careful voice was low and intense. I decided to skip finding out what the "right people" were going to determine about my life. The talk needed leavening. "I apologize for joking about Frank. He should have been named Lance or Errol, something like that. Anyhow, I should just feel lucky I don't have an ex-wife."

The topic of politics had flushed out the stern Aztec look. It lingered there, then abruptly vanished. She replaced it with a bright, distracted smile, which looked as if it had been thrown on. The voice was better, light and ironic. "You're right. You've probably been spoiled by the women you've known."

Dinner arrived. "Watch it, Mary. It's hot." I handed her another beer.

"Have you?" she insisted.

"I don't know. 'Spoiled' is a relative term. Anyhow, it strikes me as a little archaic, like 'helpmate' or 'the little woman'—words like that."

She smiled. "Or like 'using your education in the home'?" She plunged into dinner with unconcealed zest. Then she rushed the beer to her lips and took a hasty sip. "You're right. Wow. But it's good." She closed her eyes and moved her head from side to side. "You know, you're great at not answering any questions," she said when she had recovered.

"I guess you're right. It's my profession taking over. Ask a lot of questions and don't give away any information."

She shook her head. "On you it goes deeper than that," she started, then dropped it abruptly. "How did you find this place?"

So I told her how. About my crazy friend from college who used to get stoned and come here to plot the liberation of Thailand. And a few other stories, while we finished dinner and killed the eight-pack of beer. Which got her to laughing, a good strong laugh that lit her eyes. So she broke down and told me some funny things about Frank. We solemnly agreed that they were better off divorced, and laughed about it all the way to the car. We drove back to Georgetown in a quiet mellow mood. Mary slouched in the other seat, her long legs stretched out. We chatted easily all the way.

I parked the car and walked her to her door. She opened it, then turned around and looked at me. "I'd ask you in, but it's very late."

I hung there in adolescent confusion. "Some other time." I tried to think of a graceful exit line.

"Call me from Boston about that subpoena to Lasko."

I nodded, feeling as if I had lost the mood. Then with a quick movement she slid her hand behind my neck and pulled my face down to hers. Her mouth felt strong, almost angry; her fingers played with the hair which touched my collar. Then they slid away and she backed up against the door, wearing the amused half-smile. "Good night, Christopher Kenyon," she said, and softly shut the door behind her.

I drove home and packed for Boston.

EIGHT

I was in Boston the day he was murdered.

I landed at Logan Airport about a quarter to twelve, which left me almost three hours. I got off the plane and jammed some change in the phone, hoping to beat the noon hour. Mary was in her office. Yes, she said, Woods had okayed my Lasko subpoena. Could she reach me later at the Boston office if necessary. I didn't know, I hedged. OK, she would see me when I got back. Not much inflection; no mention of the night before. All very professional. I told myself I had what I wanted, and hung up.

I called our Boston office. They would pick up the subpoena and serve it on the company this afternoon. I went toward the baggage claim, got my bag, and hailed a taxi.

Boston was unseasonably cool, grey and gloomy. It had been grey when I'd left Boston, after losing something I had wanted to keep. Since then, I'd liked myself a little less. I felt the same way about Boston.

It was only 12:15. So I checked into the Ritz-Carlton, dropped off the subpoena at the desk, and went to the men's grill at Locke-Ober for a solitary lunch. I ate it over some solitary thoughts. They lasted me until 2:15. Then I caught another taxi, manned by a bearded Harvard dropout who earned extra cash appearing on daytime quiz shows. No, I really couldn't blame him, I agreed. He dropped me on Arlington Street across from the hotel and in front of the Common.

The rolling green of the Common was surrounded by the same black iron fence. I walked through the iron gates and into the Public Garden. The asphalt path snaked aimlessly under oak trees and through grass and flower beds. I looked ahead for Gubner. But there was no one between me and the swanboats which sat on the distant pond. The swans looked as still as a painting with no heart in it. The Garden seemed lifeless, a stillborn fantasy. I turned away.

Gubner sat on a wood bench, about thirty yards to my left. He was alone. It appeared that he had been watching me, but hadn't moved. I walked toward him. Gubner sat frozen, looking as unreal as the swans. But he rose when I reached the bench. The handshake was firm, but the smile was less jaunty than usual. He had the pale, sandbagged look of someone who had just been punched in the kidneys.

"Hello, Chris."

"Hello, Marty." I looked past him. "Where's your friend?"

"Over at the Ritz." He stood hunched against some unseen threat, his hands jammed in his pocket. "I'd like to talk with you first." The voice was off, a tinny shallow rasp. Someone else's troubles were leeching Gubner like a parasitic plant.

"This bench looks good enough." I sat down gingerly, feeling somehow that it was an act of commitment.

It was Gubner's turn to stare at the swanboats.

"Let's have it," I said.

He turned to face me. Gubner usually looked raffish; today he seemed strained.

"His name is Alexander Lehman," he began. "He was my friend, at Brandeis, twenty years ago. My best friend. Still is. I was in his wedding, things like that. None of which you give a shit about. But he's also the controller at Lasko Devices. It looks like he's involved in some pretty bad things. And you're about to help him cut his own throat."

"How so?"

Gubner's face hardened. "That subpoena your boys sent scared the piss out of him. So now he wants to spill his guts. And when you vultures are through, he'll be out a job—with no career, and maybe no marriage."

"I'm just doing my job. I didn't ask your boy to do these 'pretty bad things.' And I didn't ask for this little chat."

"Fuck you, Chris," he said without feeling.

I let it pass. "Look, Marty. I'm sorry your friend went sour. But it's no good holding a wake. Make sure I get everything he knows, and I'll try to help him."

Gubner tugged at his thick black hair as if trying to find a handle on himself. "You can't promise for McGuire."

"Would you rather tell it to him?"

He shook his head. "No. I want you to carry the mail for him. Remind people that he helped."

"I'll suspend judgment until I hear his story."

"What about immunity for testimony?" It was a gesture; his voice wasn't hopeful.

I shook my head. "You've got no cards, Marty. Anything else?"

"No, I'll let him tell it himself. I'll be hearing most of it for the first time anyhow."

I was surprised. "Why are you letting him talk before you know what he's going to say?"

Gubner looked away at nothing. "Christ, I'd almost rather shoot him. But he's got some hangup— he'd rather tell it to the government. Says he doesn't want me in the middle. I'm just holding his hand." Gubner's anger mingled Lehman, himself, and me in a disillusioned mix. I wondered why Lehman inspired that much grief.

"Ready?" I asked. Gubner got up without a word. We walked with our separate thoughts out of the park and over to the Ritz. I had missed something in Gubner. He had always projected the studied cynicism of a shell-game artist who dared you to find the pea. I supposed he had his reasons. But Gubner had done himself a disservice; he was better than that. I wondered if as much could be said for Alexander Lehman.

The Ritz bar was a soft-lit room off the lobby, as understated as a grey pinstripe and as quiet as a bank vault. The marble tables focused on a large window which looked back to the Garden. Most of the tables were empty. In one corner two middle-aged gentlemen sat in quiet conversation. Both wore grey suits with handkerchiefs carefully arranged in their breast pockets, and talked with the attentive gravity of serious men discussing money. I liked the place well enough. But today it seemed funereal. I half-expected to find Lehman stretched out on a table, made up for burying.

But Lehman was alive enough. Gubner steered me toward a man who sat facing the window. I moved toward the table, feeling edgy. This seemed the wrong place to be doing our business.

Lehman's back conveyed queasiness like a contagion.

I reached the table and stood over him. My imagined Alexander Lehman was tall and slender. The real one was short and pale, with brown hair and the boyish roundness of a child comic.

"Mr. Lehman?"

"You're Mr. Paget." He said it with the sad expectancy of a man who had been formally introduced to a terminal disease. "Please sit down." The voice went with the face; it had the youthfulness of an adolescent's. But at second glance there was something older in him, like seeing your paperboy grown up and disappointed. His eyes were a sad light blue which looked as though they had the life bleached out. We sat down.

His eyes searched me, as if trying to learn whether I were really fatal. "Marty has explained the situation?"

"Generally. We're both waiting to hear it from you."

"I wish I shared your sense of anticipation." Lehman seemed to be gliding elliptically around his problems. I waited. I noticed that he had long piano player's fingers, which noiselessly drummed the table. They seemed constantly in motion, like nervous antennae feeling out his relation to the world.

"I don't expect you to understand how I got involved in this," he finally said.

"I can listen, Mr. Lehman." I seemed to have been chosen; as the one to whom Lehman would make his personal accounting. I was all wrong for the role; I was neither wife, friend, nor psychiatrist. It struck me that he was a lonely man.

"I knew what Lasko was doing when he hired me. That's the worst part. I was in debt and my business had gone bust. I'd quit my old job and started a fast food chain in New Jersey that didn't fly. Borrowed $10,000 from my wife's parents. This was a couple of years ago. So, I was broke and out of a job. He found me through one of those executive placement deals. When I came to Boston, Lasko went through my finances with me. More even than my qualifications. Then he offered me the job. You can see how it worked out." He stopped abruptly, like a man reaching a rest point in a grubby and unpleasant job.

I had a notion how it had worked out, but didn't say so. I chose some neutral words. "I'd appreciate it if you would explain."

Lehman looked both eager and reluctant, as if unsure whether he would be helped or humiliated. Gubner broke in softly. "Go ahead, Alec."

Lehman nodded slowly. "My wife was afraid. Hell, I was afraid too. I was a middle-aged, broke business failure in a buyer's market, with two kids."

His words picked up speed. "Lasko was pushing me to come to Boston. He even offered to loan me down-payment money and to guarantee any mortgage. And I owed my in-laws $10,000. Have you ever owed your in-laws money?"

"I'm not married."

"Hell, I'd sooner owe money to the Mafia. They might kill you, but you don't have to eat dinner with them." He looked at me to see if this little joke had taken. I was beginning to get a handle on him. At the center of him were other people looking back. And now it was me.

"The thing about being dead, Mr. Lehman, is that there's no future in it."

His smile was bleak. "So I took it all. I took the job, which was better than I'd expected, and I moved to Boston. Then, I took the loan. Lasko kept pressuring me to get a good house, so I did. A nice old white frame house in Newton, with oaks in the front. My family loved it. And Lasko gave me the loan and set up the mortgage, and I was controller of Lasko Devices, with a house in Newton." The sad face made it seem as attractive as acquiring leprosy. Lehman's features were astonishingly mobile. I wondered if it came from practice.

A not-so-wild guess hit me. "Mr. Lehman, were you the one who called McGuire a week ago to talk about stock manipulation?"

He looked surprised. "No. What manipulation?"

It was my turn for surprise. But Lehman hadn't finished his confessional. "The thing is, I knew why Lasko wanted me. I used to be a CPA with a national accounting firm. You learn pretty fast to figure out your clients. I knew Lasko wanted someone that he owned, that sooner or later I would do something I didn't like. But I bought into the whole thing a long time ago. The house, the job, all the expectations. All the deferred gratifications."

"And when it didn't work, you folded up." I said it quietly, looking at him.

He stared at the table. "There wasn't enough in me. You know, I knew that I was a born lackey." The voice had gone starkly bitter. "In college I was the class clown." Gubner smiled faintly in rueful recollection. "Between then and now I must have kissed enough ass to fill a stadium. The one time I tried to get out from under myself is when I started my own business. I was going to be a boss. But I wasn't cut out for being a boss. I kept looking for someone to please, for someone to tell me what to do. Or what to be." He paused, then pronounced judgment on himself in a final tone. "And that's the bottom line on me, Mr. Paget. I'm someone else's boy."

And now he was my boy. The thought must have shown in my face. "What do they call you, Mr. Paget?"

"Chris."

"Tell me, Chris, have you ever wanted to please someone else, even when you thought it was wrong?"

"More often than I'd like."

"What keeps you from doing it?"

I thought. "I honestly don't know, Mr. Lehman. I guess I'm afraid to."

Lehman nodded; he knew what I meant. For a moment, we were almost friends. But he was a witness, and I needed to use him. I decided to put a cap on self-analysis. "Let's just say that I understand what you've told me."

But Lehman was looking beyond me at some middle distance. The bar reverberated with the echo of a long-ago psychic explosion, of which the current Lehman was the remains, a crazy quilt of roles with no stuffing. The act of contrition was the only thing which was making Lehman real to himself. But I was going to have to push it to the end.

"Let's talk about what you've got for me," I said.

Lehman snapped to as if wrenched out of hypnosis. "I don't know about any manipulation. But I've got proof of something different. A lot worse." Whatever it was lent an awed tone to his words. "I've got a memo at home that will deliver the whole thing." He looked around. "But we can't talk about it here."

I felt impatient. "Look, you've got to tell me sometime."

Lehman's voice was thick with knowledge. "Mr. Paget, you don't want to talk about this here either. I know I'm doing a mental striptease. But I didn't want to sit in a government office, like a criminal. You've been very decent. Come to my place after dinner tonight, and I'll show you what I've got. You can handle it the way you think best." His voice slowed to a low emphatic rhythm. "And you are going to want to think about it."

It was a strange scene and sad. The man had wanted to see me—be friends—before he put his future in my hands. But I couldn't give him that. "You know, Mr. Lehman, I can question you, under oath, any time. And have you sent up for perjury if you lie."

Gubner cut in sharply. "He knows that." I looked from Gubner to Lehman. He nodded.

"All right, Mr. Lehman, 7:30 tonight. And I hope it's good."

Lehman stood up, smiling in a lifeless way which made my words sound foolish. "It's better than you imagine. Or from my perspective, worse." He paused. "You should remember, Mr. Paget, that Lasko is a very ruthless man."

He should know, I thought. But Lehman seemed like a weak reed for Lasko to be trusting. "One thing bothers me. Just why does Lasko trust you with whatever this is?"

The bleak smile held. "Because I'm his controller," he said with irony. "Besides, he's got me by the balls."

I could see that. "Then why are you here?"

He exhaled, staring at his feet. Then he looked directly at me. "Because this is my last chance to like myself."

I nodded. He turned to Gubner. The two friends looked at each other for a moment. Gubner wore the rueful half-smile. Lehman saw it and reached out with one hand to touch Gubner's arm. Then he turned and walked from the bar. Gubner stared after him, as if regret had turned him to stone.

I let him stare for a moment, then spoke. "Marty, I'll buy you a martini. They're good here, and you could use one."

Gubner turned, then sat down heavily. I ordered two martinis, straight up. They arrived in record time. I pushed one toward Gubner and picked up mine. I felt pretty good, sort of. But not perfect. Lehman appeared in the window, walking with the comic stagger of a penguin. He looked as if he had been shot, but didn't know he was dead. Which he was, in a way. I sipped on the martini and watched my new star witness walk across the street.

I saw the black car before I knew what it meant. It seemed to have pulled out from the sidewalk. Lehman was crossing Arlington, not looking. From the bar, I saw the car accelerating silently toward him. I half-rose, a strangled yell in my throat which tasted like gin.

Then Lehman saw the car. He stood stock still for a split second, as if he had expected it. Then he gave a pathetic little skip, stretching forward to the sidewalk. The car smashed into Lehman in mid-stretch, his hands reaching toward the Garden. I saw him flying above the car in slow motion, arms flailing like a spastic rag doll. He seemed to snap in mid-air as the black car moved by. Then he fell in a precipitous dive, hit on his head, and folded into a shapeless heap. The heap didn't move.

Gubner's mouth was hanging open. I ran from the table, shouting for an ambulance. I smashed into someone in the entrance of the bar and bounced him off the wall. I kept moving. Lehman lay where he had fallen, alone. A few pedestrians stared at him from the sidewalk. A sticky splotch of blood spread like oil from his head. I reached him and felt for his pulse. Nothing. Then I looked at his face. It was a garish nightmare. But out of it stared one pale blue eye. It still looked sad.

NINE

Gubner was squatting next to me, chanting "Oh my God" over and over, like an incantation. I got up, feeling sick. A lump of passers-by were gawking at me. I went for the nearest one, a thin middle-aged man, and grabbed him by the lapels. "Be useful, you moron. Go to the Ritz and make sure the cops come." The voice I heard was clear and very cold. It was mine. The man nodded soundlessly, gaping at my bloody hands. I stared at him for a second, then dropped him from my grasp. He clambered off to the Ritz. I watched him to the door. Then I went to the iron fence, grabbed it, and threw up.

After a moment I stood, staring at the swans and the flowers in the Garden. Then I turned back to the street. Gubner was still stooped by Lehman's body, standing guard. The squad cars arrived in a squeal of sirens, with an ambulance. Three police-men got out and squatted around Lehman. A white-coated man probed him with his fingers. Then he and another man laid Lehman on a stretcher and bore him to the ambulance. The ambulance moved away. No sirens and no hurry.

Gubner and the cops drifted to the sidewalk. It all had a strange, dreamlike quality, as if I were stoned, watching a movie. The street was eerily empty, like a stage without props and actors. The only trace of Lehman was the splotch of blood.

I liked being alone. But I forced myself to cross the street. A crowd had gathered. One of the cops was asking questions, a big sharp-eyed man with dark sideburns and mustache and a low voice. He turned to me. I pulled myself together, and told him who we were. What had I seen, he asked. It was a Cadillac. I thought, late model. I hadn't seen the hit-skip driver. Or the license plate. I guessed the car was going thirty-five, forty, and accelerating fast.

He was watching me closely. "Anything else?"

"Yeah," I said. "I think he was murdered."

The cop's eyes narrowed. He turned and barked something to another cop. Then they trundled Gubner and me into the back of a squad car. A crew-cut drove while the sharp-eyed one asked some more questions. We didn't speak unless spoken to. I couldn't shake the feeling that I had stumbled into a surrealistic film. Gubner leaned against the corner of the car, white and waxen. We had stepped outside of our profession. And Lehman was dead.

The police station was down Berkeley Street in a squatty grey building. The police ushered us into the main room. It was sterile and badly lit, a paranoid's cop-house. A fat sergeant with lifeless grey eyes sat at a desk behind a rail. The sharp-eyed cop disappeared. When he returned he told us we were seeing Lieutenant Di Pietro. He steered us down a dark corridor to an office on the left, and opened the door.

The room was light green, except where paint flaked off the walls, which was all over. Di Pietro sat behind a beat-up metal desk, next to a picture of a plump woman and three black-haired kids, and in front of a map of his precinct. He asked us to sit.

He was in his forties, with dark, curly hair, swept back. He had a kind of ridged, Castilian nose, hooded eyes, and a thin mouth set in a seamed face. "You gentlemen are both lawyers?" he said abruptly.

We nodded. The word "lawyer" had a dry sound, as if Di Pietro had just swallowed something disagreeable. I sensed bleakly that he would have preferred two run-of-the-mill murderer-rapists. "Sergeant Brooks"—he gestured at our sharp-eyed guide—"says that you think this is a homicide, Mr. Paget. I'd like you to tell me why."

I felt Gubner's eyes on me. "Do you know a man named William Lasko?" I asked.

The hooded eyes turned vague; evidently Di Pietro was not a reader. I went on. "Lasko's a big industrialist here in Boston. We got a telephone tip a few days ago concerning some illegal transactions in his company's stock. Then Lehman contacted me through Mr. Gubner and asked for a meeting. I flew up to Boston and met with both of them at the Ritz. Lehman was controller of Lasko's company. He didn't know about the stock. But he said he had something on Lasko—something worse. He never got to tell us what it was."

Di Pietro inspected me wordlessly. I talked at the impassive face. "The thing is this. Lasko doesn't need problems with the government. If he does, Justice may stick by its antitrust suit. That means Lasko may lose part of his company. And Lehman had something bad on him. As I recall, that's known as motive."

"What else?"

The stiff face was beginning to anger me. "Look, Lieutenant, how many pedestrians get run down in front of the Ritz at forty miles an hour? By hit-skip drivers in late model Cadillacs that accelerate instead of brake? Show me another and I'll buy two tickets to the Policemen's Ball."

Di Pietro snapped at the holes in my argument. "Mr. Paget, I was thinking about motive when you were in prep school. Tell me this. What was Lehman going to tell you? Who drove the car? Whose car was it? How did Lasko find out about the meeting, or where it was going to happen?"

It was the last question that made me sick. "If you find the Cadillac," I parried, "the rest may come easier. Lehman had to have left some marks."

Di Pietro looked from me to Gubner. "Was Mr. Lehman a friend of yours?" he asked.

"Yes," Gubner replied in a far-off voice. In our own ways, Di Pietro and I had started to look forward. Gubner was still looking back.

The contrast seemed to impress Di Pietro. He turned to me. "We were talking about motive. We're not geared to come up with a motive on a man like this Lasko. I'm not a stock market wizard." That was obvious. Still, the admission seemed to cost him something; the voice had trailed off unhappily. It struck me that he had been talking like a cop talks to a lawyer. And that I hadn't helped.

"And I'm not a criminologist. But I can keep pushing and give you what I get."

Di Pietro nodded stiffly. Then he stepped back into the safety of his own routine. "First you and your friend give us a complete statement. And don't leave anything out."

This last was said to me with the unblinking stare. Either I was touchy, or Di Pietro guessed that I was holding back on something. The possibility suggested dimensions to him that I hadn't considered. I switched subjects. "I'd like some help from you, too. Sort of a trade-off."

His voice was noncommittal. "We'll see how it works out. But don't get your ass in a wringer, playing detective. You're not a cop."

The thought seemed to give him some satisfaction. He stood up. We exchanged telephone numbers and a wary handshake. Gubner did the same, belatedly. Then Sergeant Brooks led us away.

They took our statements in a pale green room with a metal lamp hung from the ceiling. Then the crew-cut cop drove us back to the Ritz. Gubner brooded out the window. I wasn't much better. My game with McGuire had turned into murder.

Giving the statement had made me feel more organized. But it didn't help with anything else. Lehman's chances had run out.

I figured Lasko had killed him. Nothing else made much sense. The question was how he had known to do it.

There were a couple of possibilities. I didn't like them at all.

TEN

Gubner and I got out at the Ritz and wandered aimlessly through the lobby. We passed the bar without looking in, both of us carrying the weight of unsaid things. I decided to get them out.

"Let's talk, Marty."

He gave me a resentful look, like a trapped animal. Then he nodded. "OK, my room. But not long."

We went to his room. I selected one of two matched blue chairs and turned on all the lights I could reach, to push away the police station. Gubner fell into his chair with a thick-bodied slump. He looked like a man who could use a drink. But this wasn't the kind of tough day you could ease away with gin. I felt sad and helpless.

"This is pretty worthless, Marty, but I'm sorry."

Condolences didn't interest him much, especially from me. The useless words hung in the air.

Gubner looked at the wall with an air of deliberate choice.

"OK, let's have it." The defensive sharpness in my voice surprised me. He turned on me with tired distaste.

"How did they know about the meeting?"

I wondered how he was so sure of the answer. "You can turn off your spotlight. I didn't tell anyone outside of my agency. Try Lehman or yourself."

"I didn't tell anyone," he said distinctly.

"That leaves Lehman." I said it with the hollow feeling that Gubner had an answer.

"I talked to Alec once. He called from a pay phone on the Mass. Turnpike. No tap possible. Sorry." His voice wasn't sorry at all.

I decided to play out the string. "What about meeting you? That could have looked strange."

Gubner's eyes flashed impatience. "I had lunch with Alec about seven, eight times a year. Almost every time I came to Boston. I was an old friend. Everyone knows that. And Alec swore he hadn't told anyone else about meeting you. Not Valerie. Not anyone."

I believed him. I could see Lehman cowering in a lonely phone booth before I could imagine him calling Gubner from his office. His sad afternoon apologia had the freshness of catharsis.

"Do you know anything more than what he told us?"

He shook his head. "Not about what he had on Lasko."

I got up. "I can't help you, Marty. But I may want to talk to you later—to get your help."

His eyebrows raised in bitter inquiry. "Why should I?"

"You'll have to answer that question yourself." I let myself out, went down to my room, flopped on the bed, and stared at the bare ceiling, trying to pull my scattered thoughts together. A slow, sick anger spread through me like nausea. Lasko, Catlow, and a friend of theirs paraded around in my stomach. The phone rang.

It was McGuire. I looked at my watch. 7:30.

"Chris. I was at the office late. How was your wild goose chase?" His voice sounded reedy through the bad connection.

"Not good."

"Cop out on you?"

"Not exactly. Someone ran him over."

Silence. "You're kidding me."

The anger rose and gripped my throat. "You want pictures? He's dead."

The phone conveyed reedy awe. "Jesus. What happened?"

"He got hit-skipped in front of the Ritz-Carlton. He didn't look like anything human."

"Who was it?"

"Alexander Lehman. Controller at Lasko Devices."

"That's awful." It was hard to tell how he felt. "What's being done?"

"The police are looking into it."

"Can you help them?"

"I've given them a statement."

"Did you find out anything?"

"No."

"What happened exactly?"

I told him. He was silent. "Well," he finally said, "there's nothing for you to do then except come home."

"I guess not."

"OK. Come see me as soon as you get in."

I hesitated. "I may take an extra day in case something comes up."

"Listen, it's a horrible thing. But don't fool around up there unless the police want you. We need you back here."

"I'll see you later, Joe." I slammed the phone down, and started thinking.

My thoughts began to mesh. McGuire had never called me out of town before. I remembered that he had let me meet Lehman after a sham argument. And there was the lunch with Catlow. Whatever I was going to do, I didn't have much time to do it. I jumped up and left the room.

Gubner was still in. He let me in, his dull stare

following me to the chair. I steeled myself. "I want you to take me to Lehman's place tomorrow."

Hostility changed to shock. "You're out of your mind." The stock phrase seemed to be all he could think to say.

"It's the only way. Lehman said he had a memo and I don't want anything to happen to it."

Gubner half-rose from his chair. "You fucking ghoul. You honestly think I'd let you bother Valerie and the kids after this?"

I stayed calm. "If I have to, I'll subpoena her to Washington."

His voice shook with disbelief. "I'll take you to court on it."

"Which will only upset her more."

He stood up. "You know, I hadn't realized what a prick you really are." He said it as if he had just turned over a rock and found me there, looking up.

"Save the bouquets. You've been sitting here sniping at me to indulge yourself. You've got a dead friend, and you won't help. I tell you, man, it's pathetic."

My words stung his eyes. "I don't give a shit about your investigation. Alec's dead. What else matters?"

"Is that your position on Buchenwald too, Marty?"

It was a raw remark. Gubner stood staring at his clenched fist. I got ready to dodge the punch which had been coiling all evening. But it never came. I figured I knew why. I spoke with a toughness I didn't quite feel. "There's something else, isn't there? Lehman got killed because you didn't bring him to Washington. Maybe you blew it." Gubner shot me a look of pained anger. I went on. "You figured that if his information was good, you'd threaten to have him take the Fifth unless we gave him immunity for testifying. That you'd have me come up here and then run back to McGuire, all excited. It might have worked. Except now we're out of luck, especially Lehman. And you're trying to push it all off on me. That's a chickenshit play, and I'm not going to play along. Try a psychiatrist."

Gubner's face collapsed in a tired, confused look. I chose a more even tone. "I'll apologize now, Marty. You can decide to or not, later on. I really don't care. But Lehman's death isn't your personal possession. And sitting on your ass is a crappy memorial."

Gubner had decided not to hit me. But my agency was in the way. He shook his head slowly.

I had to commit. "OK, you think someone at my place tipped Lasko. But there's no way you could ever find out. I'm going to try."

Gubner sat down as if someone had sucked the starch out of him. He sat, elbows on knees, with his head half-covered in his hands. Then he raised a blank, weary face. "I'll call Valerie in the morning. Whatever she wants. If she'll see you, OK. If she wants to fight you, I'll fight you. Either way."

"All right."

Gubner looked back at the wall. "Now take off, Chris. I don't want to see you again tonight."

I knew what he meant. I left without a word.

I paced my room restlessly, unnerved by the stillness, the sense of being alone. I had lawyer's nerves and instincts, for maneuvering and bluffing. But always within the rules. The rules made lawyers safe; they cut you off from the nasty parts of life. Such as murder. Lehman's mangled body had made me feel worthless and frightened.

I tried thinking. The first thing I thought was that I was afraid of dying, afraid that if I kept up someone would kill me. That didn't say much for me, but there it was. I tried thinking about someone else.

There was McGuire. He was in touch with Catlow. Feiner and Mary Carelli had known I was in Boston; only McGuire had known I was going to the Common. Perhaps he hadn't counted on murder. If he wanted to be a commissioner, that might be reason to call Catlow. And then Lasko would know where to look for Lehman.

Then there were Woods and Mary. And Woods was close to the White House. Which was close to Lasko. I would have to move carefully. Robinson wouldn't help me with that. No one would.

Finally, I thought about Lehman. I felt a belated, worthless sympathy for the man who had been. Perhaps he had been pathetic, but he had been alive, and trying. Then he had chosen to meet me. Not about a stock manipulation, but something else. And now he was dead.

It was down to that. Maybe if I hadn't seen it, or hadn't been using him, I could have walked away. But I had helped get him killed. So I would try to find the reason. I needed to.

The empty room around me was strange and hostile. I couldn't sleep.

ELEVEN

The next morning it rained, a bleak grey drizzle. I called room service for coffee, but skipped the paper. I didn't want to read about Lehman. The cold print would remind me of what I had seen without telling me what I didn't know.

I finished the coffee, showered, shaved, and packed. Everything I did seemed banal—rote skills learned in another life. I caught myself. The notion that Lehman's death had made me unique was insane, as indulgent as self-pity. I waited for Gubner.

He called about 12:30. Lehman's wife would see me. I felt relieved and unhappy at once. Barging in on new widows to riffle their husband's papers wasn't appetizing work. Just necessary. So I rented a car and met Gubner in front of the Ritz. It was 2:15.

Gubner was less than cheery. He exhausted his supply of chit-chat by giving me the address. I picked my way out of Boston toward Lehman's home.

Lehman had lived in a white frame two-story in an oak-lined neighborhood full of them. The affluent conformity spoke of executive good sense and sound property values. It seemed safe and very polite, right down to the green lawns, as flawless as astro-turf. Murder seemed as alien as crab grass. It jarred me that this insipid Valhalla was the pay-off for Lehman's little Faustian bargain. I wondered how his wife would find it now.

Gubner and I parked in the asphalt driveway and followed the walk which cut through Lehman's perfect lawn to the front door. Gubner paused glumly, then jabbed the doorbell. Lehman's wife answered. Gubner embraced her silently, then said a few soft words. I watched them. The hug was stiff, more reverential than personal, as if done in honor of Lehman. Gubner disengaged, his arms hanging awkwardly at his side. I sensed that his affection for Lehman did not extend to the wife. I stepped in.

"Mrs. Lehman," I said softly, "I'm Christopher Paget."

She turned. "Hello, Mr. Paget. I'm Valerie Lehman. Please come in." She extended her hand. Her eyes were hollow, but her hand was cool and dry, like the rest of her. Her neatly coiffed hair had gone silvery grey. She had a fox-pretty face, and her trim figure spoke through the silk blouse and tailored slacks of exercise and self-denial. She was so put together it was spooky. She could have been going to a bridge club.

"Mrs. Lehman, I'm sorry to be here and sorrier about your husband. Very sorry." I spoke slowly, hoping my words would sink in. I gave them time. "I appreciate your letting me come with Marty."

Her face had a curious blankness. "Thank you."

I forged on, feeling useless. "If I can do anything for you, I'll be happy to. Otherwise, I'll just stay out of your way."

I was hoping to disappear to wherever Lehman kept his files. But her mannequin calm had turned to tautness. "You want Alec's papers, Mr. Paget. Why?"

I picked my words. "Your husband was helping me with an investigation. Apparently he was aware of some things that concerned him."

Her brows knit at the word "concerned." "Alec never liked his job. He never liked this house." Her voice had an odd accusatory tone, as if their disputes had survived her husband.

I preferred not to pursue it. We stood in the hallway, looking into the living room at the fruits of installment credit. The Lehmans had decorated at some cost. In one corner was a roll-top desk, antique. The rugs were a quiet expensive beige. An off-white couch sat behind a rich mahogany coffee table. I peered past it into the dining room. Under the crystal chandelier stood an ornate carved dining table. Probably Italian, minimum three thousand dollars. Not my taste, but costly. Lehman's death gave it all a curious museum quality.

His wife had followed my inspection. Her low ashy voice carried abstract fury, anger at Lehman for his desertion. "This job saved Alec from being a failure. But I had to push him to take it, as if it were bad to be successful. He acted so resentful sometimes." There was a submerged question in her voice, as if she were vaguely aware that she had gone wrong somewhere. But she would never quite figure it out. And it wasn't my place to assist her.

"Perhaps if Marty could show me where your husband kept his things."

But she wasn't through yet. Her distracted mind skipped along the surface of things from one point to the next. Her eyes locked on me as if I were the answer to her confusion. "Was Alec killed, Mr. Paget? The police were so vague."

Real grief lit the bewilderment. Her moods were quicksilver; she hadn't decided how she really felt. After they buried him, the reality would hit her hard. I didn't want to make it worse.

I shook my head. "All I know is that he was hit by a car."

Gubner moved close to her. "I'll show Mr. Paget to Alec's study." He nodded at me.

"Thank you, Mrs. Lehman," I said. She stood,

looking confused, as if life had moved too quickly.
We left her there.

Gubner steered me through the hallway toward
the stairs. On the way, we passed the family room.
Two boys, about twelve and ten, were sitting with a
stout grey-haired woman. They were staring at a
color television, looking lost. I followed Gubner up
the stairs, feeling a little like a B-52 pilot brought
down to view his work. It was easier when you
looked from a distance. I told myself that I hadn't
asked Lasko to do whatever he'd done, or Lehman
to be weak. It didn't help.

Lehman's study was a footnote to affluence, hidden at the end of a long hallway which ran past the
bedrooms and bathrooms. Apparently it had not
been part of the family house and garden tour; it
was a compact cubicle, with a scratched maple
desk, one dingy green chair, and an old Royal typewriter. It was probably the most honest room in the
place. Gubner surveyed it silently, standing with his
hands shoved in his pockets.

"Show me his papers and you can go back
down," I said finally.

He gave me a sharp, reproachful look, as if I
were a grave robber. "Valerie says that they're all in
his desk drawers," he said in a flat tone. "Enjoy
yourself." He turned and left.

I switched on the metal lamp and eyed the drawers. There were four stacked on the left side and

one over the middle, where the chair fit. I didn't like it much. I was too late to save a life and too early to be a historian. So I felt like a Peeping Tom. I waited until the feeling was overrun by curiosity, then reached for the bottom left drawer and started.

It was a lot of junk. Stock prospectuses, financial statements, annual reports, and the like. Occasionally the task was brightened by an upbeat company bulletin, like the one on the annual management seminar weekend. Last year the boys had taken their wives to New Hampshire for three classes, two speeches by Lasko, a cocktail party, and a meeting of the wives' club. The trip was memorialized by an eight by ten glossy of the management team and their ladies, wearing the discomfited looks of sixth graders corralled for the class portrait. Lehman had the sheepish grin of the kid who had been caught smoking in the boys' room. She was looking great—good outfit and a bright picture smile. Their bodies leaned away from each other. Lasko was to their left, smiling broadly.

I checked the stuff carefully for markings and marginal notations. I didn't find any. It was the same with the three other left-hand drawers. The last paper in the top drawer was another company bulletin, announcing that Lehman was joining Lasko Devices. The article praised Lasko's drive to assemble a "permanent management team." Apparently Lehman's permanence had been revoked. I wondered how the writer would handle that little problem in the next bulletin. I jammed the drawer shut, frustrated.

The last chance was the middle drawer. I jerked it open. There was only one thing inside: a plain manila envelope, gummed shut. I grasped it with hasty, awkward fingers and ripped it open.

Inside was a handwritten note on a blank piece of paper. The writing was rough, strong, and somehow familiar. I made out the words "For A.L." in the upper right corner. The rest was scratched out in the middle: "95—Move whole package across the street—J859020. Justice is blind."

I figured "A.L." for Alexander Lehman. The rest was foolishly cryptic, a child's riddle. But it had probably meant something to Lehman—enough to kill him.

I stared at the writing. Then I reached into the left-hand drawers and pulled out an old annual report to stockholders. I turned through the glossy pages of bold print and colored pictures until I reached the one headed "Chairman's Page." It contained a three paragraph message of moral uplift, probably ghosted by Lasko's PR firm. Below it was a replica of Lasko's signature. I held the memo next to it. They looked the same. I combed the signature

for a unique letter. I hit on the curiously looped
"k." It matched the "k" in "package."

I put the annual report back in the drawer, and
the memo in its envelope. Then I slid the memo
into my attaché case. I rose and left the room, closing the door after me. It felt as if I had just shut the
door on Lehman's life.

Valerie Lehman was perched on the couch, talking to Gubner. They both seemed uncomfortable,
like actors at a first rehearsal. Her role of grieving
widow was undercut by her fear that she might
have to play it in rags. Her eyes moved around the
living room, from piece to piece. Gubner's support-
ive old friend part hung on him like a bad suit. I
guessed that he had disliked her for years and now
was trying to hide it from himself. The rain seemed
reflected in the room's gloomy pall. I stepped in.

"Mrs. Lehman, pardon me for interrupting." She
peered up with pretty blankness. Guber seemed almost glad.

"What is it?" he interjected.

I spoke to her. "I'm almost through and I'll be
gone. I just need to talk to Marty for a second."

She hesitated, head half-cocked, as if awaiting
the English translation. The shock was showing in
her reaction time. "Marty would like a martini,"
she said with bright irrelevance.

That called for a response, I guessed. "No thank
you, Mrs. Lehman. I appreciate your kindness." I

wanted to say something more but nothing came out. Gubner rose and steered me into the hallway. I glanced back. She was staring around the living room, at nothing at all.

"Did you find anything?" Gubner asked.

"Nothing sensational," I hedged. Gubner seemed too distracted to press it. "Are you staying or going?" I asked.

Gubner's face was sober. "Staying. This is going to get worse."

"I think so too."

"About talking, Chris—I think I'll take a pass on your company for a week or two."

I could see it. "Fair enough, Marty. See you around."

I let myself out. Then I got in the car and drove to the airport, through the rain, away from the white houses and the perfect lawns.

It was evening when I got there. I was tired. I checked in mechanically, thinking about everything and nothing. Then I went to a phone. I thought about calling the office, then didn't. I had started to absorb the bleak idea that talking to the office was worse than useless.

Instead, I called Di Pietro. His voice on the phone was all parsimony. The cops had found the Cadillac abandoned on a side street off Commonwealth, with a little bit of Lehman on it. It had been stolen from a shopping center and the license plate switched. No fingerprints. I suggested that meant it had been swiped to kill Lehman, then be untraceable. Di Pietro countered that maybe some punk had stolen the car and couldn't afford to stop. He said it in less time than that. It was as if each sentence was being docked from his pay, at five bucks a word. I thanked him a lot and hung up.

I boarded the plane. I was in the taxi home before I remembered that I'd never paid the Ritz for my martini.

The taxi stopped at my place. I got out, still holding the memo that had killed Lehman.

TWELVE

I walked slowly through the hallway to my door, dragging my suitcase. I put the key in, turned it, and pushed. I started to step inside. Then I froze in the doorway. A light was on, casting dim shadows on the wall. Someone was waiting.

Mary stood by the bookshelf, very still. "I heard about Alexander Lehman," she said simply. "I'm sorry."

Somehow I was angry. "So is Lehman's wife. How did you get in?" My voice belonged to someone else. It was dry and scratchy. I realized how scared I had been.

"The manager gave me a key."

We both waited for the other to speak. She looked at me directly, not stirring. I wanted her to move.

She stepped away from the books, and snapped the spell.

"I shouldn't have come."

"It's OK." I paused. "Would you like a drink?"

"Are you?" I nodded. "Yes," she said. "Thank you. Scotch."

I pulled a bottle of Scotch from under the bookshelf and went to the kitchen, suddenly glad to be doing something mundane.

"How did you hear about Lehman?" I asked over my shoulder.

"McGuire. He said it was pretty gruesome."

"Gruesome" seemed arch, like "untidy." "That's a way of putting it. 'Sickening' is another." I wanted to shake her; the man was dead.

I splashed ice in the drinks, suddenly alienated by the illusion of routine: " 'And how was your trip, darling?' 'Oh, fine, dear, but poor Alec got squashed by a car.' 'Too bad, I liked Alec. But fine otherwise?' " Something about the scene was out of sync, like roses at an execution. I half-shook my head, as if trying to throw off a tangible strangeness.

I left the kitchen and returned to reality. She was sitting on the living room couch. Her shoulders were turned in and knees together, as if hunched against the cold. I handed her the drink. She clasped it against her lap with both hands and stared into it. I sat down.

"What did you do?" She looked up from her drink.

"I threw up."

"Do you care to talk about it?"

"No." She looked hurt. I tried to explain. "Look, yesterday I was sitting with Lehman. He was scared and sick of himself. But he was alive, trying to get something back. When it happened, I was sipping on a martini, stroking my self-esteem. Then there was Lehman, flying through the air. When I got to him, he looked like something people feed to their dogs." Her fingers squeezed the glass. I rummaged for the words. "It's not just the finality. It's that it's so arbitrary." It was a meaningless word. I gave up.

"You think he was murdered?"

"I think he was murdered."

"By whom?"

"Lasko." And someone else.

"Did you find out anything about Lasko?"

"No. Lehman was killed before he told me anything." My attaché case sat against the couch, a mute reproach.

"What are you going to do?"

"I don't know."

In the light her face was softer. She grazed my knee with her hand, then rested it there. I looked at the hand, then her.

"You look tired," she said. It was a fill-in, as though words would hide her hand.

I pushed Lehman aside. "Did you mean what am I going to do about Lehman, or about you, here?"

"I don't know," she said quietly. Her eyes were wide and watchful. I saw Lehman swimming through them in slow motion. I wanted him to leave. Lightly, I pulled her to me and kissed her once, gently. When she was undressed, I held her for a long time. Then we began to make love.

Afterwards we slept. My sleep was jagged, with strobe light dreams. They were fragments of madness, unbounded by time or place. I kept introducing Mary to Alexander Lehman. My childhood friends came, and we all put on masks and played hide-and-seek. Then Lehman lay in a funny heap. I woke up sweating, to a sudden, angry noise I couldn't place.

I started and bolted upright, fully awake now and stiff with alarm. My head cleared. The telephone. I hit the lamp switch and squinted at my watch. Four o'clock. It rang again. I answered it.

"Do you know what the hell time it is?" I snapped at the receiver.

No answer. I tried again, calmer. "Who is this?"

Silence. I thought about hanging up. But instinct kept me on.

The voice was very quiet. "You like getting laid, Mr. Paget?"

It didn't sound like an academic question. My fingers tightened around the telephone.

"She looks like she'd be good. I hope you can do it again." It was a tone totally without emphasis, as if I had dialed a recorded message. Somehow that made it worse.

I finally tried my voice. "I suppose there's a point to this." I already knew half the point; someone was watching my apartment.

"Leave the Lehman family alone, Paget. Otherwise you might spoil your looks." The voice paused. "Maybe you'd like to look like Lehman."

I waited for more. There wasn't any. I had the strange sense of a hand slowly, carefully placing down a receiver. The phone clicked dead. I was still holding it to my ear when the dial tone began.

Mary was stirring drowsily on her side, black hair half-falling across her face. She flicked it away with her fingers, eyes still closed. "What was that?" she murmured.

"Wrong number."

She reached absently for my shoulder, then fell back to sleep. I looked at her a moment, then flipped the switch.

There were no more callers. I lay back on the bed and wondered how long I would be sleeping with Lehman's corpse.

In the morning I found her in the kitchen, scrambling eggs. She was wearing a borrowed white dress shirt which turned suddenly into long legs. I watched her, then took my thoughts to a window.

Mary leaned out the kitchen nook. "Is this what they call post-coital *tristesse*?"

"Hardly that."

She looked faintly pleased, an almost imperceptible smile. "You know, you're not much like Frank." She turned back to her eggs. "In bed or out."

"Is that good?"

She smiled quickly back over her shoulder. "Very."

Our breakfast was quiet. We sat at the round white table under the last living room window. Squares of sunlight hit the table and warmed her face. I tried concentrating on that. She looked fresh and good to touch, black hair falling around the collar of the borrowed white shirt. We talked about small things. It had changed between us. But we pretended for a while that the change hadn't happened. It didn't quite work. It never does.

We talked softly. She learned where I was from and what I had done in college. I was content with that. But Mary leaned on the table, shirtsleeves carefully rolled back from the slim wrists, looking for more in me. I didn't have more to give, right then. I was tired, and the scene raised faint ironic echoes of other mornings in another place. I kept hearing the voice on the telephone. And Alexander Lehman was dead.

The last thought crept over me like paralysis. She asked me what it was. I looked at the sun squares on the table. "A lot of things. That Lehman is dead. That I'm alive. And that because of these things, the sunlight looks brighter, as if I hadn't really looked at it in a while."

Her eyes consumed me in a deep-black gaze. "You can't bring Lehman back to life."

"Ashes to ashes and all that?" I asked.

"Please don't do that with me, Chris. You know what I meant."

I wasn't at all sure. But I was glad to let it go. I analyzed the sun squares some more. I could feel her on the other side of the table, edgy under the cool. The silence swelled.

"Have you ever really cared for anyone?" Her voice was quiet, but the words came with the suddenness of a champagne cork bursting under pressure.

I was caught with my brains on vacation. "Yes. Once. In prep school, for a sheep. Runs in the family. I can still recall running my hands through her wool. My parents found out and transferred me to military school. When I came back at Thanksgiving, all that was left were three lamb chops and a wool sweater. I carried it for years . . ."

I stopped myself, unhappily. Her face had closed against me. I broke in through a silent impasse. "OK, that was tacky. I'm sorry."

It didn't salvage me. She was angry. "Are you always so flip?"

"I'm not flip. I just don't go in for indecent exposure. And this morning is wrong for 'This Is My Life.'"

She tilted stiffly back in her chair, arms folded. "Why does my asking throw you off so much?"

"You don't give up, do you?"

"Just what is wrong with you? You play it cagey about your Boston trip. You can't talk about anything personal, anything that gets close to you."

"I'll bet you were a psych major in college. Anyhow, my mother loved me."

"It's not contagious."

I was about to lose her again. There were reasons that I didn't need that. I reached for her arm. It felt rigid under my fingers. But she didn't move it. "Mary, there are certain things that are personal to me. I live better that way. Maybe that makes me unfit company. It isn't intended to." I gathered my thoughts. "Some things I can't cheapen by making them seminar subjects."

"Is that what I'm asking?" Her voice was shaded by the night before, but crossed with self-control. The question came out intense and uninflected, at once.

I made patterns in the sun squares with my free hand, and thought some unhappy thoughts. She watched me and waited. Finally, I contrived an abridged version. "In Boston, four years ago, I lived with a woman. I wanted to keep her." I felt somehow that it was slipping from me. Keeping her to myself had pushed away the finality, as if I still had her. "I knew too much about what I wanted and not enough about what she needed. What I should have understood, I saw as things she did to me." My patterns in the sun had quickened. "It ended badly, in a fight where nothing we said was quite true or quite fair. I invited her to leave. She took me up on it." Mary's arm had turned under mine, her fingers touching me. I finished it. "If we ever get to the point where we really need to get into this, perhaps I will. But we're not there yet."

"What happened to her?" she asked in a subdued voice.

"The other guy was smarter, and more patient. So now she's a psychiatrist's wife in Boston. I never see her."

"Is that why you came to Washington?" Her eyes had softened into curiosity.

I shrugged. "Not necessarily. I had a lot of reasons."

Mary looked down at the table. She finally spoke. "I'm sorry, Chris. Perhaps I've acted badly this morning—under the circumstances."

She sounded as if she weren't sure. But then it was a new situation. I thought. For her and for me. And she didn't know all of it.

Her fingers held my arm now. I stopped drawing

my squares and circles. I reached and pulled her up, suddenly wanting to cheat the voice on the phone. My white shirt fell in the corner. Her hair lay on her shoulders, where the collar had touched. The sun made her skin rich olive. It looked warm.

THIRTEEN

McGuire sat staring at Capitol Hill, where new commissioners were confirmed. His fingers were rubbing the armrest and his feet inched the chair back and forth on its rollers. I wondered if he ever sat still.

He looked up at me. "Sit down, Chris." I pulled up a chair while he tried on his rubbery smile. It looked sick, like a minister's smile at a big contributor's dirty joke.

"You're late this morning," he started, then fished for some banter to match his smile. "You out getting laid or something?"

"That's very droll. Particularly under the circumstances."

"You can't lose your sense of humor."

That would be a shame, I thought. "Why don't you call the Lehman household, Joe. They're starving for a joke."

"Look, I'm as sick about this Lehman thing as

you are." He waited. I didn't answer. "Did you find out anything in Boston?"

"Not really."

"Then where the hell were you yesterday?"

"Out getting laid."

His smile evaporated. "Don't bullshit around. Where were you?"

"I was at Lehman's house."

The chair stopped moving. "I didn't say you could do that. What were you doing there?" His voice quickened into staccato.

"I was hoping to find something."

"The day after the guy was killed?" McGuire sounded both appalled and intrigued.

"That's right."

"Christ, do you realize how we look? One of our guys bothering people after the husband gets killed. That's just awful." His mind shifted. "Find anything?"

So much for compassion. I wondered who else wanted to know. The attaché case sat at my feet, the memo still in it. "Nothing much. Old financial statements, junk like that."

His eyebrows converged anxiously. "Are you sure?"

Something was wrong. "Did something happen here that I should know?"

The question brought on his cheerless smile.

"You're meeting with William Lasko this afternoon. At 3:30."

Lasko again. The news hit my stomach like an indigestible lump. I didn't trust myself to say anything. So I tried to stare out an explanation. His frozen smile was a ghastly rictus of embarrassment.

"Lasko's attorney called this morning and asked for a meeting." He paused. "A Mr. Catlow," he added vaguely.

The last was very cute. I figured McGuire must have almost forgotten Catlow's name, since Monday. I wanted to remind him, then knock out his teeth. But I didn't. I waited for more.

He gave it in a reluctant voice, as if the words were extracted by my silence. "Lasko thinks this case clouds his reputation. He's asked for a meeting to answer any questions we may have."

That was straightforward enough. But something in McGuire's voice tipped me.

"Do you have a stenographer to take it all down?"

That was it. McGuire shook his head at the floor, not facing me. "No. This is just an informal meeting." He tried to say it casually, as if this were our standard routine.

I wanted to do something. Anything but sit. But I sat, and let the anger simmer. When I spoke it came out dry and precise. "I don't need to tell you that this meeting is worse than worthless, do I, Joe? I mean, you do know that?" He stared back at me, looking both trapped and outraged. I went on. "With no transcript, we'll never prove perjury. He'll lie to us anytime it suits him."

"He's the President's friend. Remember that. And he's coming to us voluntarily."

"Little wonder. You know damned well why he's coming. In return for lies that will never hurt him, he'll find out exactly what I know. He'll listen to the questions. If I ask him about Sam Green, he'll find out about that. If he's tied with Green somehow, he'll get to Green before we do. If I know something from Lehman, my questions will tell him that. If he lies to me about fact 'X' and I can't follow it up, he can figure I don't know about fact 'X.' That's the way it works. Maybe I should just start reporting to Lasko direct."

"The man has influence, damn it. And you don't have a fucking thing on him."

"I think Lasko had Lehman killed."

His eyes flashed. "Look, I don't want you talking that kind of irresponsible garbage." He spoke with the emphatic contempt of a drill sergeant. "I've put up with your shit around here, for the time being. But you start smearing anyone else and you're out on your ass." His voice held a sort of submerged dread beneath the anger, as though silence would make murder less real.

So I said it again, very slowly. "I think Lasko killed Lehman."

He flushed. "Say that outside this office and you're fired."

"Does that include to the Boston police?"

"Especially the Boston police."

I stood up, not trusting myself to continue. "Is that all?"

His voice rose in anger. "No, it isn't. You horsed around at Lehman's house without authority. You've gone over my head on the Lasko subpoena. Now you've appointed yourself a detective. If you think Woods is going to keep covering your ass, forget it. When I fire you, I'll have all the reason in the world. And no law firm will hire you to run coffee."

I was almost out in the open, I thought. I balled my fists in my pockets to steady myself. "I wouldn't fire me just yet, Joe. It would stink too much." Our eyes locked. "Are we through now?" I asked.

McGuire's gaze broke. He nodded, his eyes angled away from me. An uneasy mix of anger and chagrin haunted the gesture. Against the bare wall, he looked as solitary as the last tenant in a condemned building.

I picked up my case and walked to the door. I opened it, then leaned back. "By the way, Joe, have you started making funny phone calls?"

I was looking for recognition in his eyes. All I got

was anger—and puzzlement. I slammed the door and left.

Suppressed rage overcame me. I moved half-blind through the corridors, back to my section. It was still there, the clatter and greyness, as if nothing had changed. A mail boy delivered a stack of memos and the agency newsletter. Three of the secretaries sat at Debbie's desk, talking and stirring their coffee with the serene complacency of civil servants. It was a big day. One of them had won the ECC bowling championship.

I looked around the fringe of offices, feeling like a visitor from Botswana. Feiner stared out of his office, saw me, and looked away. A strange face brushed by me, attached to a flying shirttail. They had hired someone new. I went toward my office.

Debbie glanced up and followed me inside the office. She just looked at me for a while. "Are you all right?" she finally asked.

"I guess."

Her eyes were still and serious. "I'm sorry about your witness," she said simply.

Somehow, it was the most normal reaction I'd seen in three days. Then it struck me that Mary had said much the same thing. I tried to puzzle out the difference. I couldn't. "Thanks," I finally said.

She nodded. "If you'd like to talk—" The sentence drifted off, as if to tell me it was optional. I told her I'd do that, and ran out of things to say.

She went back to her desk, closing the door behind her.

I threw my attaché case on the desk and sat down. I was still staring at the case when Robinson knocked on the door. His face was keen and sympathetic. "What happened, for Christsakes?"

He sat down while I told him—about everything but the memo. It helped, getting it out. But the memo stuck in my throat. So, somehow, did the phone call. Perhaps in daylight it seemed childish. Anyhow, I held it back.

Robinson was weighing it all. "So you think Lasko killed Lehman?" he asked.

"Yeah."

He nodded. "It makes some sense."

The grimness of the thing filled the room, as if Robinson had confirmed Lehman's death. Robinson felt it too. He fished awkwardly for something to divert me. "You know," he said finally, "there's only so much you can do by yourself."

"How do you mean?"

He leaned back with the air of a man telling a parable. "A few years ago, I had a secretary who'd always fall asleep at her typewriter with her nose running. One day I took a good look at her. Needle tracks all over. So I tried to have her canned. She found out and filed a complaint with the Equal Opportunity Employment counselor, claiming I was a racist."

"What happened?"

"I got my ass chewed out by personnel, and had a talk with some pompous shit about my latent racism. The upshot was that I was ordered to have weekly counseling sessions with my secretary, to help her along. They lasted three weeks. The fourth week I couldn't take it any more. I recommended her for a promotion. She's now supervising a typing pool of thirty secretaries, between naps."

I shook my head. "The point is," he added, "that it goes with the territory."

The story seemed to have some vague but depressing relation to my work, perhaps even to Lehman. Robinson's acceptance bothered me. I tried to think of something constructive.

"The Boston office served the subpoena for Lasko's financial stuff on Wednesday. Think you can get them to air express those down today?"

"Some of them."

"Let's look at them this weekend. There has to be something else going on that ties in with all this."

"I'll do it," he said crisply. "Anything else?"

My mind was still on the memo. "You do know we're meeting with Lasko at 3:30?"

His eyes looked puzzled through the thick glasses. "So I hear. I can't say I like the rules."

"It wasn't my idea, Jim."

He nodded. "I had guessed that. Did you talk with McGuire?"

"We had words about it," I said dryly. "I had my second almost-firing this week."

Robinson's bemused look returned and focused on his fingernails. "Ever wonder why he doesn't can you?"

"Yep. My answer is that it's too much trouble to boot me in the middle of this."

"Then the question you should ask is why he put you on this one in the first place. Anyone else would have been less trouble."

It was as if he had sniffed out my suspicions and was conducting a veiled debate. With me and with himself. I wanted to tell him about McGuire and Lasko's lawyer. And about the memo. But that would put Robinson in the middle, between McGuire and me. He didn't want to be there.

"I'll think on it, Jim. And I appreciate your help." I felt as if I were closing out his friendship, selling him short. But he didn't need my problems, and I couldn't make him hold out on McGuire. I let him go.

I got up and closed the door after him. Then I pulled the manila envelope out of the attaché case. Lehman's memo. I fingered it, wondering if the absurd scrawling could somehow kill me too. I stared for a long time. Then I opened up my desk drawer and looked in. The bottom of the drawer was two layers of metal. I took my letter opener, jammed it between the layers at the front of the drawer and pried. It lifted minutely, making a crack between the two layers. I pulled it back out, and took the memo out of the envelope. I copied the cryptic words on a note pad, ripped it off, and stuffed it in my wallet. I replaced the memo in its envelope. Then I re-pried the layers with the opener. I took the envelope in my left hand and tried to slide it between the layers. It fit. I slowly shoved it all the way in.

I thought for a while. It was a turning point, I knew. I could hide it, or give it up and try to walk away. But I had probably come too far the first time I read it. I closed the drawer and locked it.

I leaned back in my chair and waited for William Lasko.

FOURTEEN

I picked up Robinson about 3:20 and went to the conference room. It was done in bargain chic: a cheap wooden table and Swedish modern chairs, covered in yellow, maximum life three years. There were glass windows on two sides, covered by cheap orange burlap curtains. A green plastic schefflera, in a pot, completed the room.

We sat in the disposable chairs, joking uneasily about the decor and waiting because Lasko had the suck to make us wait and knew it. Robinson's bemused look had turned glum. My defensiveness was mixed with fear; I thought I was meeting Lehman's murderer, the man behind the quiet voice on my telephone, the author of the memo hidden in my desk. It was a new experience. I gazed absently at the curtain, trying to rehearse my plan.

I looked at my watch. It was 3:40. Lasko was making a point. It was effective. Each second measured itself out, separately. Robinson's forefinger made invisible grooves on his notepad. I caught myself tapping the table with my pen, Gene Krupa style.

The phone rang. The downstairs guard told me that Lasko had arrived, with his lawyer. I said to send them up to the conference room, third floor. We waited. Then the door cracked open.

Lasko's pictures hadn't prepared me. He filled the doorway, at least six-four, two-thirty, and giving a sudden impact of darkness and controlled force. He entered and strode around the conference table, smiling broadly, with the air of a man securing a beachhead. He got close, where he could look down at me, and administered a bone-crunching hand-shake.

"I'm William Lasko." His eyes riveted mine, gauging my reaction.

I tried not to have any. "How are you, Mr. Lasko. I'm Christopher Paget."

He stared a second longer, then turned to Robinson, repeating the ritual. He had a Southwestern look: high color, fleshy face, and black eyes, hard and intelligent. I gestured at the table. Lasko appropriated a chair with a decisive grasp and sat down. He had a kind of self-conscious presence, as if he were watching himself in the mirror, approvingly. It was oddly impressive. I felt puny, aware of my unimportance.

It was then that I noticed Catlow. He was standing in the background, the perfect self-effacing counselor. The contrast with Lasko was striking, Catlow was slight, sandy-haired, and sallow as a Dead Sea scroll. He introduced himself in a dry, thin voice and parceled out a fleeting handshake. His liveliest feature was the sharp, careful grey eyes. Unobtrusiveness was Catlow's business. I looked back at Lasko. He was black-haired, with a blunt nose and a thick full mouth. Obscurity wouldn't suit him.

We all sat, Robinson to my right, the other two to my left. Lasko leaned over the table, as if it were something he had bought. They stared at me, waiting as I considered how to start.

The phone rang. I picked it up. An overseas operator rasped at me, asking for Lasko. I handed it to him. His baritone voice was rich with satisfaction. "I've got some acquisitions in the fire. I can't get away—people always needing to talk." He spoke into the phone. "Leo. Where are you? Japan? What the hell time is it over there? Yes, I'm with the ECC. What's up?" Lasko was conducting both sides of the conversation, for my benefit. I wondered how poor Leo liked getting up at midnight to call the boss.

Lasko kept talking to Leo, watching me. I watched back to keep him happy. "Yeah, OK. Thirty-five a ton? That's a holdup." His eyes followed me jealously, demanding my attention. "Lis-

ten, Leo, that's bullshit. You ask that Jap where else
he's going to get coal like that for his crappy little
island. Then take a walk. In two weeks he'll be
crawling." I got the message: Lasko was a very important man. That was his way of relating to people. What was important was to be important.
Lasko needed importance like a junkie needs
smack. And Lehman had somehow threatened the
supply.

Lasko finally rang off. I looked at him, waiting
him out. He finally spoke. "Well, Mr. Paget, what's
on your mind?" His voice had a pushy heartiness,
to prod me back in line. Catlow sat, hands on the
table, completely still.

I answered politely. "I was thinking, Mr. Lasko,
that you might throw out some suggestions as to
what we can accomplish here."

Lasko answered smoothly. "All right. I think we
should let our hair down. I'm being practical. Your
investigation is bad for my company." He spread
his hands in a gesture of openness. "Ask me anything you want. I'll answer all your questions until
you're satisfied that you've got absolutely nothing
to worry about." The amiable words were surface
amenities; the speech was imperious. Lasko figured
he owned me, like Lehman. His contempt was as
palpable as the August heat.

I made myself smile. "I appreciate that." I fished

around for what was strange in the meeting. Then it hit me. No one had mentioned Alex Lehman.

I spoke diffidently. "Ready to go?"

Lasko smiled back, opening his hands again. "Ready."

I spoke very slowly. "Did you kill Alexander Lehman?"

Each word dropped like a stone. Catlow's eyes widened, almost imperceptibly. His right hand fluttered. The smile lingered on Lasko's face a second after his brain tried to erase it. Then his features set in a cast as primitive as I had ever seen, the primal face of a predator. It was my answer. His formal response was an anticlimax, delivered in a monotone selected to be meaningless.

"No."

"That's a relief." I turned to Robinson. "Do you have anything else for Mr. Lasko?"

Robinson stared at me, then shook his head solemnly.

Catlow cut in. The strain showed in his parched voice. "Surely you must have more questions. Mr. Lasko has made himself available, at considerable trouble, in the middle of three acquisitions. You should do a better job than this."

McGuire just couldn't get good help anymore. I waved Catlow's words away and turned to Lasko. "Consider yourself cleared, Mr. Lasko. Can I see you out?"

Lasko's baritone carried an icy tremor. "Mr. Paget, you're making a serious mistake." Condescension cut him to where he lived, pushed him to ultimates. His face said the rest—that I was making Lehman's mistake.

I couldn't let Lasko see my chill. I spoke quietly. "You're a taxpayer. Write your Congressman. You and I are through—for now."

Catlow touched Lasko's sleeve. "Wait for me downstairs, Bill. Mr. Paget and I are going to talk." Lasko didn't answer. Catlow went on in the same calm tone. "This"—he nodded at me as if I were the potted plant—"is why I'm your lawyer." Lasko was still staring at me. The atmosphere was as murderous as fallout. Then Lasko wrenched out of his chair, raked me with a last hot glance, and stalked from the room. The man's strange force lingered; the room seemed suddenly empty.

Catlow remained where he sat, eyeing us coolly across the table. He turned to Robinson. "Would you excuse us? Mr. Paget and I need some discussion time."

Robinson glanced at me. I nodded. He left, looking dubious.

Catlow and I were alone. "You'll have to excuse my client," he said.

"Pretty broken up about Lehman, isn't he?"

Catlow lit a cigarette, an appropriately cautious low-tar brand, and reached for an ashtray. His movements were spare and abstemious. He looked up. "I imagine that you're feeling quite heroic. Every young government lawyer probably dreams of his moment in the sun. 'Young Mr. Paget, valiant for truth.'" He exhaled smoke, and appraised me through the haze.

He was quietly patronizing, but his words were close enough to be comfortable. "Something like that."

He gave a thin, satisfied smile. "It's very foolish, Christopher. This case will come and go and in a year will be nothing more than a footnote in a budget request, gathering dust. Even if there is a case, it will settle for a consent decree, and nothing will have happened. Except to you." He looked at me with level grey eyes, choosing his words with care. "Putting aside what was said here this afternoon, the consequences to you could be considerable. You will make enemies needlessly. You will be an undesirable, not because you've made people angry, but because you've made people angry in a way that reflects on your judgment—over nothing."

His calm was oddly deflating. "Go on. I'm all ears."

"There was also careless talk this afternoon— your careless talk—about matters which are not the province of your agency. The police have made no accusations. You have no one who, in the final analysis, will support you in this game." His voice was mournful now, the dirge for my dead career. "You're all alone. So there is nothing to be gained. Think on it."

He was watching me expectantly. I noticed that a blood vein showed in his pale forehead. I watched him inhale. It made him look gaunt, like a death's head. He was Mr. Outside to Lasko's Mr. Inside. Catlow would take care of my career and handle the agency while Lasko commissioned the heavy stuff— traffic fatalities and death threats—at a safe distance. It was all very effective. And I was sick of it.

"It's a good analysis, Mr. Catlow. But you've made one invalid assumption. You assume that I want to be like you. The truth is, I'd sooner flunk my Wassermann test. That's not heroics. It's just a fact." My voice picked up tenor. "Now I'll give you some advice. Your client's performance today was one of the uglier things I've seen. But not as ugly as Alec Lehman, bleeding all over Arlington Street." The vein in Catlow's forehead was throbbing now; it made him seem as pale as ivory. I finished. "Lasko is a tar baby. You're going to get tar all over you."

Catlow stared for a moment; I wasn't behaving right, not at all. Then he stood briskly, primed to leave. No final threats. Catlow was not a man to waste words; he would use them elsewhere. "Goodbye, Mr. Paget." The good-bye carried echoes, as if I were going somewhere.

My voice stopped him. I spoke in a conversational tone. "You know, when I got to Lehman, his face was smashed in and his skull was crushed. One eye was closed and there was a sticky pool of stuff on the outside of his head that used to be on the inside."

The vein pulsed; his eyes were knife-points of anger. I had spoken crudely, not like a lawyer, of forbidden things. Things that formal language made less real. He left quickly.

I slumped down in my chair. The party was over, and I was left to clean up the mess. I felt more tired than I could remember.

FIFTEEN

Robinson was fidgeting with the contents of his "in" box when I walked into his office. It was something he did when he was excited and wanted distraction.

"What happened?" he asked. His eyes were bright with curiosity.

I slid tiredly into the chair in front of his desk. "Your guess, Jim." I said it in a casual tone, to assure him that he hadn't missed anything.

Robinson smiled faintly. "I think I can give you a synopsis. Big Daddy told you that you had been bad, and would be punished. Exiled to the Bureau of Fisheries and Hatcheries, to think about proper spawning conditions for salmon." His tone said that he half-expected it to happen.

"That's fairly close." I was coming down fast; my voice seemed to arrive at my ears from great distance.

"And you told him to stick it."

135

I nodded.

Robinson's face sobered. "That was a pretty amazing performance. The first time I've actually seen you do something stupid."

"You just haven't been looking. How do you read Lasko?"

"I think Lasko wanted you to know that he killed Lehman. He wanted you to get the sweats at night, thinking about it. And Catlow will be trying to put the fix in."

"I don't think I'm the next pedestrian fatality. Too messy, and unnecessary. I don't know anything." I spoke with more conviction than I felt.

"Lasko can't be sure of that. Let me tell you what I think." His voice turned firm and authoritative. "Even granting your assumption, you don't have long on this case. About once every five years, we get into something that stands to hurt someone really powerful. It usually works out about the same. There are ways of pressuring this place through the people who run it, the ones who want to get what politicians or maybe someone with money can give. This is that kind of case, and you're in the middle. But this one is worse—somebody's gotten killed."

"So what would you do?"

Robinson looked down at his desk. "I'd leave it alone." He spoke quickly, as if anticipating an argument. "Look, I'm not defending any of this. But I think this place does some good, and it's not a perfect world. Realistically, your chances of getting anywhere with this—except hurt—are about zero. Let the police do it."

I shook my head. "It's too late for that."

"Damn it, Chris, it's too late for this. It's too late for Lehman."

"Lehman's death wasn't where it ended. It was where it began."

He paused, as if weighing the finality in my voice. "All right," he said at length, "if Lehman makes this one worth the risk, OK, although I can't see why. But you need another friend to help— Woods, McGuire, I don't care who. Otherwise, you won't have authority to spit. Catlow will cut your nuts off. If Lasko doesn't do worse."

I shifted in my chair. "I guess it has to be Woods."

"Whoever, Chris, you'd better get on it. And no more going off on a tangent, investigating your own agency."

I stood. Robinson's round worried face belied his sharp tone. "Good luck," he added mildly. "You've always shown a genius for making friends in high places."

I left and went looking for Woods.

The tranquility of the Chairman's suite was unnerving. Up here, my meeting with Lasko seemed unreal. I asked the receptionist for Woods, and

sank to a soft chair. Woods was out. But Mary was
in. She peered around her office door.

"Good afternoon, Chris." She didn't smile, but
the words carried a faint, wry allusion to the morning. The receptionist sensed it somehow, and
squinted, as if she were picking up distant signals
on a crystal set. It would have all been very funny,
some other day.

"Are you free?" I asked.

"Yes," she said crisply. "Come in."

I sat across from her. Her navy silk blouse made
her tan rich brown. Her hair was pulled back.

She saw my eyes and smiled pointedly. "I didn't
have time to wash my hair this morning."

I grinned. "It looks fine." But I had to get to it.
"I've got a problem for Chairman Woods."

"What is it?" Her wispy smile vanished.

"McGuire set up a meeting this afternoon between me, Lasko, and his lawyer, a man named
Robert Catlow. No stenographer. Lasko wanted to
pick my brains. I wouldn't play. It's fair to say that
I did not leave them laughing."

Her face went glacial; right then, we could have
fooled the receptionist, or anyone else. "Why didn't
you tell us before the meeting?"

Because I'd rather do it myself, I thought. "I
don't know."

"And now you want Jack Woods to clean up after
you."

"I want his help." I hesitated. "And yours."

Her voice was cool and distant. "Just how much help do you expect, Chris? You're not a day ahead of me anymore. I've caught up." Not quite. I remembered the dead man's memo, hidden in my desk drawer. "You used me to backdoor McGuire on the Lasko subpoena. You didn't tell us that you were going to meet a witness. You tried not to tell me that you were going to Boston at all." Her recitation was dispassionate, as if she were introducing exhibits. "You've been acting as if you were an independent contractor."

"I do better on my own," I said.

She looked at me as if to learn where my words began and ended. "So far, you've done brilliantly. You've got no facts and a dead witness. All that you've managed is to make trouble for your own commission."

"Nobody's perfect."

A thin line of annoyance furrowed her forehead. "You had better decide who you work for, Chris."

I told myself that I had done as well as I could. I had taken five days' free ride: sneaked out the second subpoena, gotten to Lehman's memo, and sent Lasko away with nothing. "When can I talk to Woods?"

"He'll be in Monday morning."

"OK, I'd like to see him at nine."

She inspected me evenly. "Don't expect applause."

I stood, suddenly angry. "Look, the last three days I've seen someone killed, been threatened by a pig and his tight-assed lawyer, and been screwed by my own boss. So I don't give a shit what you think."

Her eyes widened. I looked back, knowing how little of that had been meant for her, and realizing that I could still feel her. I felt schizoid. Some other day, I'd have taken her home. Instead, I turned and left.

It was five o'clock. From my window I could see the street in front of the building. It suddenly teemed with cars and bodies. As if on cue, an army of civil servants scrambled out the doors and into the streets. I turned away and glanced at my desk. Someone had thoughtfully clipped an article on Lehman from the *Boston Globe*. The cops were still calling it a hit-skip. I picked up the phone and called Greenfeld.

SIXTEEN

Greenfeld was already at the Madison when I arrived, sitting at a table near the bar. He saw me and grinned. "You look like hell, Chris," he said in greeting.

I sat down. "That's funny, I feel terrific. After I leave here I'm planning to practice my kung fu, make love to the wife of the Brazilian ambassador, and write the first two chapters of the Great American Novel." His grin broadened. "What are you so cheerful about?" I asked.

We ordered two martinis. "You too would be cheerful," he explained, "if you'd just gotten rid of one of the great American boors."

"Who's that?"

"My brother-in-law. Living proof of the remarkable survival powers of the upper-middle class. Took five years to get through prep school. Basic intellectual deficiencies, stemming from a weak gene pool. So his father hunts up an eastern school which needs a library. Takes him another five years to get a C average in history. He's still unemployable, so then his father finds a suitably mediocre law school. It's a three-year program, but it takes him four, mostly because he spends his time drinking beer and playing the bowling machine at the student union. So Dad gets him a job with a friend. Now he lounges at the country club, drinking gin coolers and bitching that 'the blacks' don't work hard enough."

I smiled. "You must like him a lot."

Greenfeld contemplated that. " 'Loathe' isn't a bad word. 'Despise' is OK, too." He dismissed his brother-in-law. "What's up?"

"Nothing. I've had a shitty day. I wanted a good stiff drink and the pleasure of your company. I'm expecting you to emulate the bright chatter of the Algonquin round table, playing all six members, while I listen and get drunk."

He looked curious. "Were there six members of the Algonquin round table?"

"Christ, Lane, I don't know."

His grin reappeared. "Why not?"

Our drinks arrived, brought by a waiter so quiet and efficient he blended into the bar. The bar itself was small and pleasantly dark, with small squares of silver glass on the wall, picking up fragments of light. A few patrons drifted in, looking for the first drink. I picked up my martini. I like the first martini of the evening. It tastes clean and new, especially if you get it before the bar crowds up and the air gets noisy and stale with smoke. I sipped. The martini almost felt like a fresh start.

Greenfeld put his drink down. "What's happening with your Lasko case?"

"Nothing much. I met Lasko today, though. He and Catlow were over at the commission."

His eyebrows raised. "Did you learn anything?"

I shook my head. "Nothing, except that I don't like them worth a damn."

"What did they do?"

"Mainly tried to walk all over me."

He smiled. "That's not unusual." The smile faded. "You know, I saw that one of Lasko's executives was killed by a car the other day. In Boston."

I nodded. "I read the article." I spoke as casually as possible. I couldn't prove murder. And to suggest it to Greenfeld might wind up losing me the case. But my little game felt pretty bizarre, like denying that Lehman had ever existed.

I couldn't tell whether Greenfeld was looking dubious, or just thoughtful. I sipped my drink, picking around for a change of subject. "What do you hear about Justice's antitrust case against Lasko? Is it going ahead, is the White House dropping it, or what?"

He shrugged. "I don't know. Does the White House know about your Lasko thing?"

I could give him that much. "I'm sure they do."

His thin smile appeared fleetingly, then vanished in thought. "That puts your agency in a touchy position, doesn't it?"

"So it would seem. Have you anything that can help me?"

He stared at me questioningly. "You sound like you need help."

I grinned, trying to sound careless. "I always need help."

He thought. "I've heard one thing, thirdhand, from my fabulous selection of sources. Lasko is supposed to be busy in the Caribbean, buying secretly into banks, dummy corporations, things like that. Someplace like the Netherlands Antilles, with no regulation, where your boys can't get them."

"Does your friend know what for?"

He shook his head. "Getting information out of the Lasko organization is not the easiest thing in the world. But hell, Chris, that's your line of work. Have you ever heard of a Netherlands Antilles corporation that was straight?"

I smiled. "Maybe two or three."

"So what does that suggest?"

"I don't know. Lots of people have used them. Bernie Cornfeld and the boys from Investors Overseas Services, for instance. But I'd have to know more, like how that relates to stock manipulation, if at all."

"So you think Lasko did this stock manipulation?"

"I don't know that either. Honestly."

He accepted that, and ordered another drink. I did the same. The subject of Lasko was dropped by tacit consent. "I'm taking a nice-looking woman to dinner," he announced cheerfully. "Why don't you get a date and join us? We're going to Nathan's. Then there's an old flick on the box tonight. *The Big Sleep*. Bogart doing Philip Marlowe."

Greenfeld was a film nut. "How many times have you seen that one, Lane?"

He stared at the ceiling. "At least five," he concluded.

I grinned. "Thanks anyhow. I think I'm going to sack out."

Greenfeld wagged his head in a burlesque of disappointment. "You're missing a great film. Probably not a bad dinner, either." His voice turned wry. "Are you between meaningful relationships?" The ironic phrase seemed somehow directed at himself. It reminded me of Lynette.

"I guess so. I seem to have backed into something that's very strange and doesn't know where it's going."

He smiled reflectively at his empty martini. "I know the kind." I was curious about Lynette. But not curious enough to ask. We paid the bill and left.

"Have a good sleep, Chris," he said when we reached the sidewalk. "I'll probably know by nine which one of us is better off." He roared off toward the evening in his Alfa-Romeo, silver-white. I dragged home in someone else's Checker taxi, dirty yellow.

I locked the apartment door carefully, and stared at the messy bed and the borrowed shirt that Mary had flung on a bedpost. Two nights of half-sleep and three days with Lehman's death caved in on me. I fell into bed and a black, bottomless sleep.

I woke up somewhere in the Netherlands Antilles, thinking about Lasko. The clock wrenched me into lucidity. 10:15. Robinson would already be in, looking at the Lasko documents. I took a quick shower, threw on blue jeans and a T-shirt, and looked out the window. It was sunny. I headed for the agency on foot.

East Capitol had stirred to life with young people, doing their Saturday things. Across the street a bearded type was carrying a bag of laundry. A short blonde woman came toward me, clutching a bottle of wine for tonight's dinner. She nodded as she passed. Up ahead, rising between the trees, the Capitol dome gleamed in the sun. Tourists clambered over the Hill peeking and peering like archaeologists on a dig. I cut through the Supreme Court grounds, passed the Senate Office Building, and got to the office. I took the elevator and walked through the empty corridors, the slapping of my feet bouncing echoes off the wall.

Robinson was already there, sitting on the floor amidst brown cardboard boxes which had been ripped open—the financial data from Lasko, scattered all over. I apologized for being late and took my place among the boxes. "Find anything interesting?" I asked.

"Not really. Have any luck with Woods?"

"Wasn't in." I remembered Greenfeld's informant. "Anything here on new foreign acquisitions?"

He pointed at a box. "There was something like that in there."

"Think you can find it?"

He nodded and dug through the box. After a while he emerged with a clutch of papers. He took off his glasses and rubbed his eyes. "You know what electronic chips are?"

"Sure. They're little chips which are electronic conductors. Lasko would use them in his computers, stuff like that."

He fiddled with his glasses, looking like a myopic professor puzzling over his notes. "Lasko has been importing most of his chips from Japan. Gets them from an outfit known as Yokama Electric, according to what I read here. About a month ago, he buys a little company called Carib Imports." He pointed to the stack of papers near his feet. "The sales agreement is in here some-where. You can look at it. The business of Carib Imports is importing electronic chips. Its location is some little island in the Caribbean—St. Maarten. That's Dutch, isn't it?"

"Yup, I think it's in the Virgins." I took a handful of documents and thumbed through them, stop-ping to read over the contract. I finished the rest with rising curiosity.

"Say anything to you?" Robinson asked.

"The whole thing is interesting. I can't figure what a company on some two-bit island is doing importing computer chips. I don't see why Lasko would buy it. There's no business reason. He can probably get the chips from Yokama for less. And the timing of it is strange too. He bought it about one week after Sam Green acquired all that stock. And paid $1.5 million exactly. I'm wondering what the connection is, if any."

"Maybe we should ask Sam. He's due Monday."

"I wouldn't want to do that yet. It would just get back to Lasko." I thought. "Who is this Peter Martinson?"

"The seller? You've never heard of him?"

"No."

Robinson rubbed the back of his neck. "Neither have I." He kept rubbing. "Slept wrong last night."

"Any indication that Lasko had a piece of Carib Imports prior to sale?"

"Not according to the sale agreement. Incidentally, under the agreement Martinson stays on to run Carib at $100,000 a year."

"Do we know when Carib was incorporated?"

Robinson shook his head. "Can't tell from this stuff. Can't tell much."

"What do you think, Jim?"

"It's a little peculiar. But St. Maarten's Dutch. We've got no jurisdiction."

My instincts picked up a faint message. "I think I should go down there and look it over. See Martinson. Find out when the company started, how it does business."

Robinson's smile was wintry. "Maybe Woods will advance you the money out of his own pocket."

"At least it gives us something else to talk about."

"I suppose it's a waste of time to tell you that you're looking for trouble again, going down there."

"I guess you'll have to count on Woods' good sense."

He stood and stretched. "OK, Chris. I'm going to take two aspirins and go home. Anything else?"

"Nope. I appreciate it."

"Any time." He smiled. "I hope Woods is as interested in this as you are. Whatever it means."

He left. I picked up the pile and went home to do some research on St. Maarten.

St. Maarten turned out to be a flyspeck in the

West Indies, east of Puerto Rico, with a French side and a Dutch side. My encyclopedia said it was 37 square miles, stuck on old volcanic rock, and turned out some salt, cotton and livestock. Population 6,540. The Dutch side had white beaches and the cruise ships stopped there in winter. Its capital was Philipsburg, for lack of competition. And Carib Imports was there, probably for the same reason.

My almanac added one more fact. St. Maarten was on the northern tip of the Netherlands Antilles.

SEVENTEEN

Monday morning was hot, cloudy, and dense with exhaust fumes. The city felt and smelled like a locker room, and the ECC building looked dismal. There is almost nothing as grey as a government building on a dark morning. It matched my mood.

Woods was waiting for me in his office door. He whisked me past the receptionist before I could open my mouth. I looked around on my way in. Mary was nowhere in sight.

I took a seat. Woods walked to his desk with a purposeful air and sat, staring at me. It seemed to be a symbolic gesture, his desk the armor of rank and power. He spoke. "I think we'd better start with what happened with Lasko on Friday and work back to your dead witness." His voice was cold with withheld anger.

"I'd rather begin with Lehman."

He examined me, as if appraising a slide through

151

a microscope. "If you think it will make any more sense."

I began. "OK. Tuesday, Marty Gubner calls me and asks me to meet his unknown client. Gubner's client turns out to be Alexander Lehman, who's controller at Lasko. Lehman's never heard of any stock manipulation, but says that he's on to something else. Which he doesn't explain. I arrange to talk with him about it that evening." Woods' eyes held a bright cynical glint. I went on, editing out the memo. "Lehman walks out of the Ritz and gets run down." Suddenly I was angry at my own defensiveness. "You know, it's fine to sit here as if I were rationalizing the loss of a chess game. Except you're missing the flavor of the thing. Maybe I should dump Lehman's body on your desk, so you could look it over."

Woods leaned back in his chair, head tilted, as if to consider me from another angle. "All right, I wasn't there. Go on."

"The point is that I had to consider what it meant. Two questions occurred to me. First, why was he killed? Second, how did it get out that I was meeting with him? The last one concerns me a lot. Gubner swears that neither he nor Lehman told anyone. That leaves three people aside from Jim Robinson and me: Joe McGuire, Ike Feiner, and Mary Carelli."

Woods had frozen somewhere in the middle of

my speech. "Let's make sure that I understand. Are you suggesting that Lasko murdered Lehman after someone from this agency warned him?"

"I'm suggesting the first. I'm considering the second."

He stared at me, then half-raised his hands as if calling time out. The hands framed a thin, wry smile. "OK, Chris, you've been under a lot of pressure."

I didn't like the drift of that. "I don't think I'm quite ready for civil commitment."

He dropped his hands on his trousers with a slap, then leaned on his desk in a friendlier attitude. "Look, you've been in a hell of a mess. But you've got a long way to go before you convince me that anyone here is involved. You don't know anything that even makes that kind of suggestion responsible." His voice was rich in nuances; it conveyed loss of respect, and regret, all in one sentence. I wanted to reclaim his regard. But accusing McGuire wasn't the way. I dropped it.

"As for the Lasko meeting, it caught me by surprise. All that I could think about was facing him down, sending him away with nothing. I didn't think to tell you—it felt like my problem. I apologize for that."

"What happened?"

"He came expecting to pick my brains. I asked

him if he had killed Lehman. He said no. I sent him home."

"Why in hell did you ask him that?"

"I'm not sure."

Frustration burst through his voice. "I expect more from you than adolescent macho. You should have told me about the meeting. I could have cancelled it, or maybe insisted that it be done under oath. Instead, we've got a goddamned confrontation and a goddamned mess." He stared angrily at the desk, as if the mess were sitting on it.

"I'm sorry," I said, and regretted saying it. It sounded pitiful.

He looked up, continuing as if he hadn't heard. "The White House called me this weekend. They wondered if I knew what was going on here. Which I didn't." He leaned back. "You know, Chris, you're on the way to becoming famous."

"I'd just as soon pass it up."

His face was cold. "Listen, all I expect is some sense of responsibility. You've given Lasko the perfect excuse to snipe at us. Now we've got the White House on our ass. Without support from the Administration, Congress could slice our budget—hamstring us. The problem is a lot bigger than one case."

"OK. That's understood."

"Good," he said crisply. "Another thing. No more playing both ends against the middle. Any big discussion will include you, McGuire and Mary—or me. Whatever you and McGuire have going, I don't want it to screw up this agency."

I found myself staring at his books and paintings. His voice broke in, in a different tone. "OK, Chris, I'm not going to pull you off, in spite of what some people may want. I want to do it right, as long as we don't ruin this place in the process." His eyes held me, seeking trust.

It wasn't much of an opening. But I took it, and told him about St. Maarten. His face held bleak amusement. "You're not exactly dealing from a position of strength," he said. "It also seems to me I just finished telling you not to go over McGuire's head."

"I know. But I've been looking for a reason for the stock manipulation and haven't found any. There has to be a connection between the stock thing and Lasko buying this nothing little company. The timing is too perfect. Besides, Lehman didn't die because of the stock manipulation. Something else killed him."

"You're just guessing. And we're authorized to look for stock manipulation, not comb through Lasko's affairs." His voice turned dry. "Don't you think we should keep our heads down a little? Besides, we're running out of time on this one. Better to stick to what we know."

I felt a little desperate. "Have you ever met

Lasko?" I asked. He shook his head. "I have. He's pretty close to the evolutionary tree. He may kill someone else if we don't wrap this up."

His face assumed a youthful gravity, the look of the boy genius faced with a tough exam. "We're not the police." He paused. "When did you want to leave?"

"As soon as possible."

He shook his head. "I can't see it. But I'll ponder it and give you a final decision. One more thing." He jabbed his finger at his desk for emphasis. "Calling Lasko a murderer is dangerous. We've no proof. If we ever do, I'll take it to the proper authorities. That's not your job. Understand?"

I nodded.

"OK," he continued, "you've got Sam Green this morning. Go do it."

I decided to leave on a higher note. "Thanks for your time."

He gave a shrunken version of the lopsided grin. "Just keep out of trouble." I left.

On the way out I ran into Mary. She was looking good, slim in tan cotton slacks.

"Good morning," she said, as if she hadn't seen me in a very long time.

"Hi."

Her eyes seemed to appraise my mood. "Have time for coffee?"

"A minute or two."

"Come on in." I followed her in and sat.

The receptionist brought us two cups. Mary reached in her desk for creamer and sweetener. "How was your weekend?" she asked, looking at me for the answer.

"Terrific. I brooded over my sins."

She handed me my cup. "Cream and sugar, isn't it?" She had learned that Friday morning. A small spark of warmth lit her eyes. "I'm sorry about Friday afternoon."

"So am I." It occurred to me that we spent half our time apologizing. I told her so.

Her brows knit. "You know, I looked for you Friday after you left."

"I had drinks with a friend. We concluded that women are difficult."

She smiled. "Who is this misogynist?"

"Fellow named Lane Greenfeld."

She sipped her coffee. "Doesn't he work for the *Post*?"

"The very same. You know," I added, "this place doesn't help. It seems that our peachy professional relationship keeps interfering with the other, or vice-versa."

She gave a small, helpless shrug. "I can't help my job."

"Nor I mine." I looked at my watch and stood up. "I've got Sam Green in ten minutes. Let's try communicating again in a couple of days. We might surprise ourselves."

She smiled her good smile. "All right. I'll look forward to it."

I went to my office and asked Debbie to make St. Maarten reservations, for luck. Then I met Robinson back at the conference room.

I sat down and told him about Woods while we waited for Green. The shorthand reporter arrived to set up her machine. She was my favorite—face as bland as a baby's and her eyes as glassy as marbles. I had seen lawyers screaming and swearing all around her, while she tapped on her machine, a dizzy half-smile directed at some inner space, getting it all down. Right on schedule, five days later, the transcript would arrive, all its threats and "screw you's" neatly typed, recorded for posterity. In my fantasies, she left her machine at five and went home to a scruffy apartment where she sold smack and was known as the Potomac Connection. It was a nice theory.

Green and his lawyer showed up just when she had finished. I looked Green over. He was a walking definition of the word "seedy." It wasn't his clothes; Green was just one of those people who looked second-rate. He had a ferret face and the kind of furtive eyes that seemed to dart away. His thinning hair was styled in the wet look and his skin was fish-belly pale. Robinson and I shook his hand reluctantly and turned to his lawyer.

It was the lawyer who was a surprise. Green usually came equipped with a low-rent item named Johnson, with a scar on one cheek and a dull, nasty look that made you wonder where he had gone to law school. But this time Green had stepped up in class. All the way to Edmund O'Hair.

O'Hair shook my hand, and sat next to Green. He had white hair and a red Irish face, gone Establishment around the edges. I knew a bit about him. He was a boy from Hell's Kitchen turned Wall Street hired gun, and he'd never looked back. Now he was chief trial lawyer for a hundred-man law firm, with a tough, atavistic pride in his work, and clients like General Motors. Green wasn't in his usual line. That suggested possibilities I didn't much like.

Robinson and I sat at the opposite end of the conference table. I asked O'Hair if his client was ready. He nodded. The reporter's fingers poised over the machine. I began my litany: right to counsel, Fifth Amendment, and the penalty for perjury. I came down hard on the last.

Then my questions started. Yes, Green had purchased 20,000 shares of Lasko Devices on July 14 and 15, through three different brokers. Yes, he still had the shares. I moved in, feeling O'Hair's watchful eyes.

"For what reason did you place those orders?"

Green's eyes slid off toward a corner. "I thought it was a good investment."

"Did anyone specific suggest it?"

"I don't remember."

"Do you know a man named William Lasko?"

He stared at the curtains. "I can't recall."

"Have you ever spoken to a William Lasko?"

"I don't remember having done that." He had a thin, reedy voice. Lying didn't improve it.

"Speak up, Mr. Green. Did you discuss your purchase of Lasko stock with William Lasko at any time prior to July 15?"

"I'm not sure." His whine took on a phony, insulted quality.

"It's a simple question," I snapped. "Yes or no?"

He shook his head stubbornly. "I can't. I don't know."

"How did you finance your purchases?"

"I'm trying to think." He spoke to the ceiling in feigned recollection. "I believe I borrowed the funds from the First Seminole Bank of Miami."

"How much?"

"Four hundred thousand."

"When did you borrow the money?"

"About the first week of July."

"With whom did you make the arrangements?"

"A Mr. Billings. He's a vice-president." The sentence had an incomplete sound.

"Did you discuss the First Seminole Bank with someone else at any time prior to the loan?"

"I can't recall doing so."

"What about discussions with Mr. Lasko?"

"I can't remember."

I shifted abruptly. "Who's paying for Mr. O'Hair's services here today?"

O'Hair broke in. "I'm directing my client not to answer that. It's privileged."

"The hell it is."

"Then take us to court and try to compel an answer."

I stopped, frustrated. O'Hair stared back impassively. He would stick to it. Green was either more afraid of someone else, or O'Hair figured I could be fixed somehow, or maybe stopped before I ever got that far. And he knew that I didn't have proof. I asked several similar questions and got similar answers. I noted for the record that Mr. Green would be recalled at a later date. Then I quit.

O'Hair and Green rose. Lying made Green nervous. He looked weary, and he left quickly. O'Hair got ready to follow, but I stopped him. "When we call Green back, Mr. O'Hair, it won't be so much fun. I know you'll remind him of that."

O'Hair shook his head with a slight smile and walked out. So did the reporter, with her own half-smile. I turned to Robinson. "Being lied to always makes me hungry. Can I buy you lunch?"

"Sure." He smiled. "You know, that kind of thing makes you wish for thumbscrews and rubber hoses."

"Damn O'Hair anyhow, the smug bastard. It's clear Lasko put Green up to it. Or else Green would have denied it without the weasel words. But all we have on the record is the First Seminole Bank. Can you dig around to see who owns the big interests in the bank?"

"OK. I've got a friend I can call at the Florida Corporations Commission. I'll meet you downstairs in fifteen minutes."

We walked out together. Robinson headed for the telephone. I went back to my office.

The phone rang. It was Woods. "I've been thinking about what you said. Still want to go to St. Maarten?"

That threw me off. "Sure."

"When would you go?"

"Tomorrow."

Woods paused. "OK," he said, "go ahead. I'll tell McGuire." His phone clicked.

I stared at the phone, surprised. But there was no use puzzling over a break when you got one. I hung up.

EIGHTEEN

By two the next afternoon, my airplane hovered over St. Maarten. It was green and white, surrounded by vivid blue. I wished it were winter, and vacation.

I felt the searing heat as soon as we landed. By the time I got my bags and checked through the customs, I was moist and enervated. I walked toward a line of cars parked expectantly at the end of the airstrip. The nearest one was an old Oldsmobile. The driver leaned against it with elaborate casualness. I don't give a damn for you, his face said, but you're a living.

I didn't give a damn either. "Give me a lift to Philipsburg?"

He nodded and tossed my bags carelessly into his trunk. I opened my own door. Welcome to friendly St. Maarten.

We drove in silence through low green brush on a choppy slash of dirt and rock, past huts of wood and corrugated metal. It wasn't hard to see: tourists arrived each winter like migratory birds and were chauffeured past the huts, chattering about the white sand and blue water. They didn't see the stony faces or shabby huts; if they had, they wouldn't have chattered. The ones that saw felt guilty, and went to Palm Springs next year. And the natives despised them all and took their money. And despised them more. Which was stupid, in a way. Looking at the black rock, you knew the natives needed the tourists, not the other way around. We passed another hut, with a sad skinny goat tethered to it. Like a lot of things, it was tough to get moral about it, either way. But I was probably going to Palm Springs next year.

We came up on Philipsburg. It was not a likely spot for a Lasko enterprise. The town was mostly one-story stucco, with some metal and wood signs that needed paint, scattered along a few cramped streets. It had a desultory, absentminded look, as if it had been thrown together a little at a time. The asphalt streets were crowded by trucks, jeeps, and some cars, most of them old enough to enhance the junkyard ambiance. The streets themselves were quiet and veined with cracks and lent the parked cars and trucks an abandoned quality. A few palms stood on scattered patches of grass, along with some leafy shade trees I couldn't identify. The main thing was the heat; it was so wet you could almost see it. It seemed to have seeped into the wood and the metal and the cracks in the sidewalk. And into the movements of the few islanders—a listless amble. I felt a little like that myself.

The driver dropped me at the Government House, where the police were. This neighborhood was better—some large two-story white frames, freshly painted. The government building had a red tiled roof and a long covered porch. I pulled back the screen door and stepped into a pale green reception room presided over by a serious young black man in gold-framed glasses. I put down my luggage and asked for Inspector De Jonge. He directed me to a wooden chair in front of his desk and picked up the phone.

I waited for about five minutes. Then a bulky man in khaki slacks and a short-sleeved shirt jogged down the stairway. He came up to me, and shook my hand.

"Mr. Paget, I'm Henrik De Jonge. Would you care to come to my office?" His voice was soft and lightly accented.

"Yes, thanks."

I followed him up the stairs and around the corner, into a broad hall that had once been the second floor of someone's home. De Jonge's office was on the left, also light green. It was small but neat, with a large overhead fan. He had a wooden desk, very uncluttered, and one chair stuck in front of it. The fan and shade made the office bearable, no more. I took the chair and looked around. The walls were bare save for an official portrait of a much younger Queen Juliana and Prince Bernhard, pre-Lockheed. De Jonge's age was harder to peg. He had a full thatch of dirty-blonde hair, a creased young-old face, and clear blue eyes, but he slumped tiredly in his chair. I put the slump down to the white man's burden and guessed late thirties. I kept wondering how he got there.

De Jonge was playing with a meerschaum pipe, watching me watch him. "Well, Mr. Paget, what can we do for you?"

"It's really no more than I explained on the telephone yesterday. As far as I know, we're not investigating any Dutch nationals. Just the one American. William Lasko."

He pulled a tobacco pouch from his desk drawer by feel, still looking at me. "And you want to visit Mr. Lasko's company here."

"That's right."

He carefully pinched some tobacco into his pipe. "And this relates to what, precisely?"

"We suspect—we don't know, but we suspect—that the acquisition of Carib Imports may relate to some stock market activities of Lasko, done in America and illegal under American law." I searched for a formula that sounded safe. "All my agency really wants is information as to where at home we should look. There's a man at the company I'd like to talk with—a Peter Martinson."

He lit his pipe, glancing sideways at the picture, as if Juliana were watching him. "After you called, I spoke to the Governor-General's office on Curaçao. I can assist you to the extent of visiting the company and getting you the records you requested." He sounded very cautious, like a bureaucrat. The thought must have crossed my face; his tone changed abruptly. "You understand, Mr. Paget, that these islands are very poor. We encourage foreign investment. The philosophy is—and it is not my choice—that one does not have to be a saint to do business in the Antilles."

That was hardly a sunburst. But it was an explanation of a sort, the best he could make. I didn't have his job and didn't want it. "I understand, Inspector. We appreciate any assistance you can give." I looked at my watch. "Have you time to visit the company now?"

He stood. "I can manage it. We can find a jeep and driver downstairs."

The driver was a young black policeman named Duval, with sharp eyes and a strong grip. He steered us to a jeep and piloted us expertly through the narrow streets to the outskirts of Philipsburg. A corrugated metal warehouse stood in a patch of dirt and rock behind a scrofulous strip of cement.

The warehouse was long, low, and singed with rust. A metal door was the only front entrance. We got out and approached it. Screwed next to the door was a heavy bronze sign, incongruously new, reading "Carib Imports." I looked at the warehouse, a little amused. Pictures of this one would never grace the company bulletin.

We stepped inside, into a passageway between metal partitions. The partitions looked new and formed three offices on each side. The offices were empty. The passageway led through them to a large warehouse area, grubby bare cement half-filled with boxes and half-lit by hanging fluorescent tubes. A couple of workmen in sleeveless T-shirts were restacking boxes in a corner, clearing space. On the far wall of the warehouse a half-opened door admitted a crack of sunlight and some wet air. In one corner a wooden stall stood open, a dirty toilet visible. I craned my neck, searching for someone who looked like a Peter Martinson.

I settled for the only white face I saw, a stocky blunt-featured man with thinning red hair. He wore a blue short-sleeved shirt and leaned in a far corner idly watching the workmen. We stood at the end of the partition until he spotted us. His gaze across the warehouse seemed to flick past the two police, then settle on me, as if I were expected. He gave the workmen a last careless inspection and sauntered over with a kind of calculated aggression.

"Yes?" he asked. His tone was as expressionless as his face.

I let De Jonge do the talking. He gave the man an even stare, neither impressed nor unimpressed. "I'm Inspector De Jonge," he began, "and this"—he nodded at me—"is Mr. Paget, who is here representing the United States government. We wish to speak to Mr. Martinson."

The man spoke with a heavy Dutch accent. "Mr. Martinson is not here."

"When may he be expected?"

"I don't know." His voice seemed to push us toward the door.

"Who are you?"

"My name is Kendrick." Kendrick was definitely not interested in talk. Each word had a grudging quality.

"What is your position here?"

"Working. Not talking."

De Jonge's voice was patient. "Nonetheless, we would like to talk for a moment."

Kendrick shrugged and led us silently to a partitioned office nearest the door. He moved behind a bare metal desk and sat. De Jonge and I took two chairs across from him. Duval stood apart, marking Kendrick with sharp eyes as if filing him away. De Jonge was talking to Kendrick. "I think," he said, "that Mr. Paget wishes to make some inquiries."

I nodded. "My agency is curious as to the business of this company." Kendrick looked back at me in silence. He didn't ask what my agency was or why we were curious. I didn't like that, any more than I liked Martinson's vague absence.

"What exactly is the business of Carib Imports?" I asked.

He folded his arms. "I am not authorized to speak for the company. You'll have to ask Mr. Martinson when he returns."

"Hasn't anyone told you?"

The sarcasm stirred him a little. He flushed. "It should be obvious. We import electronic chips."

"From Yokama Electric?"

His eyes flickered. "That is not a familiar name."

"Perhaps if I spell it."

His voice turned emphatic. "We do not deal with Yokama Electric."

"With whom do you deal?"

"Various companies. You'll have to ask Mr. Martinson. I just run the warehouse."

"For how long have you done that?"

"Just a month."

"How long has the company been in business?"

His eyes were sudden pinpoints of hate. "I told you that I'd just been here a month."

I felt a cold returning anger, at him and at the

situation. They had known I was coming. I wanted Kendrick on my ground, under oath, where I could pick him apart. But I couldn't do that on St. Maarten and he knew it. I looked at De Jonge. He was leaning back in silent disassociation. This wasn't his case.

I turned back to Kendrick. "Where is Mr. Martinson?"

"I don't know."

I felt a sudden sharp fear that I had killed Martinson, as surely as I had killed Lehman, without knowing the reason.

"Why not?" I snapped.

"He left me in charge. He said he was worn out. Mental strain. He was taking a rest. He wouldn't tell anyone where."

"What if you need to ask him who you do business with?"

He flushed again. "I told you I didn't know."

"When did he leave?"

"A few days ago," he said vaguely.

"You mean yesterday?"

He blinked. "I don't remember. Ask him."

I paused. This wasn't going anywhere. I smiled apologetically, in feigned embarrassment. "I know this is off the subject," I said to Kendrick, "but do you have a toilet here? I've had a very long trip."

He hooked a disdainful thumb at the warehouse. "Thank you," I said. "Excuse me."

Kendrick half-rose, as if debating whether to stick with me or the police. He chose the police and sat down.

I strode to the warehouse area, looking back to make sure I wasn't watched. The workmen were still stacking boxes in the far corner to my left. The toilet was in the opposite corner to the right of me. Next to it lay two boxes. I walked to the stall and glanced around. The workmen had their backs to me.

I grabbed one of the boxes and dragged it into the stall, closing the door. Then I stooped and ripped open the top. Inside were two dozen brown paper sacks. I opened one. Black metallic fragments scattered into my cupped hand. Electronic chips. I lifted the flap of my left outside coat pocket and sprinkled the chips inside. Then I tore up the empty sack and flushed it down the toilet.

I looked out. The workmen were nowhere in sight. I hauled the box back and stacked the other box on top. Then I rejoined the others. They were still where I had left them, silent, as if frozen by my departure.

De Jonge looked up blandly from his pipe. "Do you have anything further for this man?"

"No. I think we've exhausted Mr. Kendrick's usefulness."

Kendrick stared at me in sullen relief. De Jonge stood to go. "Thank you, Mr. Kendrick." Kendrick said nothing. We walked out of the office, opened the warehouse door, and got in the jeep. The chips rubbed silently in my pocket.

NINETEEN

We went back to the Government House and waited while Duval checked on Martinson. He came back with a number and the address of a rented house in the hills above Little Bay. Did I intend a visit? De Jonge asked warily. No, I said, but if I changed my mind I would let him know. De Jonge detailed Duval to take me to my hotel. We drove off in silence.

The ride was hot and dusty under the glaring afternoon sun. I couldn't stop worrying about Martinson. Woods hadn't listened about McGuire, and I'd asked for St. Maarten anyway. Now Lehman might get Martinson for company. All compliments of my own vanity and stupidity.

I was an albatross, hunting men so Lasko could find them. And Lasko had always been one step ahead and out of sight, from that first day when McGuire met with Catlow, dispenser of plum appointments. When I met Lehman to see him killed.

When my search for the cryptic memo turned into quiet threats and Lasko came to pick my brain. When Sam Green sprouted an expensive lawyer, who gave me next to nothing. And now Martinson had disappeared. It was a grim way to confirm his importance. I wondered what he was like, whether he had a family, what things had put him in my path.

We drove up a small hill and the view suddenly opened into salt-white beach and water bluer than azure, rich and clean looking and glinting in the sun. The hotel squatted behind the beach, three long two-story units of white stucco. Summer was well off-season and the hotel looked deserted. When we reached it, I thanked Duval and got out. He looked solemn. "I am sorry, Mr. Paget, that we did not do more."

I realized that the silence had been embarrassment. I tried a smile which almost took. "Then do me a favor sometime. Beat on Kendrick for me."

Duval grinned back. "I have that one marked." He pointed to his skull.

I laughed. "I noticed that." We shook hands. "Good luck," I said.

"Thank you, sir." The jeep rumbled off, and I walked into the hotel.

The lobby was bright, modern, and deathly quiet. A heavy Dutchman checked me in with grave courtesy, tips on restaurants, and a few ponderous quips. I wasn't in the mood. Did he have an envelope and a safe, I asked. He nodded. I threw the chips in the envelope and watched while he put them away. I got a key and went to my room.

I had a top floor room with an ocean view, and a sliding door which opened onto a cement deck. The beach stretched for miles to my right, below green hills. It was bleach-white and sheltered by low palms. We were on a bay; the far hills curled back out to reach for the sea. A tame surf crept in, lulling and regular, with a deep satisfied sound. Out beyond, the sun caught jets of white in the dark azure, glistening like mica. I watched it for a while. Then I shook myself, showered, and put on a fresh suit.

The phone was next to my bed. I lay down, leaning on my elbows, and thought for a long time. I started to reach for the phone, then stopped, thinking of Lehman. Then I stretched for the phone and had the switchboard place the call. I could hear the phone ring, a shocking metallic rattle that made me start.

Then it stopped. "Hello." It was a woman's voice, American I thought.

"Mrs. Martinson?"

"Yes. Who is this?" Her voice sounded timorous, as if she feared bad news.

"I'm Christopher Paget. I'm an American, a government lawyer. I'm trying to locate your husband."

"What do you want from Peter?" The question was both edgy and hopeful.

"Just to talk to him. I think he could help me." I tried to make my voice suggest that helping me conferred honor on the helper. Lehman knew better, but he wasn't talking.

"What do you want to talk about? I mean, why can Peter help you?"

"I'm doing a government investigation of an American company. Lasko Devices."

Her voice went flat. "Then Peter can't help you."

"Can't or won't?"

"He can't help you," she insisted.

There was trouble in the words. I decided to push. "Mrs. Martinson, is your husband home?"

Silence. "No."

"Is he in some sort of difficulty?"

"What do you mean?"

I forced myself to speak with cold precision. "I'll put it another way. Do you even know where he is?"

"I—don't—know." The crying broke then, as if my question had pulled the plug on her self-control.

My hand squeezed the phone, trying to hold her on. "Mrs. Martinson?" I tried.

"Yes."

"Can I see you?"

She caught her voice. "Yes."

"Let me think." I hesitated. "Have you eaten anything today?"

"No." The answer was delayed, as if she had shaken her head, then remembered I couldn't see her. I understood. Her voice on the phone was more real than the room around me.

"I don't want to be seen going to your place. Do you know La Porte?"

"Yes."

"Can you meet me there in an hour?" There was a long silence. "Mrs. Martinson, please come. It could be very important."

She sounded drained. "All right, Mr. Paget. I'll meet you."

"Thank you," I said. She hung up abruptly.

I rented a car and got to La Porte a little early, about 7:15. A slight Frenchman led me in with elaborate politeness. He seated me by the window at the end of the small room. I told him that I was expecting a lady. He scurried away, looking pleased. Through the window, the sea looked rich blue in the waning sun. The decor around me was dark and simple—French rustic, graced with white linen and pewter. I liked it. And I hoped Martinson was alive.

The Frenchman reappeared, leading a tall blonde young-looking woman dressed in white slacks and turquoise silk blouse. I stood, surprised.

"Mrs. Martinson?" She nodded, eyes resting on

me. "I'm Chris Paget. Please sit down." The Frenchman whisked out a chair and deftly steered her to it. I took a second look. The woman was perhaps thirty-five, though age had only touched her eyes. The rest of her was youthful—pretty cheerleader face and slim body that moved with the carelessness young girls have before life becomes a harness. She looked back across the table. The sad puff around her eyes rebuked me. Being glad she was pretty was more than pointless. I wondered where Martinson was while I dined with his wife.

"You're very young," she said.

I smiled. "Old enough. Can I get you a drink?" She hesitated. "You could probably do with one."

"All right. Thank you. Whatever you're having." Her natural tone was high, a girl's voice.

I ordered two rum and tonics and turned back to her troubled gaze.

"Let me explain why I'm here." I spoke carefully, trying to feed some confidence into her eyes. "I'm a lawyer with an agency in Washington, the ECC." I took out my ID card and laid it in front of her. "One of our jobs is to investigate fraud in companies that sell stock in the United States. I'm working on a case involving Lasko Devices. I flew here this morning to talk with your husband. I visited the company and saw a man named Kendrick. He said that your husband had gone on vacation because of some sort of mental strain. He wouldn't tell me when he had left, where he had gone, or when he would come back. My guess is that he disappeared within the last twenty-four hours, and that he's not on the island."

She shook her head, the blonde shag grazing her shoulders. "No."

"No what?"

Her voice quavered as if something was shaking her. "No, he's not crazy. He went away because they told him."

"Who told him?"

"I don't know. Someone from the company. He called me this morning. He said he had to go away for a while, right away, that someone was looking for him." The two thoughts collided in her eyes. "It was you." Her voice accused me. It made as much sense as anything else.

"Probably. Why did he go?"

"They told him to. He was afraid. He's never been afraid before, of anything. I asked him please not to go. He kept telling me that he had to. Then he hung up. It was so frightening. It doesn't make any sense at all." Her shoulders drew in. It gave her a breakable look.

"What else did he tell you?"

"That I shouldn't tell anyone—but I'm afraid for him."

"Why are you afraid?"

"Because Peter's afraid." The words had strange

echoes, as if she had lived for years on her husband's reactions. But I was afraid too.

"Did he tell you why?"

"No."

I could feel her trust slipping from me in the sterile inquisition. I sensed that she hadn't decided who to be afraid of. Our drinks arrived. She sipped listlessly, watching me over the rim.

I tried something else. "Mrs. Martinson, this case seems to be very important to someone. I want your husband safe. Anything that you can tell me about his business here would help."

Her eyes clouded with doubt, then tears. She stared at her lap. I waited. "Can you help protect Peter?" she asked after a time.

"I hope so."

She looked up at me. "All right," she said quietly.

"Let's start with how your husband got here."

"Well, I guess the thing was that nothing quite worked out. Peter—well, it's not that Peter isn't smart, he's very clever, really—he just hadn't found the right spot." The words had a pat, formula sound, as if she had repeated them to herself until memorized. "When we finished college, Peter wanted to go to Europe. I couldn't have children—" Her voice caught; perhaps children would have made her husband a grown-up. "Anyhow, Peter is a manufacturer's representative for international companies. We've been everywhere in the last twelve years. I've got beautiful memories. And Peter speaks three languages." The tumble of words stopped abruptly. I thought of a cheerleader again, turned older. She was still leading cheers, but the team was behind and would never catch up. The knowledge showed in her eyes. They moved between innocence and hurt. "I'm not helping, am I?" she asked.

I tried to look encouraging. "Just keep on talking. Where did Peter work last?"

"Japan."

"For Yokama Electric?"

"That's right. How did you know that?"

"I'm beginning to put some things together. About when did you come to St. Maarten?"

"July." She stopped. "Just last month." It seemed to surprise her, as if it felt longer now.

The Frenchman arrived to take our order. She looked distracted. I asked some questions and ordered for her. It felt strange. Perhaps her husband did that too.

"Why St. Maarten?" I asked when we had ordered.

"Peter was asked. He did a lot of his business in Japan with Lasko Devices. They liked him. Peter told me that. William Lasko asked him to come here personally."

"What was your husband supposed to do?"

"Mr. Lasko wanted Peter to run his new company for him. Carib Imports."

"Does your husband own any part of Carib Imports?"

She shook her head. "No. Peter is just running it for him."

"You're sure of that?"

"We didn't have the money to own a company. This was really a break for Peter." The sentence started in pride and trailed off in embarrassment.

"If you don't mind my asking, what is he paid?"

"Well, it seemed fantastic. He got a $100,000 bonus and $75,000 a year for two years. We're renting a beautiful home in the hills."

"I can imagine." I could—but not the way she thought.

She read it. "Mr. Paget, what's going to happen to Peter?"

"Nothing. But I need to find him. Have you any idea where he is?"

Her voice shrunk. "He wasn't to tell me." she hesitated.

"Damn it, Mrs. Martinson, help me out." I shook my head. "I'm sorry. I know it's not the same, but I'm involved in this thing too." Lehman's unspoken presence thickened my speech. "You'll help your husband best by telling me everything. Especially that."

She gave me a candid gaze. I decided that her

eyes were very nice. "Mr. Paget, I love Peter very much."

"I won't forget that," I said quietly.

She touched my hand. "All I know is Peter said he would be somewhere safe. Near Boston."

It figured.

The Frenchman brought us dinner. She picked at it. I encouraged her, pointing out things that looked good. I asked a few more questions and turned up nothing. She was not a stupid woman, not at all. But she had abdicated responsibility for the world of men. Or, more accurately, had never presumed to have any. She was all victim, hurt and hopeful at once. And I liked her.

We finished dinner. "Do you have a picture of your husband?" I asked.

She fumbled in her purse and produced a wallet-size snapshot. "This is Peter," she said. The warmth in her voice was crossed with fear, as if Peter might be only the picture.

The picture showed a lean man with sharp features and dark curly hair. He had all the elements of good looks. What stopped me was a sort of spurious winner's smile. Somehow he reminded me of a guy who would show up for tennis with a graphite racket and a $100 outfit, and flash all the strokes you wish you had. And then leave you wondering why he lost.

"Can I keep it?" I asked. She nodded. I placed it carefully in an inside pocket.

The Frenchman returned, casting a doleful eye on the woman's picked-over plate. It had a messy, abandoned look, as if someone had begun surgery and then decided to quit. It affronted his sensibilities. I cheered him up by saying that duck à *l'orange* this fine was tough to come by. She watched the byplay with empty eyes, as if it were no more or less significant than the rest of her day. I flashed on Valerie Lehman, staring in pretty bewilderment at her nice furniture. We passed on dessert. I took her arm and steered her out the door.

The night was a dark cocoon of privacy. We walked across the street to her car. There were no buildings or people near us.

We stood by the car. "You know," I told her, "I don't know your name."

It took her a second to understand. "Oh," she answered. "It's Tracy."

I smiled. "I'm a believer in the importance of names. Tracy Martinson is a fine name."

She put her hands on my lapels, half-leaning. "Please find Peter for me."

"I'll try not to let you down," I said quietly. She looked up at me as if she knew what I meant. Someone else had let her down. A soft breeze blew her hair against my shoulder. I brushed it away, across her cheek. She shivered and clung to me. But this wasn't my kind of occasion. Or hers. I waited. She pulled back.

I asked her to wait. I scribbled my hotel, office, and home numbers on a scrap of paper. I pressed it in her hand. "Will you be all right alone?"

She answered slowly. "Yes." But she wouldn't, at all.

I was looking at her, thinking that, when the headlights cut across her face. I turned toward the harsh glare and sudden roar of an accelerating car, racing toward us from the once-quiet street, maybe fifty feet away. In the dark it looked like a huge malevolent bug. Tracy screamed in my ear. I froze. The crazy thought bolted through my brain: "Just like Lehman." Twenty feet. I wrenched out of it, grabbed Tracy, and hurtled sideways onto the hood of her car, feet trailing. The car squealed past as we kept rolling, off the hood and onto the grass on the other side. I held her there, face down in the grass. We heard the growl of the motor as it sped down the choppy road.

I pulled her up, and dragged her by the hand across the road. We got to the restaurant and then she leaned on my shoulder, crying softly. The Frenchman scurried up, alarmed and sympathetic. There had been an accident, I said. He sat Tracy down and steered me to the phone. I reached Duval at the Government House. I was glad of that.

He arrived in two minutes, wondering what he could do. I glanced at Tracy, sitting at the table.

"Can you watch her house?"

He nodded. "Surely. But what of you?"

"I'll be all right. This was a warning, I think. If they had wanted to kill us, there are better ways, like two bullets in the head. But I'm not quite dangerous enough for killing. I think what they want is for her to shut up, and for me to lay off."

"This is to do with her husband then."

"Yes. He's missing."

"And you saw nothing?"

"Nothing except the car."

We talked another moment, while I explained as much as I could. Then he retrieved Tracy. She was still white and dazed.

"It's all right," I told her. "The Inspector will guard your house."

She nodded distractedly and started with Duval through the door. She stopped and turned suddenly, as if she had forgotten something.

"Thank you, Mr. Paget."

It was a thanks I didn't rate. I could have left her safe at home. "I'll try to find your husband," I promised. But I wondered if I would.

She turned and walked with Duval to his jeep. She got in and gave me a last quiet look. Then they drove away. I watched until I couldn't see her any more. Then I drove back to the hotel.

TWENTY

I parked in front of the hotel and got out. The night was still and a tropic breeze blew in from the ocean. Some other time I'd have put on cut-offs and walked along the water at the edge of the beach, listening to the surf. But not tonight. I headed for the room, feeling stiff and bruised.

I was still shaken and feeling the vague disquiet that goes with being somewhere you hadn't expected to be. I stopped for a moment at the hotel steps, looking up at the stars.

I heard the rustle of clothes the last second before he hit me. A thick arm flashed. Then the pain tore through my head and buckled my legs. I fell into a sudden dark hole.

I fought through fog to a vicious ache that pounded my head. My stomach churned and my legs were numb, as if disconnected from my nervous system. I lay there regaining consciousness in gauzy chunks.

I was sprawled on my back looking at the stars, and I suddenly knew that I would have been dead if someone had cared. Christopher Paget, the last act on the Amateur Hour. My pockets were turned inside out.

I staggered up and dragged myself up the stairs, falling, then half-crawling, then righting myself to walk the last few steps.

My key was in the door and the room was open and torn up. I edged to the doorway and leaned there. The whole thing was like television, I thought. But it wasn't, not at all.

I stepped in. No one home. I locked and latched the door and inched woozily around the room. Nothing seemed to be gone. I lay down on the bed.

I fished inside my coat pocket. My wallet was still there. I opened it. No money missing. I slid the words of Lehman's memo out of its crevice. It hadn't been touched. They weren't hunting for a scrap of paper, I thought. It was the chips. They were looking for the goddamned chips.

I had just enough strength left to call Tracy. She answered in a hopeful voice. She was OK, she said. Duval was there. Was there anything new? Nothing at all, I said. Just checking. I wished her good night and hung up.

Something made me think of the words on the

scrap of paper. But they kept swimming out of sight. I fell asleep, still clutching the scrap.

I was jolted awake by the savage tropic sun streaming through the windows. My head throbbed. I cleaned up and packed in a fever of delayed anger. I checked out and picked up the parcel of chips. Then I went to town and called on De Jonge.

He looked up from his neat desk with a phlegmatic gaze. "Good morning, Mr. Paget. Are you all right?"

I wanted to dump over his desk, mess up his office and chuck Bernhard and Juliana out the window. But I didn't do any of those things. I didn't sit either.

"Good morning, Inspector. I've come to report a case of white flight. One of your businessmen is missing. Your economy is threatened. And I've got a headache."

He sat up in his chair. "What is this all about?"

I started with the attack and break-in, while I gathered my thoughts on how to cover Tracy. I assured him I wasn't hurt any more than anyone who'd been beaned with a brick. No, I didn't know who did it, although I wondered what Kendrick did for fun. No money lost to speak of, and no valuables. I left out the chips I had stolen.

De Jonge was apologizing and looking embarrassed. There was nothing in that for me, so I moved on to Tracy, leaving out what she had told me.

"Mrs. Martinson couldn't help," I summarized. "But I think he's disappeared—because I was visiting."

He flushed. "I told no one."

"I believe you, Inspector." I did, provisionally. "I'm asking you to take this seriously. The woman needs some police protection."

De Jonge's face was strained. "Please sit down for a moment."

I cooled off and sat. De Jonge's voice became sympathetic. "Whatever you may think, Mr. Paget, we are concerned when someone disappears. The police will ensure that nothing happens to Mrs. Martinson."

I rose. "All right. Thanks."

He held up his hand. "Mr. Paget, you are not a patient man. You asked me yesterday to check some records. Would you like to know what I found?"

He was right about me. "Peter Martinson hiding in a filing cabinet?"

He gave his pipe an offended look. "No. But I did learn when Carib Imports was founded. Just this July. Peter Martinson signed the papers." He eyed me. "I hope that is useful."

I retracted the irony. "It is, Inspector."

He stood and stuck out his hand. "I'll contact

you if we discover anything." He paused. "I'm sorry that we were not more helpful."

He probably was. I shrugged and took his hand. His eyes turned back to Juliana. I said good-bye and drove to the airstrip.

The airstrip had one building, the naked cinderblock shelter that housed customs and baggage. There was a telephone inside. I used it to call Robinson. His long distance voice was fuzzy. "How is it down there?"

"Lousy. I got beat up last night. And I can't find Martinson."

"Christ. What happened?"

I made my decision. "I struck out. No information. No nothing. Listen, did you find out anything about Green?"

"One thing. Lasko controls a substantial interest in the First Seminole Bank."

I thought. "We'd better get Green back in, quick."

"I'll do that. You all right?"

"I think so."

"Well, that's something."

I thanked him and hung up. It was a long wait and a long trip to Washington. It was night when I got there. The Capitol dome was spotlit against a black sky. St. Maarten seemed very far away.

TWENTY-ONE

I sat alone in my office early the next morning, trying to make sense of it all. The thing was: I couldn't trust anyone. If I showed them Lehman's memo, Lasko would find out. If they knew I'd stolen the computer chips, Lasko could see where I was headed. And if I said I was tracking Martinson, he might end up dead. If he weren't already. The one way to be sure was not to talk much—even to Robinson. It wasn't that I didn't trust him. But I couldn't ask him to hide the ball. If he went along, it could be trouble for him. If he let it slip, it could be trouble for me. I fingered my skull gently. It still hurt.

The isolation was oppressive. I was the only one who held the pieces—the sham company, Lehman's memo, Martinson's disappearance—even if I couldn't fit them together. And I couldn't let the pieces go. It would have helped to level with someone. Preferably someone who nodded when I mentioned murder and leaks in the agency, and cheered when I lied and hid things in my desk. But that wasn't going to happen. I was wondering about Martinson when Robinson opened the door.

He blinked at the sunlight which came through my window. "How are you, Chris? Hurt any?"

I reached for the blinds. "My head, some."

"You're a little white. Seen a doctor?"

"I may do that."

He nodded, satisfied. "So what happened?"

He got the abridged version, the one without the chips, the memo, or Tracy's story. I was getting pretty good at it. Robinson sat, listening intently. "And you couldn't find Martinson?"

"No."

"Think he's hiding out with Lehman?"

"Christ, I hope not."

Robinson shook his head. "I'm not used to this."

"Who is?"

"What I can't figure is why Lasko, who's got serious problems with Justice on this antitrust suit, needs more with us." Robinson pondered his own question, then switched tacks abruptly. "How much trouble are you in?"

"You mean how many intimations of mortality am I having?" He nodded glumly. "Well, I keep telling myself that killing me is like killing a cop. So I figure that they won't unless they have to."

"The corollary of that is if they have to they will."

"Don't depress me."

"I'm trying to depress you."

It was a conversational blind alley. I looked at my watch. "When do we see Green?"

"9:30."

"Then you had better tell me what I should know."

Robinson shrugged. "OK. Lasko owns 25 per cent of the stock of the First Seminole Bank. Actually he doesn't own it. His companies do—Lasko Devices and its subsidiaries, through their various pension funds. Made it sort of hard to trace. Anyhow, the 25 per cent is effectively his. That makes him the largest single stockholder, not enough to control the bank itself, but enough to have real pull."

"That's nice. Talk to anyone at the bank?"

"No. I figured you'd worry that it'd get back to Lasko."

"Anything else?"

"Just that I called up O'Hair, reminded him the subpoena was still good and invited Sam back. I didn't say why."

"OK."

"How are you going to handle this?"

"I'll give O'Hair a veiled offer of leniency, then threaten a perjury prosecution. He's got to believe

I'd do that, although I wouldn't. Then I'll try to make him think we've gotten to the bank, which we haven't. From there on, I'll see what turns up."

"Hope O'Hair buys it."

"So do I. Listen I've got a couple of things to do."

He got up. "OK. I'll see you down there."

"Yeah." I was feeling a little guilty. "Jim, thanks for your help. I mean it."

"Sure," he answered, and shut the door behind him.

I stared unhappily at the phone. Once I picked it up I was committed to going it alone. But I hadn't left myself any choices. So I made the easy call first.

Greenfeld was in. "Lane, I've got a pure favor to ask you. No strings."

"You can always try," he answered in a dry tone. "What is it?"

"Do you have sources at IRS?"

"Sure."

"If you can do it without getting them excited, check IRS for a list of any mental hospitals or sanitariums to which the Lasko Foundation has contributed. Especially around Boston. Can you do that?"

"Do I get to ask why?"

"Sure. You just don't get answers."

"Isn't this something you can do through your channels?"

"No. Not this one."

"What the hell is going on over there?"

"Can you do it?" I persisted.

"All right," he said in an aggravated tone. "I'll call you back." The phone clicked off.

There was one more favor to ask. I readied myself to reach back in time, mix past with present. Then I made the call.

"Mr. Stansbury? Chris Paget."

"Chris," the vigorous voice answered, "where are you?"

"Here. Washington. I work here." And have for three years, I didn't add.

"That's marvelous. You'll have to visit."

"I had that in mind. I think perhaps you can do me a favor."

"I'd be delighted." His voice warmed suddenly with old hopes. They had been my hopes too, and they had died hard. But I had buried them.

"It's business, I'm afraid."

His tone faded a bit. "Surely, Chris. What is it?"

"I remember you were an electrical engineer, before you went into the business end. How are your skills?"

"Pretty good still, I think."

"I need an expert opinion on some computer chips. Can you look at them today?"

"Surely. Retirement has left me with nothing but time. Too much time. Can you find the place?"

"Sure."

"I'll look forward to it."

"Thanks much, Mr. Stansbury."

"See you later then." There was a question in his voice. I hung on for a second, but he didn't ask it. I was just as glad. I rang off and felt absently for the chips in my pocket. Still there. Then I went off to question Sam Green.

Robinson was already sitting in the conference room, with Green, O'Hair, and my favorite reporter. She set up her machine next to the potted palm, still smiling like the Mona Lisa. Green was perspiring. The room was cool enough; the sweat was from wondering what we had. O'Hair was next to him, looking ostentatiously calm.

I moved to the head of the conference table and sat next to Robinson. Green stared at an empty corner, as if that would make me disappear. I shuffled some papers, to let him stew awhile.

O'Hair thrust forward. "On behalf of my client, I demand to know why he's been recalled."

I excused the reporter, then turned to O'Hair. "Because we're interviewing mental defectives this week. We got Green for today's special."

"What kind of crap—"

"You can take your demand and shove it. Someone's already dead, and your boy here has been horsing us around."

O'Hair picked a lower key. "My client is aware of his constitutional rights."

The bargaining had started. I asked Green to leave. He rose clumsily, almost tripping, and stumbled out. I looked after him. "I hope his constitutional rights console him at Danbury. With his record, he'll do some time."

"You said yourself you couldn't prove perjury." O'Hair tried sounding aggrieved, as if I had broken a promise.

"I've changed my mind. I figure no jury will believe that he can't remember one month later who got him a $400,000 loan."

"So why don't you prosecute?"

That was tactic number one. Trying To Get The Prosecution To Admit Your Client's Importance. "Because Green is a piss-ant, of no importance. To be honest, I don't much care what he does. If he talks, that's another witness against Lasko. If he doesn't, I just prosecute them both."

"You haven't shown me a thing."

I shrugged. "It's your choice, Mr. O'Hair. Green can take the Fifth, or he can cooperate. But he'd better not try perjury."

Robinson was playing his part, regarding O'Hair with a faint, superior smile. O'Hair stood. "I'll talk to my client."

We stared back at him. He left.

Robinson turned to me. "That was raw," he observed. "And I thought McGuire used to be a prick."

I shrugged. "Some night, when this case is over and I have time to review what a shit I am, I'll drink a martini and feel bad about it. Right now, I can't afford to. Anyhow, no one forced Green to be a crook."

Robinson nodded. He knew that was right; he was just glad that I'd played the heavy. That was a normal reaction; sometimes it bothered me that I didn't mind. It didn't bother me on this one.

O'Hair returned. "Can you guarantee that Mr. Green's testimony will be confidential?"

For at least two or three hours, I thought. "Are you asking for special treatment?"

"I can't tell my client to do something that'll be public knowledge."

I tried to look blasé. "You know our rules. No investigation is made public before a case is brought."

My answer was beside the point. In the Lasko case, our rules were worthless. And O'Hair might end up a creditor of Green's estate, fighting it out with the First Seminole Bank. But O'Hair ducked back outside.

I heard vague mutterings in the hall. Then Green came in first, wearing the fretful look of a weak-willed man who had just been cornered by a high-pressure salesman. He didn't know what he had bought and wasn't sure he'd enjoy finding out. O'Hair just looked inscrutable. "Go ahead," he nodded.

The reporter trailed after them, and smiled at her machine. I caught her eye, then began.

"We are continuing the testimony of Samuel Green in The Matter Of Lasko Devices, Home Office File Number 774." The reporter's fingers twitched on the keys of her machine. "Mr. Green, you testified previously that during this July, the First Seminole Bank of Miami loaned you approximately $400,000. Please describe fully and completely the circumstances of that loan."

"Yes, Mr. Paget, I would be pleased to." The written transcript, I thought idly, would never do justice to how unpleased he sounded. "In late June I was contacted by Mr. William Lasko."

"By what means?"

"Telephone."

"And what was that conversation?"

"I'd heard of Mr. Lasko—you know, in the papers, the *Journal* and all—but I'd never met him. Just maybe seen his picture once or twice. Anyhow, I asked him why he was calling me and he said how he got my name wasn't important but he had a business proposition for me. Well, since last year when I had trouble with Mr. Robinson here and the others, I haven't done too well. So I said sure. I mean it wouldn't hurt to listen, right?" Green stopped, looking moist and irresolute.

"Go on."

Green gave his hands a wan, antiseptic glance, as if he had just spotted dirt under the skin. "Well, so I met with Mr. Lasko and he said that he knew that I wasn't too flush so he would help me if I would help him. You know—" Green's threadbare quality permeated his speech. I waited for him to say "one hand washes the other." He let me down: "Sort of 'you scratch my back and I'll scratch yours.' Mr. Lasko said he would get me four hundred thousand in capital and set me up to play the market again. All I had to do was buy Lasko stock. He said if I couldn't repay he'd make good on the loan, and if Lasko stock went up, well I could sell the stock, pay the loan back, and keep the profits. So I couldn't lose. He called me twice, once on the fourteenth and once on the fifteenth and asked me to buy. He told me how much to buy and where to place the orders. I didn't use all the money so he said to do with the rest what I wanted to, so I bought a couple of other things." Green stopped, out of breath. Under the light he was pale and spindly. O'Hair stared out the window, as if he saw something interesting.

Green realized I was waiting. "That's all," he said.

I nailed down the rest. He'd met Lasko in New

York for lunch. Lasko had plied him with white wine, oysters, and a whiff of money. We went through each purchase. Lasko would call before the market opened each morning. He hadn't known why Lasko wanted all this, he claimed. That, I thought, was about as likely as Green intending his profits for the March of Dimes. But I didn't much care. I had what I wanted. I closed the record. The reporter smiled, folded her machine, and left.

Green was eyeing me warily. O'Hair glanced from Green to me. "I hope you appreciate that you have Mr. Green's full cooperation."

"That's wonderful," I said gravely.

O'Hair looked benign; Green, hopeful. They both decided it was time to leave. The empty ring of their footsteps faded and disappeared.

"Well," I said, "we've got Lasko for manipulation." The problem was I couldn't make it fit with anything else. Martinson, Lehman, and St. Maarten were a jumble of puzzle pieces.

Robinson slid in his chair. "You know, they've got a pretty good argument for immunity."

I nodded. "Green will always do OK as long as he can trade up. That's the way it works. Hell, look at the guy who ratted on Tricky Dick. Three easy months and then he's a star at literary luncheons."

Robinson smiled and said nothing for a while. Then he spoke. "I wonder why Lasko would settle for a cheap operator like Green?"

That bothered me, and there was something else. My triumph was beginning to ring a bit hollow. I wasn't used to winning on this case. "Did O'Hair strike you as entirely too agreeable?"

Robinson looked interested. "I've seen him tougher."

"It was almost as though he didn't mind us pinning the manipulation on Lasko."

"That would make sense if he was Green's lawyer."

"Yeah, but I think he's Lasko's lawyer, here protecting Lasko's interests. And why would Green stick his neck out? Lehman died over something like that."

"Where does that take you?"

"Maybe that Lasko is willing to let us find out about the stock manipulation and settle the case on that basis. Maybe he wants the agency to close out the investigation, to keep us from finding something worse."

Robinson considered that. "I don't see why, offhand." He tilted his head backward, as if he had forgotten something and would find it on the ceiling. "He would have to have something big to hide."

My skull was throbbing. I decided someone should look it over. I excused myself. Then I took the chips and taxied to the hospital, wondering if Stansbury could tell me what I needed.

I was pretty clear on one thing. Stock manipulation wasn't what this case was all about. I had a long way to go yet and not much time to get there.

TWENTY-TWO

The hospital kept me until about 3:30, a fair amount of which I spent filling out forms, ours and theirs. No fracture, they told me cheerfully, and they had pretty much ruled out brain damage. I was delighted.

Normally I would have flagged a taxi in front. Instead, I found a pay phone in the lobby and called a cab to meet me in the rear. Ten days before I would have laughed at that but now nothing much was funny.

I waited inside until the cab showed up, then got in and routed the cabbie toward Old Town Alexandria on the George Washington Parkway, paralleling the Potomac. As near as I could make out, no one was following.

The Parkway ran abruptly into Alexandria and turned into Washington Street. The cabbie turned left and steered through cramped lanes onto Duke Street. Old Town was mostly brick townhouses,

very old, with small yards stubbing the sidewalk.
As Georgetown, it would never quite make it. Not
enough trees and no restaurant I cared for. But it
was peaceful for the most part, and not jammed
with weekend tourists hell-bent on making it im-
possible to live in. That had its charms.

Stansbury lived on Pitt Street, named after William Pitt. The Elder. His house had a front yard,
large for Old Town standards, and crammed, but
neatly, with the kind of lush stuff you can grow in
Washington. The house itself was brick, painted
grey, with a freshly painted black door and new
brass knocker. I could have picked it out without
an address.

I told the cabbie to wait and went to the door. I
skipped the door bell and gave the brass knocker
two good raps, thinking to please him.

The door opened and Stansbury stood there,
looking as clean and trim as the house. He smiled
broadly. "Chris, how are you?"

"Fine, Mr. Stansbury. You certainly look well." I
shook his hand.

He waved me in with a pleased expression. I
looked for signs of aging and couldn't find any.
Sixty-eight, maybe. Grey hair. Skin leathery but
still almost unlined. The one price of age was in his
voice, a sort of manly croak.

He steered me toward the living room. I looked
around. Furniture sparse, mostly antiques, very

tasteful and not too much. A lot of it I remembered from the old house.

"You've done a nice job with this place," I said.

He nodded his thanks. "It's given me something to do since Martha died. That's when I decided to move here. Cheryl's husband is with the State Department, you know, and they've just had a second boy. This is close enough to Chevy Chase to see them and far enough away not to be a bother." And farther away from Boston, I thought, but didn't say so.

He was taking stock of me. "You look well, Chris. Older. Old enough," he added with a smile, "to have a drink. Gin and tonic?"

He was proud of those, I remembered. "Fine," I said, and followed him into the kitchen. We chatted, catching up while he worked on the drinks. He made them carefully, measuring and stirring, as if sealing an act of hospitality. Then he cut the lime into slices, and squeezed them with a careful, practiced twist which feared the first betrayal of old age. It was that, oddly, that reminded me that I had missed him.

He was still peering at the drinks. "Do you ever hear from Brett?"

I shook my head. "No. How is she?"

"I don't really know." He glanced up sideways. "No, I suppose I do know. That's one reason I live here instead of there."

Brett was his favorite, I knew. I tried joking. "Vietnam is over now. I would think you're out of things to argue about."

He smiled fleetingly. "I tell myself that wishing for past things is the first sign of senility. But I remember that you and Brett talked, communicated." His voice lingered on the last word. "She and Roger just play act."

I looked down at the drink. "There were a lot of things about it that were my fault. But that's not one of them."

He gave me a quick, questioning glance, then touched my shoulder. "I'm sorry to bring it up," he said in a dismissing tone. "What can I help you with?"

The chips were in a sandwich bag in my pocket. I pulled them out and spilled them on his kitchen table. They scattered with a hollow rattle. He raised an inquiring eyebrow in their direction.

"I need them analyzed."

"With what in mind?"

"Are you familiar with chips manufactured by Yokama Electric?"

He nodded. "I worked with them at the company."

"Can you get a hold of some Yokama chips and compare them? I need to know if these are the same."

"I can. But I probably can't answer until Monday. Why do you need to know?"

"I wish I could tell you, but I can't. I'm a little out of bounds on this one."

He made a satiric face. "Top secret?"

"Something like that. To do this, does anyone at Yokama need to know?"

"Not if that's important."

"It is."

"All right then. Can you stay?"

I shifted uncomfortably. "I'd like to, but I can't. I'm under some pressure right now."

Concern grazed his face. "Anything I could help with?"

"You already have."

We talked a moment longer. Then he walked me to the door and gave me a firm handshake. "I've missed our talks, Chris."

So had I. "I'll come out again."

"Good." He waved as I went down the pathway, then turned back to the empty, quiet house and shut the door.

I rode back to the agency, trying to think of the case. It made me face something unpleasant: that I was wishing it was someone else's problem. Sometimes I didn't know whether I was trying to avenge Lehman, save Martinson, or catch up to my troubles before they caught me. I went to my office—thinking of Brett, then the case—depressed.

Debbie was waiting with a message. McGuire
had called a meeting the next morning. Woods,
McGuire, Feiner, and me. I was pondering that
when some rodent who processed travel vouchers
came quivering through my door. He was wearing
plaid pants and white patent leather loafers and
blinked a lot, for no particular reason except
maybe the glare from his shoes. He was very disturbed by my expense report for Boston and
couldn't reimburse me until I explained. Why, he
wondered, had it been necessary to stay in Boston
overnight? Because the blizzard had closed the airport, I countered. He started to lecture me on the
difficulties of his job, which I should take more seriously. I amused myself by wondering what
Martinson was up to while I performed such so-
cially useful work. Then I explained that my witness had been run over by a car. I was sure he
understood that made my job more difficult. First
I had to help remove the body from Arlington
Street, and then the tiresome police wanted to re-
hash it all. So I hadn't been able to see the widow
until the next day and, of course, I'd wanted to give
her a proper mourning period. Did he want a
memo explaining all this, I wondered, or would au-
topsy photos suffice? By this time he was green,
and I felt a little sorry for him. Dealing with mad-
men wasn't in his job description. He said he

would think about it and backed out, looking worried.

Robinson passed him on the way in. "What happened at the hospital?"

"The doctors say I'm OK. No fracture."

Robinson looked pleased. "That's good." He checked his watch. "Let's call it quits, Chris. I'll run you home. You've earned it."

That sounded good. But I hadn't talked to Woods yet, about Green or St. Maarten. Robinson waited while I called him. I struck out. Woods was testifying on the Hill on corporate payoffs, then giving a speech in New York. He would be back in the morning. I gave up and accepted the ride.

We walked to the garage, got in his car, and headed toward my place. "So what are you going to do about all this?" he asked.

"I've got a meeting tomorrow. Woods, McGuire, and Feiner. Maybe I can get someone to wake up."

"You might try being nice to McGuire." I looked over at him. He wasn't joking. "You know, Chris, you're a natural target. There's nothing about you that asks for help. You go your own way. Your better side most people don't see because you're so damned private. And you've got no use for the little accommodations people make for each other so they don't have to look at their lives."

I felt touchy. "Just where is all this getting us?"

Robinson glanced over. "Just this. A requirement

for liking you is for people to like themselves. If they don't, there's too much in you that feeds the tapeworm most people carry with them. Look at you and McGuire. You're comfortable with yourself in a way that McGuire will never be. You've never scrapped for money, questioned your right to what you wanted, or worried about pleasing anyone. McGuire's had to do all of that. And you sit there with that you-be-damned expression telling him that it hasn't meant shit."

I wanted to tell him what I was holding against McGuire. But I couldn't. "Look, I never said I was inherently noble. But it's not my fault that McGuire's turned into Silly Putty and the reasons for it—whatever they are—won't make Lehman less dead."

"Have it your way."

"Come off it, Jim. I've got a dead witness and another man missing—maybe dead too. And I can't even find out why. I'm quite a threat to the social fabric."

Robinson pulled up in front of my place. "Look, you've already half-killed yourself. Just what do you want, perfection?"

I opened the door, then leaned back. "No. Just something to halfway justify the splendid opinion I'm supposed to have of myself."

Robinson gave a tired smile. "OK, Chris. Just

take it easy with McGuire. And don't be too disappointed the first Easter after your death."

I was amused in spite of it all. And I wanted to talk with him. But the things on which we parted company were the reasons I couldn't. So I smiled, slapped the hood on his car, and went into my apartment.

I mixed a martini, put on some Chopin, and sat, staring into the empty fireplace. I turned the facts around, but couldn't quite fit Martinson and Sam Green. What thoughts I had kept evanescing. Martinson could help, if I could find him. If he were alive.

That night there was another call. No words. Just silence, to remind me they were there. I hung up. They didn't call back.

TWENTY-THREE

The meeting was scheduled for the next morning. I got to the office and called McGuire's secretary. It was still on, she said. I was thrilled.

I was stepping out my door when the phone rang. I picked it up.

"Good morning," Greenfeld said. "Still want the stuff from the IRS?"

"Sure."

"OK. The Lasko Foundation contributed heavily to only one mental health facility in the Boston area. The Loring Sanitarium, outside of Boston. Gave it a half million last year and three hundred thousand the year before."

"That's a lot."

"Lasko's a nice guy. Don't know what use you can make of it."

"I'll try to think of something. Maybe it'll come to me the first Easter after my death."

"What?"

"Nothing. Listen, I appreciate this."

"Not good enough. You owe me a squash game, at least. 12:30?"

Tuesday, beatings and speeding cars; Friday, squash games. Somewhere my life had stopped making sense. But I owed him.

"OK. I've got to run now. Got a meeting."

"Enjoy yourself."

"I always do," I said, and hung up.

I made it to the meeting on time. I could tell they were serious; a banged-up coffee pot and Styrofoam cups graced McGuire's conference table. I poured a cup and glanced around.

Everyone was already there. McGuire occupied his usual place at the head, looking grim and fidgeting with his belt buckle, as if it wouldn't fit. Feiner perched next to him, wearing a martyr's grimace and managing to hover while just sitting. Woods sat a little apart and to the middle, as if to get a better view of the battlefield. His expression was one of concerned unconcern, as if he'd been working on it. They seemed to circle each other like strange dogs, without moving at all. I slid in at the far end, facing McGuire.

The coffee tasted foul, and the atmosphere smelled of raw nerve ends. I rarely came out of these meetings as well off as I'd entered, and this one felt even worse. I could sense Lasko's unseen presence. A harsh sun cut through the window and into my eyes, forcing me to squint.

McGuire cleared his throat. "As you know, Chris broke Sam Green yesterday. We now have testimony that Lasko goosed the price of his stock."

Woods gave me an approving nod. Feiner picked that up with a nervous half-twitch of his neck. I figured he was still antsy about being one-upped by an anonymous tipster. McGuire droned on. "Lasko apparently found out from Green. His attorney contacted me this morning to discuss settlement." The flat voice tried to make it all sound like nothing.

I jumped in. "Hang on, Joe. This is a criminal case. Just what are they offering?" Woods' eyes tracked the exchange like he was watching Ping-Pong. He turned back to McGuire.

McGuire looked at me for the first time. "Lasko will take an injunction restraining him from such future conduct, without admitting responsibility for Green's actions."

I turned to Woods for help. His eyes deflected the glance. I began to feel very hollow. "What's your recommendation?" I asked McGuire.

"I say we should accept."

"Are you sure we're not being too tough? Maybe we should just revoke his visitor's privileges at Disney World. We could call it 'Son of Hartex.' "

"Don't be cute."

"I'm just curious. Will he agree to any limit on the number of witnesses he kills in any one year?"

"I'm sick of this," McGuire snapped.

"Look," I said to Woods, "there's more to this than stock manipulation or even Lehman." I paused: I couldn't reveal the memo, the chips, or my talk with Tracy. That would tip Lasko, perhaps even push him into another murder. But I decided to open up a little, wondering whether each word made me less safe. "That Carib Imports in St. Maarten looks like a dummy. Lasko started it this July, with a guy named Martinson fronting. Lasko paid Martinson a million-five for it. But I can't find Martinson. He turned up missing as soon as I got there."

Woods took that in. But McGuire cut me off before he could comment.

"And just how does all this connect?"

"I don't know. The point is," I added for Woods, "that this isn't just a stock manipulation."

Woods spoke for the first time, to McGuire. "On what basis do you recommend settlement?"

"On practical grounds." McGuire's gravelly tone was urgent. "We've identified the problem publicly and prevented its recurrence. But we haven't embarrassed the White House more than neccessary. They'll remember that at budget time."

I had to hand it to McGuire; he had the cold-eyed pragmatism bit down pat. And he could usually sell it. The reason for Green's cooperation was clear. Lasko had let Green give us just enough of a case to settle, to keep me from going after the rest.

"What about Chris's other stuff?" Woods was asking McGuire.

McGuire shrugged. "It's all speculation. We've got police for Lehman. And the rest of it's off the subject." Forget it, his voice said. I wondered how many times he'd rehearsed this with Catlow.

Woods raised his eyebrows in my direction. "Chris?"

It was no use accusing McGuire of Martinson's disappearance. Woods wouldn't buy it, and they could always point to De Jonge. I spoke to Woods. "The night I was in St. Maarten, someone tried to run me over. Later, they knocked me out from behind and ransacked my room."

Woods sounded shocked. "What happened, for Godsakes?"

I told them. Woods' expression changed to pained sympathy. "I'm sorry, Chris. Are you all right?" The others mumbled their concern.

I said I was fine. "The point is, there's violence running through this case, and now there's a missing man. This Martinson has disappeared."

Woods leaned over the table. "Any idea where he is?"

I glanced at McGuire, picking my words carefully to protect Tracy—and Martinson himself. "No, I don't. But it's clear that there's a lot to this case, and whatever it is is dangerous."

"But you don't know this Martinson is in danger," Woods said.

"Not in the sense that I can prove it to you. But I believe it."

"Just what do you suggest?" McGuire asked.

"I think we keep digging until we solve this." I turned to Woods. "You told me that cases like this were the measure of an agency. Do you think this deal rates a supplement to *Profiles in Courage*?"

Woods looked troubled. "It has its merits."

"Not many, even overlooking the special handling for Lasko."

"That's hardly unique," he said in a defensive tone.

"And neither are you if you sign off on this."

He shook his head. "The thing is, Chris, we're not criminal investigators. This case has gone beyond what we do. What's happened to you is proof of that. I don't want you hurt. It's time for someone else to take it on."

I kept trying. "But I'm on the right track, if you'll keep me on it. We can't just settle and forget it. That's what Lasko wants. I think he's let Green confess to give us enough to settle the case. There's something else here that Lasko is desperate to keep hidden."

Woods thought for a moment. "What bothers

me," he said to McGuire, "is dropping the rest of it." McGuire didn't reply, and Woods continued. "What I propose is that Chris report all this to the Department of Justice and let them look into it."

McGuire nodded. Feiner looked pleased. And I was out of a case, just like that. The pit of my stomach seemed to drop two feet. I could almost sense Lasko at the table, smiling. I made a last stab in Woods' direction. "You know damned well Justice will sit on this. If we feel pressure over here, look at them. The Attorney General is a cabinet member, for Christsakes."

"I don't accept that," Woods replied calmly. "And it's the best thing we can do. Your investigation has been unconventional, to put it mildly. This case belongs at Justice." His voice was very final.

I hoped no one knew I was hunting Martinson. Then it hit me that I wasn't anymore. I forgot myself and remembered Tracy. Someone would have to find him for her—Di Pietro, I hoped. "I'd like to brief the Boston police before I write this up," I said.

"What for?" McGuire asked.

"Because Lehman is their business. You said so yourself."

That stung him. "Don't you think you've done enough?"

Woods spoke over him. "If Chris confines himself to facts, I think that's acceptable. We can't pretend facts don't exist."

McGuire flushed and was silent.

"All right," Woods said smoothly. "If you recommend settlement to the Commission, I'll support it. I'll set up a meeting. Chris will make his report and brief the police on Monday, if he likes. Then this case is closed."

"It isn't good enough," I said to Woods. "It's not even close."

Woods looked at me evenly. "I'm sorry, Chris. You've been through a lot, worked hard, and done well. But I think this is the right thing for you and for the agency." He glanced around. "Is there anything else?"

They all turned to me. My eyes moved over them slowly one by one. Then I stood, slid my chair in carefully, and left them sitting there.

I stalked back to the office and called Di Pietro while I could still think. He agreed to meet me Monday, with no particular enthusiasm. That only made me angrier. I wanted to leave right then. But to go before Monday, without orders, could only give away my plans and endanger Martinson. I had to wait—and hope. And I needed Di Pietro. So I thanked him for his time.

I had been standing with the phone in hand, talking. I slammed it down and slumped into my plastic chair. For some reason, I began staring at the one thing there I owned: my bookends, onyx, carved with fierce Aztec faces. I called them mine. They were Great-grandfather Kenyon's really. He'd picked them up in Mexico in the last century, while he was picking up part of Mexico. I looked at them glumly. The only thing I could say for McGuire's settlement was that it might make me safe—as safe as the nicest little bureaucrat at the sleepiest agency in town. I wondered why it felt so bad.

I was still staring at the bookends when McGuire opened the door. I was surprised. He'd never done that before.

"Don't you think you've done enough?" I parroted.

He ignored that. "You think Woods is your friend, don't you?"

I wondered where that came from. He stood in front of my desk, his face completely expressionless. "Are you going to be my friend, Joe? That's a real comfort."

His eyes narrowed, as if debating whether to say more. I watched him, feeling as friendly as the Aztec carvings. "I'm just telling you to watch your step," he answered quietly.

I shrugged. "I guess you know what happens to people who don't watch their step." I looked up at him, but what I saw was Tracy—and Lehman in the street.

His eyes sparked, then turned blank. "Shut up,

Chris," he said, very softly. He wheeled and snapped the door behind him, as if kissing me off.

Life goes on, I thought. Cases come and go and widows get over it. Husbands get lost and stay that way. I couldn't worry about that. After all, I had important things to do. Greenfeld and I were playing squash.

TWENTY-FOUR

The green ball ricocheted off the white walls, pursued by an echo, a rubberized whine which carried into the next hit. Greenfeld and I scrambled after it, armed with wooden rackets. The only other sound was the quick, hollow thud of our tennis shoes.

Greenfeld played with tenacious alertness, as if squash were his job. The ball shot to my backhand. I wheeled and slammed it hard and low to the left corner. Greenfeld sped for the left wall. The stretched arc of his racket ripped air and missed the green blur by half an inch. He shook his head. We usually played even. Today I was beating hell out of him.

It kept up. I flowed on a savage adrenalin rush, half-conscious. The last point was low and to my right. I lunged, skidded on my chest, and hacked wildly from the elbow. The ball looped off the front wall. Greenfeld went for it and missed. Another half inch. My game.

He stared at the ball, dying in small bounces in a far corner. It gave a last rubbery whimper and rolled into stillness. He turned, hands on hips.

"You'll never do that again," he said.

"I know."

We showered and dressed in silence, then taxied toward the Hill. Greenfeld lost hard. He leaned against the right rear door, thinking it over. "Crew was your sport in college, right?"

"Yeah."

"That explains the forearms," he said, as if he'd caught me cheating.

"It also was perfect training for my current position. I sat absolutely still until someone shouted at me. Then I would stroke as fast as they told me, no faster, until someone said to stop. Then I stopped."

Greenfeld's absent smile turned inquisitive without changing at all. "What happened over there?"

"Nothing. Doesn't it always?"

His eyes sharpened. "Did they screw up your case?"

"No, we've got a splendid result. Lasko has promised never to do it again, without conceding he did it in the first place."

"You don't sound impressed."

"Are you?"

"Not very."

"Well, that makes you smarter than most of your colleagues in the financial press. Not to mention Congress."

"You'll have to go further to flatter me. Particularly after that squash game. Now why"—his voice arched—"do I get the feeling you're holding out?"

"I don't know, Lane. Paranoia, maybe."

He didn't smile. I decided to answer. "If I'm holding out, it's because there's something still at stake." Martinson, for instance. "We can't always work the same side of the street."

"I'm not persuaded," he said with irony.

"You don't know what I know."

"That's the problem."

"Bullshit, Lane. Do I know all there is to know about the *Post*? Do your readers know all there is to know about the news?"

He didn't pursue that, and neither did I. I still wanted to pump him. It was reflex, mainly; the ECC had just closed the case. But it wasn't that easy for me. I kept looking for answers. "Just out of useless curiosity," I tried, "what is Justice doing about the antitrust case? Settling like us?"

"Why should I tell you?" he jibed, not joking.

"Because I beat you at squash."

He smiled slightly. "The honest answer is I don't know. One lawyer at Justice has been slipping me bits *sub rosa*. He says they were poised to prosecute. Then your friend Catlow stepped in to negotiate for Lasko. In July sometime the word seeped down that the case was going to be settled. Just like that. My source thought that was pretty solid. Then this month he heard maybe the settlement was off, that something was holding it up. I figure maybe the something was your investigation." He paused and looked at me quizzically. "Just what have you got?"

"I just wish they'd let me find out."

"So why hold out?" It wasn't pressure now, but real curiosity.

"All I can say is that you would, too."

"Thanks." The crack needled both of us.

"You're welcome."

The taxi got to the Hill and dropped us off. We walked together. The wet sun steamed our foreheads. We loosened our ties and slung our jackets over our shoulders. Greenfeld looked over at me. "I picked up a rumor the other day from a guy who writes one of our financial columns. He says Lasko's in a cash squeeze, something about the plants they've built to handle the defense stuff costing a lot of money. Is that what you're into?"

I shook my head. "No. I haven't seen any sign, but then I haven't been looking. I suppose it's possible—if they've dressed up their financials some."

He considered that and so did I. But I didn't

want to talk it over then. "Whatever happened with the woman and your Bogart film?" I asked.

He smiled thinly. "The woman palled. The film held up nicely, though." His words held a note of irony, as if he were tired of himself. I didn't pursue it. I was tired of myself too—and the strange and treacherous world in which I worked.

We walked across the Capitol grounds toward the Senate wing, moving from shade tree to shade tree. We stopped in the parking lot. The sun baked it, soaking the asphalt and glazing windshields. Greenfeld stood sideways, still holding his coat. "You know, Chris," he said, "something hit me the other day."

"What's that?"

"That at our age, Mozart was dead."

"That's just great, Lane."

"You're welcome," he said dryly, and strolled off toward the Senate.

I walked back to the agency wishing I were somewhere else. The lobbies looked deserted, and the elevators seemed sluggish. Debbie was out. I gazed past her desk, feeling as empty as my office. No one at home in there. Martinson had to wait till Monday, and Lehman haunted me. I picked up the phone and called Mary.

TWENTY-FIVE

Mary showed up at my place about eight that evening, in a sensible green Volkswagen. She wore blue jeans, a leather belt, and a quiet, expensive crepe blouse. "Hi," she said in a soft, direct voice. "I'm glad you're all right."

I thanked her and led her into the living room. "You know," I admitted, "I haven't thought about what we're doing tonight."

"It doesn't really matter. Whatever." That was companionable, I thought. I glanced over at her. She had turned to the wall and was silently appraising the print next to the fireplace.

"That's a Vasarély," I explained.

She nodded, not turning. "I like it." I couldn't have guessed how much she knew about art. I didn't care really, except that she was always that way.

Her eyes had moved on, scanning the room with

a careful gaze which seemed somehow proprietary. "You're certainly neat for a bachelor."

"Yes," I smiled, "I'm almost totally housebroken."

She grinned back in real amusement. "I guess that was fairly condescending."

"Fairly. Care for some wine?"

"What is it?"

I went to the refrigerator and reported back over my shoulder. "A California Riesling, cheap but drinkable. At least I drink it."

"That sounds fine."

I poured two glasses and bore them carefully into the living room. She was sitting on the couch across from the fireplace. I gave her a glass and sat.

She took a sip. "I hear you're settling the Lasko case."

"They did that," I said pointedly.

"And you're unhappy?" she asked, looking over at me.

"It leaves a corpse unaccounted for, and a husband missing."

"I'm sorry, Chris." She sounded sympathetic enough. "What are you going to do?"

I realized that I was holding up my left hand as if to deflect her questions. "The Lasko case is not for tonight. Really."

"OK." She was certainly agreeable, as if her edginess were melting with the case. Maybe that made some sense. But the Lasko thing was something we weren't discussing. Not tonight, and not ever.

I had a wooden backgammon set on the glass coffee table in front of the couch. She opted for that. I put Melissa Manchester on the stereo while she set up the board. Night was coming fast, staining the corners with darkness. I turned up the dimmer on the living room chandelier and came back to the couch.

I won the first move, a six-five combination. I cleared my end point and watched her. She played with fierce concentration. I freed the other end point, then got great rolls, and strung together some points. The play moved fast. She showed me a wicked end game, smart and decisive. But I beat her, finally. This seemed to be my day for winning games. Except the one that mattered.

We talked quietly, finishing our second glass of wine while Melissa sang "New Beginnings." I had some joints rolled in the cigarette case I kept in a bedroom drawer. I offered one to Mary. She nodded her interest.

I went to the bedroom and brought back two, turning down the dimmer on the way. We both sat cross-legged on the couch, facing each other, with an ashtray in between and the half-dead wine bottle still on the table.

I lit one. Mary leaned back and took a hit. "What kind is that?"

"Something called Meshpecon. They grow it in Mexico, or Peru, or some such place." I pulled on it and passed it back. She took another hit, a good one.

"You know, I never asked where you took that vacation. The one"—she picked for a frame of reference other than Lasko—"a couple of weeks ago."

"Oh that," I said. It seemed years ago, and maybe someone else's vacation. "New Hampshire."

"Why New Hampshire?"

"An old friend of mine owns a place up there, near the Maine border. If I schedule right, I can get it to myself."

"You always go alone?"

"Usually." Except for the woman in Boston, who had belonged there. I wondered if Brett went anymore. Of course she still lived here, in a way. Every so often I'd find a trace of her in the old house, like an artifact in someone else's ruins.

"Isn't that pretty solitary?" she was asking.

I took another hit. "Not really. I saw some friends from school for a couple of days. The best day, though, was alone. I hiked up Green Mountain, which is only a couple of thousand feet. Maybe an hour and a half worth of climbing. There's an old ranger tower on top that gives you a perfect 360-degree of everything. The lakes and woods, farms, old villages, other mountains, all of it for miles. It was perfectly clear. I sat there for two hours. I hated to come down."

"It sounds beautiful," she answered softly. "It's good to be alone without being lonely."

That was right, I thought. Except for tonight. Tonight, alone would have been lonely, any way you cut it.

Mary was leaning back. She sucked on the joint, making small hollows beneath her cheekbones. "This dope is sensational."

I thought about that. "Yeah, I think that's how Pizarro slaughtered all those Indians. They were smoking this stuff."

She smiled absently. I looked at her again. She was beautiful. No question. But that didn't move me, right then. I was flashing back and forth between New Hampshire and here, past and future, the woman then and the woman now. Rod Stewart's dope-and-whiskey voice cut through the haze.

I lit the second joint. It flamed, crackled, then took hold. I passed it to her, with another glass of wine for the cotton mouth. The room was very dim. Mary's fine cheekbones left soft shadows on her face. I was floating now. Her sudden question seemed to filter through a word at a time.

"What do you want in a woman, Chris?"

It was as if she'd looked into my head and seen Brett. But her voice wasn't intrusive, just curious.

And I was stoned enough to try. "A lot of what I look for in people, I guess. Curiosity. Dislike for the easy answer. That in a good moment they can imagine what it's like to be an old woman or a small child. That they are more than what they do, or what they are."

"You don't ask much," she said, smiling.

"Not much at all." But I'd had it once and blown it.

The Jefferson Starship came on. I looked at Mary, wondering what she was thinking.

Her voice broke the quiet. "You know, Chris, you've been very lucky. You've never wanted—or needed—anything."

"I keep hearing that."

"No, I mean it. Half the girls I knew growing up were married at eighteen. Sometimes I hate looking back."

I smiled. "No need. You've done a lot. That's something else I like in a woman."

She smiled back. I reached for her then. She looked at me with a clear, black gaze. Then her arms raised in a graceful arc and pulled me down.

Afterwards a long drowsy silence, warm in the dark. An hour, maybe more. No talk needed. She stirred against me. "Again?" she murmured.

"Uh-huh. Lust is the curse of my family."

"The Pagets or the Kenyons?"

"Both."

She laughed quietly, then stretched herself against me. The Starship was singing "Miracles."

It turned out she had clothes in the car. She stayed until Sunday.

Sunday night I turned on the television. My theory was that there were other things going on in the world and that they would divert me. It worked for a while. There were famine conditions in India. OPEC had hiked the price of oil. You couldn't breathe in Pittsburgh, and another Arab had hijacked another plane. Everything was fine until a familiar face appeared.

They had caught him in the Rose Garden, in a discursive mood. "When I was young," the President was saying, "we had no money. No one in my family had ever gone to college. I scraped to get where I am." The camera closed in. "It is my philosophy that everyone in this country has the right to lead a good and comfortable life, even become wealthy, although I myself gave up many opportunities to make some money for a career in public service." He sounded somehow disappointed. "So," he was concluding, "everyone has the right to climb the ladder, and everyone in this country has the opportunity to do so. I especially urge our young people to consider that. It's one of the great things about us."

I nearly choked up with real tears. The telephone stopped me.

"Hello, Mr. Paget?"

"Tracy? Where are you?"

"At home. St. Maarten." The long distance made the girl-voice smaller. "I haven't heard from Peter." Her sad question went unanswered.

"I'm sorry, Tracy. I haven't either. I've been trying, really." I couldn't explain what had happened Friday, and couldn't explain my weekend, even if I'd wanted to.

Her voice cracked. "Please—can't you help me?"

"I'm going to Boston tomorrow. To talk to the police." I paused. "I think they'll want to help."

"Do you think so?" A small hope breathed in her words. It made me feel guilty.

"Lieutenant Di Pietro's a good man. I'm sure he'll be interested."

"Oh," she said. I could envision her hopeful imagining: Di Pietro the compassionate, restorer of husbands. "Mr. Paget, you've made me feel better."

"Please call me Chris. And if I'm not here, you can reach me through the office. Anytime you want to talk."

"Thank you, Chris," she said. "You're very nice. I'd better get off now."

I wanted to keep her on, but couldn't imagine what to say. I gave up. "Take care of yourself,

Tracy." That was the last thing she wanted to do. But she said she would and hung up.

The President had disappeared. I turned off the tube and stared out the window.

No one else called that weekend. I guess they figured I wasn't worth calling anymore.

TWENTY-SIX

Boston was sunny this time, its warmth cut by a fresh breeze. That was something. I had begun to associate Boston with drizzle, corpses, and old girlfriends, like some back-lot of the mind where I stashed half-digested fears.

I picked up my bags and went straight to the car rental. The young woman at the counter had a cute pug nose and a fey expression which turned wary when she saw me, as if I were about to make an indecent proposal.

"I'm not here to make an indecent proposal," I said, "just rent a car."

Her eyes widened slightly. "Well, that's original anyhow."

"I'll take something cheap, if it runs. You know, this job must be great for your ego."

Her smile was wry. "Not really. You should see people who try to come on to me. Wrinkles and halitosis. The one today had breath bad enough to melt my fillings. God, I wonder what they're like at home."

"God knows. My personal thing is dressing up in a wet suit and flippers and jumping out of closets. But I could tell right away you weren't that kind of woman."

"Thanks," she deadpanned. "Will a Mustang be OK?"

"If you don't have an Edsel."

"I rented the last Edsel to the guy with the bad breath," she said, and took my name down on the rental form.

She handed across the keys and told me where the lot was. Then she looked at me. "Will you be returning the car here, Mr. Paget?"

"I think so."

"Good," she smiled.

You never know. I thanked her and started to leave. "About the wet suit and flippers," she called out. "Try Radcliffe."

The things college graduates were doing these days. I grinned and waved over my shoulder. But I didn't feel all that funny.

I picked up the car and headed for town through the Callahan Tunnel. What was Mary doing today, I wondered.

I pulled up to the Ritz and left my car in front. A doorman took my bags. I stopped for a second and stared back onto Arlington. The street was quiet.

The spot where he had landed was just another patch of cement. Beyond, the Public Garden was warm with slanted sunlight and alive with people and here and there a couple. It was as if it had never happened. I looked at my watch. 3:45. I turned and walked into the lobby.

I got myself checked into a room, a quiet one and not the one I'd had twelve days ago. Coming back to the Ritz had been a reflex. But I didn't want a martini from the bar. I took the elevator down, slid into the car, and drove to the police station.

I parked a couple of blocks away and walked over. The station seemed less sullen in the sun. But the sergeant at the desk was just as fat and his eyes still as bleak as Cape Cod in January. I asked for Di Pietro. He told me to wait in a voice that went with the rest of him. So I waited, looking him over. Nothing there at all. Either he'd seen too much, or the hounds of boredom had seized his brain. I was leaning toward boredom when Di Pietro appeared and summoned me to his office.

I followed him back to the same cubbyhole and sat. He slid behind his desk, quickly for a big man, and leaned back in his chair. "What can I do for you, Mr. Paget?" he asked. The turtle stare was perpetual, I decided. I wondered how his kids liked it.

"Quite a bit."

His gaze was neither friendly nor unfriendly. "What have you got?"

I ticked it off. "One, we've got testimony implicating Lasko in the stock manipulation. Second, I've got evidence indicating that Lasko used a guy named Martinson to help set up a dummy corporation. Martinson was forced to leave a Caribbean island when I flew down to investigate." Di Pietro played with a penknife while I told him what I hadn't told the agency. "Martinson could be very dangerous to Lasko. Indications are that he's being kept in Boston, maybe at a place called the Loring Sanitarium."

He blinked at that last bit of information, as if it were unexpected. But his question doubled back. "Do you know what Lehman was going to tell you?"

"No."

Di Pietro looked sleepy. "Well, some of this is interesting, but you haven't told me anything about Lehman."

"Maybe Martinson can."

"You don't know that. Just why do you think he's at Loring?"

I reviewed it: Martinson's "mental strain," the call to Tracy, and Lasko's connection with Loring. Di Pietro pondered it a while.

"It's pretty weak," he said. "Just what do you want us to do?"

"Go out to the Loring Sanitarium. See if Martinson is there. He may be in real trouble."

He scowled. "I can't do that."

The frustration sharpened my words. "I wish I had your driving curiosity."

He cut me off in a voice managers reserve for rookies. "Look, I'm a cop, doing a job you don't know squat about. This may be your first murder, if it is one, but it isn't mine. Now one real possibility is that Lehman was killed, not just hit and run. But it's only that—a possibility. You can't tell me what Lehman knew, and I can't even begin to find out. His widow is a dead end. So all I've got are your theories, and I can't book Lasko on that. Hell, I can't even ask him anything smarter than 'who killed Cock Robin.' And like I said, we're not geared to investigate big companies."

"I'm sorry I let you down."

He ignored that. "Another thing. The Loring Sanitarium is out of Boston. I've got no jurisdiction there. We'd have to go through the locals and I'd need a reason, which you haven't given me. You know," the quiet voice turned quieter, "it's only on TV that cops have national jurisdiction. You'd be surprised how many times the Beverly Hills police don't even ask me for advice."

"That's funny."

"Not very."

He had a point. It wasn't funny. It especially

wasn't because I figured he was right. I felt reckless, at the end of my rope. "I'm just trying to keep Martinson alive while I put your case together."

I knew as soon as I said it that it was stupid. Di Pietro spoke in a cold, even tone. "You know, Mr. Paget, I don't much like you."

"You know," I snapped, "I don't much care."

He surprised me by almost smiling. "Then I guess we'll both have to get over it."

That was that. I stood. "Thanks."

He looked up at me impassively. "Sure."

I let myself out.

I walked out of the station and back toward the car, only half-aware, thinking of how well I'd done for Tracy.

I stopped when I saw a phone booth, remembering Stansbury. I stepped in and called.

"Mr. Stansbury, this is Chris."

"Chris? You sound fuzzy. Where are you?"

"Boston." There was silence. "I'm calling about the chips," I prodded.

"Oh, surely," he apologized. "They match."

"Are you sure?"

"Absolutely. I'm familiar with them and I did some tests. Those chips you gave me were manufactured by Yokama Electric. No question. I hope that helps."

"It does, and thank you. I'll call when I get back to town."

"Do that, Chris." I said good-bye and hung up.

I found the car. I got in and sat there, very still. I could be safe, or not. My choice.

There was a street map in the glove compartment. I took it and mulled it over. After a while I folded the map and turned the ignition. Then I pulled from the curb and headed for the Loring Sanitarium.

TWENTY-SEVEN

The Loring Sanitarium was in Brookline, near the country club. I picked up Boylston Street until it turned into Route 9 by way of Brookline Avenue, figuring to get there about 6:30. I felt queasy. I had crossed the line. This was my own trip, against orders, and maybe into trouble. Martinson might not be there. And I'd no fixed plan if he were.

I had the pervasive sense that I hadn't listened hard enough. That in the past four days someone had handed me the key, if I could only think. But I'd heard too much too fast, and was too unsettled to stitch it together. I got to Brookline disgusted and unnerved.

The Loring Sanitarium wasn't tough to spot. It was the kind of building that could only be a sanitarium or a high school—a stark, tan-brick rectangle with a charmless Eisenhower-years design, two stories, in a bare field set away from houses. I knew it wasn't a high school because there weren't any signs. That and the isolation gave it a guilty, furtive air: the kind of place people didn't look at when they passed.

I pulled up in the front parking lot and got out. At closer range it looked off center, like a patient too distracted to keep himself up. The lawn was long and ratty and a couple of windows were askew, like an idiot's glasses. Lasko's money hadn't gone for renovation.

An iron plate was screwed into the brick next to the front door. It read "The Loring Sanitarium" in capital letters and in small print under that was "Dr. Ralph Loring, Director." The front doors were broad plate glass. I opened one. A uniformed guard sat at a metal desk in front of a second row of doors. He gave me a pleased, suspicious look, as if being suspicious beat boredom.

"Yes, sir?" he asked, but not the polite "yes, sir" of a maître d' or a saleswoman.

"I'm here for Dr. Loring," I said, trying to suggest that Loring should be pleased.

The guard wasn't impressed. "Does he know you're here?"

"Not unless you tell him."

He didn't like that. "Does he know you were coming?" he asked roughly.

"No."

His face closed. "What's your business?"

That forced me to do what I didn't want: pose as

a federal officer whose boss knew his whereabouts. I pulled out my ID card. "I'm with the ECC, headquarters office. I'll take my business up with Dr. Loring."

That brought me another stare. But his thick hand grudgingly reached for the phone. He dialed two digits and asked whoever answered for Dr. Loring, without moving his eyes from me. I stared past him through the second doors. There was a hallway with a light green linoleum fading into chartreuse beneath darker green tile walls. There appeared to be offices on the right side.

"Yes, sir," the guard was saying. "I have a Mr. Paget here. His identification says he's with"—he looked again—"The United States Economic Crimes Commission." Whatever that is, his eyes said, but his voice didn't admit that. Security people were supposed to know these things. He listened for a moment, then hung up.

"Dr. Loring will see you," he said in a disappointed voice. I hadn't turned out to be any fun. I started for the doors. "Wait here," he growled, pointing in front of his desk.

I complied. The guard leaned back, eyes moving uneasily between me and the outer door. Dr. Loring was taking his time. I jammed my hands into my pockets and shifted from foot to foot, feeling nervous and a little silly.

My feet were wearing out when a tall, grey-haired man appeared beyond the second doors, walking with a slight stoop. He wore a tweed suit and through the glass he looked like an English gentleman hunting for grouse. The apparition came toward the doors and opened them.

"Mr. Paget," he said, ignoring the guard, "I'm Ralph Loring." He had a thin nose and a lightly pocked face, partly covered by a neat beard. The brown eyes had a liquid, volatile quality as if about to change into some unstable element. Sensitive, but not quite right. Psychiatrist's eyes, I thought.

I shook his hand and walked with him through the second doors. "I appreciate being received," I said. "Your man out there had me at bay."

It was intended as a light remark. But he gave me a sideways, troubled gaze. "I'm sure you understand our security problems."

I thought maybe I did. Loring had resumed the downcast hunch. I looked at him. He was thinner than he'd first appeared, but not wiry, just bony. His skin was pale and seemed almost translucent.

Loring led me to an office on the right corridor. It was wood paneled and fairly plain: a couple of framed diplomas and two prints by the guy who paints the children with big eyes. I didn't like the pictures much and looking at Loring I liked them less. His eyes were something like that.

I took a chair. Loring sat behind his desk, legs crossed and hands folded. He eyed me uneasily, as if I were a threat to some delicate balance in the environment.

"I'm told that you have identification," he ventured.

I took out my plastic card and slid it across his desk. He took it with two fingers, eyes half-closed, the old reluctant gesture of a man who has just drawn to an inside straight. Then he looked down at it for an overly long time, as if it could tell him something.

He looked up. "What do you want here, Mr. Paget?"

I gambled. "Peter Martinson."

His eyes flickered for an instant. "I'm not sure I understand."

I decided to go all the way. "Martinson's a witness in an investigation. The case involves fraud, murder, and your leading patron, William Lasko. I know that Martinson is no crazier than you or I and that he didn't volunteer for this rest cure. Which puts you in a crack."

I could have been wrong. And he could have said that I was delusional, or just ordered me out. The last idea seemed to flash through his eyes, then leave, along with his chance to play innocent. "Mr. Martinson is a patient of mine." The voice held a weak man's stubbornness.

"I'd like to see him."

"I'm sure you would," he said with a spurt of

righteous sarcasm, as if I were the neighborhood bully, torturing an animal. Loring, the protector. He'd probably played that role long enough to believe it.

I said nothing. He blurted into the silence. "In my opinion, seeing you would do Mr. Martinson no good."

"Would do *who* no good?"

He flushed slightly. "I can't entrust the mental health of one of my patients to you."

I decided to give Loring a dose of reality. "You have at least kept him alive?"

"Of course," he said with real indignation.

"Bully for you, Doctor. The last one in Martinson's position ended up deader than your rotten paintings."

He snapped upright. "You're not a very pleasant young man."

"This isn't a very pleasant subject. And I'm tired of sparring."

He picked up my ID card, as if something on it might help him. It gave me a chance to decipher the list on his desk, upside down.

"Christopher Kenyon Paget," he was reading. "Wasn't Christopher Kenyon a railroad owner in California in the last century?"

I was still decoding. "My great-great-grandfather, if that concerns you."

Somehow that placed me within his frame of reference. "As I recall, he sent out armed guards to kill some strikers. Nine men died, I think. Is that what makes you tick, Mr. Paget? Overcompensation, perhaps."

I was through. "You know," I said evenly, "I get tired of jerks who want me to apologize for having a middle name instead of an initial and an ancestor I didn't ask for. I'm especially tired of jerks who do it for a living. And I never heard that the old man fronted for other people's murders. Which is what you're doing." I snatched the list off his desk. "Now, Doctor, I'd like to see Martinson."

His hand jerked in a futile grab for the list. He suddenly broke down. "You must realize that I need money for our work," he stammered. "This hospital would have to close."

The list said that Martinson was in Room 19-W. I looked back at Loring. The hand was still outstretched, pleading now. "Never mind, Doctor," I said, and started to leave.

He stepped after me. "Do you have a search warrant?"

I turned back. "No."

"Then you're trespassing."

That was true. I felt as if somewhere between Lehman and here I'd stopped being a lawyer and become someone I didn't know. I pushed all that aside. "If you're so confident of your legal position, call the police. As an accessory to kidnapping you'll have their fullest sympathy."

His shoulders stooped at that. He stood in front of his desk, wet eyes seeing some inevitable disaster. I thought he looked like a man in a bomb shelter would look when he heard the first siren. I left and went hunting for Martinson.

The west wing was in the opposite corridor. It was the same green, but the dim lighting gave it a sort of restrained ghastliness. Ahead I saw doors and before that a broad beam of light coming from a nurses' station. An older nurse peered out, puzzled. I nodded, smiled, and walked on. I heard voices behind me, a woman's, then a man's. Then footsteps scrambling in the other direction. It reminded me of the lump on my head. But I didn't look back. Room 19-W was at the end of the corridor. It surprised me. No guard. Just a simple latch which locked the door from the outside. I turned the latch and opened the door.

TWENTY-EIGHT

Martinson sat in an armchair, reading a copy of *Sports Illustrated*. He half-dropped the magazine, and stared at me with fearful unrecognition. His eyes asked who I was, but his mouth couldn't form the words.

"I'm Christopher Paget, from the ECC. I've been looking for you."

"My God," he exclaimed, and his tone wasn't grateful. I looked him over then. Tracy's picture was a good likeness. He was tan and wiry, with black curly hair and chiseled features. The plain slacks and oxford cloth shirt went with the expensive loafers. A well-preserved college boy from the early sixties, catnip for gullible women. What was wrong with him began in the myopic foxiness of the green eyes and bled subtly into his features, making them spoiled and vaguely weak.

"You don't know what you're doing," he blurted. I hadn't expected this. I remembered the running footsteps in the corridor. "Why don't you tell me on the way out?"

"Where are we going?"

"To the police."

He shook his head. "Look, if I keep my head down, I won't get hurt." The words mixed fear and calculation. "You're the one who got me into this mess."

Tension raised my voice. "We'll argue that later. Come on."

Martinson's hands clamped the chair as if it were a life raft. "They'll kill me. They've already killed Alec Lehman."

That stopped me for a moment. But there wasn't time for questions. "Then you're in a jam," I said, "because now that I've found you, they'll do just that."

He hesitated, stiff with fear and resentment. I grabbed his forearm and pulled him up. He stumbled with me out the door, gaping at the bleak empty corridors. His voice was a savage whine. "Did Tracy tell you where to look?" I nodded and pulled him with me. "Stupid bitch," he mumbled.

My grip tightened. "You know, Martinson, rescuing you is a real disappointment." But I understood, in a way. He was a frightened man. I was frightened too.

The walk up the corridor seemed treadmill slow. The nurses' station was empty. I looked quickly around. Except for Martinson, the wing was vacant.

Then I heard a drum roll of footsteps. A clump of figures appeared suddenly at the end of the corridor. I picked out Loring and the guard and two large men I didn't know. The other man was tall and broad-built. Lasko. Whatever Martinson knew had flushed him out.

I felt Martinson blanch. "Jesus."

I tried to put up a front. "Just let me handle this," I said, without looking at him. Lasko was standing ahead of the group, waiting. Ahead must be the only way out.

We were within thirty feet of them now. Lasko's face was a mask of controlled anger. Something I didn't quite understand had pushed his plans awry, and it showed in his face. The two large men fanned out to either side of him, blocking our way. Loring and the guard hung back as if lost.

We got within ten feet and stopped. Lasko stared at us, eyes hard and calculating. The man to his left was bald, and watched us with a greyhound's watery eyes. The other man was younger, with a mustache and thick brown hair. I wondered if they had guns. No one moved. I wished fiercely that I hadn't come.

Lasko's voice rang commandingly in the hall. "You're very persistent, Mr. Paget, and you don't pay attention when you should. But you're not leaving."

My brain pumped words in some panicky reflex. "We are unless you're planning a mass murder." I didn't like my voice. My mouth felt artificially dry, as if the saliva had been sucked out.

A spark of interest crossed Lasko's face. "All right. You've got my attention." The carefully controlled voice made it sound as if we were discussing a business decision.

"You should have killed Martinson in the first place. But now I know what he knows." Which wasn't true. Lasko's eyes snapped toward Martinson. But Martinson didn't, or couldn't, say anything. "So when you kill Martinson, you have to kill me too. And there's a Boston cop who knows where I am."

I shot a glance at Loring. He gaped at the word "murder" like a man listening to a foreign language, hoping he had somehow misheard. I went on. "You can't trust Loring either. Kill us and the cops will be here tomorrow, poking around. He's got his license to consider, not to mention his freedom."

My voice had turned advisory. Lasko paused, as if he could hear my words coming from Catlow's mouth. The two men at his side were cool and relaxed, waiting for orders. It could go either way, I thought. I was feeling the cold reality; for whatever reason, Lasko wanted us dead.

Lasko picked for words that could never hurt him. "You're talking nonsense, Mr. Paget," he said casually. "I doubt the people in your agency have even authorized this."

I pointed to the guard. He froze in stupefaction. "The cops will track him down too. So I figure you have to kill four people anyway. I probably left someone out. I saw a couple of nurses a while ago."

Lasko's eyes turned inward, as if he were deciding whether to wait. He said nothing more; there were witnesses all around him.

I started walking, steering Martinson to the right. Five feet between me and the mustached man. My stomach felt empty. The mustached man looked back, hand in his pocket, his eyes completely blank. He stepped back three feet, to see Lasko and me at once. We kept moving. The man took in Lasko with the corner of his eyes. Then a signal moved through them.

We reached him. His hand stirred in his pocket. Then he turned sideways. We passed him and turned the corner, heading for the entrance.

Loring stood at our left in an angular slouch, like some lone desiccated bird about to become extinct. We swept by. He stared at his feet.

The inner set of doors was a few feet ahead. Silence behind us. Our footsteps echoed in the corridor. Martinson looked white. My back burned with imagined gunshots.

We burst through the first set of doors. They closed behind us with a slow sigh. I grabbed the outer door. It opened. Fresh air splashed our faces.

We walked to the car and drove away.

TWENTY-NINE

"Jesus," Martinson kept saying. I steered back onto Route 9, my mind on automatic pilot. My hands were clammy, and my mind was numb with disbelief. Martinson was shivering uncontrollably next to me, like a malaria victim.

We rolled through Brookline toward Boston. It was still light out. I was glad; I would have flinched at each taillight in the dark. Martinson was jabbering this and that, about to break into a talking jag. I reached for the car radio, trying to collect my thoughts, but all I got was a folk song that was going nowhere and feeling sorry for itself doing it. I switched it off.

"How did Lasko get there?" Martinson's voice was blaming me.

"Loring kept me waiting long enough. He probably called him."

"Then why did he let us go?"

"Two possibilities. One is that Lasko decided to

chance beating the Lehman thing and whatever you know, rather than kill someone else. Notice he didn't say an incriminating word back there. The other is that he'll take a shot at us, but away from witnesses, so he has some chance to walk away. I wouldn't mind if you'd keep an eye out the back window."

"For what?" he asked anxiously.

"For whatever looks like it's following us."

"Jesus," he said again. He turned sideways and rested his chin on the top of the car seat. His eyes seemed to strain clear back to the sanitarium.

"What happened?" I asked, as much for diversion as anything else.

"When?"

"Between St. Maarten and now?"

"What's today?"

"Monday."

His eyes crinkled. "Last Tuesday morning two guys who were with Lasko show up . . ."

I interrupted. "The ones from the sanitarium?"

"No, a crew-cut guy and one with a big, puffy nose. They said you were looking for me about the Carib deal. I asked why." His voice cut loose. "They said never mind why—that I had to take off, right then. I said I didn't want to—that I wanted to know what the story was. They said Lasko would talk to me later—not to make trouble. I said I wanted to call him. Then they told me I was in trouble too, if

I didn't move. Yeah, and they threatened my wife."
The last sounded like an afterthought. I suspected
she always had been.

Martinson stopped to concentrate on the rear
window.

"See anything?" I asked.

"I don't think so."

"Go on."

"Oh yeah, well, they kind of hauled me to some
rented car they had, like a prisoner. The bald one
stepped back in the warehouse to talk to a guy
named Kendrick."

"I met him. Why did you hire him, to bite mail-
men?"

"They stuck me with him. Anyhow, we drove to
the airport. On the way out I was sort of complain-
ing and one guy said I was just going to Boston, to
be safe. We drove up to this Lear jet, and they said
to call Tracy so she wouldn't send out a search
party. The mustached guy listens to make sure I
don't say anything out of line. I just tell her that I
have to leave. The bald guy comes up to talk to his
buddy while I'm still on, so I sort of whispered to
Tracy that I'd be safe in Boston, so please not to
make trouble. I wasn't supposed to tell Tracy about
Boston, and she wasn't supposed to tell you." He
still sounded aggrieved.

I ignored that. "What happened next?"

"They flew me to Boston, with a stop in Orlando,

I think. Anyhow, they took me out to the sanitarium. The room was all set up to be locked from the outside, in an empty wing—you saw it."

"When did Lasko show up?"

"We got there at night. Lasko came out next morning. He said the Carib deal had some illegal aspects and that I was in up to my ears. He scared the hell out of me. He can do that."

"I know."

"Then he said I just needed to keep my head low for a couple of weeks until he fixed the case. I kept saying I wanted to leave. He got angry then and hinted around that he'd already had Alec Lehman killed. I shut up after that."

It still shook me. Believing it was bad. But hearing it was worse. "I can see why he was concerned," I finally said.

His voice tightened. "What do you mean?"

"I mean you're a witness now."

Martinson lapsed into glum silence, staring out the back, while I tried to get a handle on it. Lasko was a bright man. But his actions had a harassed quality, as if something beyond his control were pushing him. I wondered what it was. Green, Martinson, and Lehman had been bad risks. The payoff was a murder and a kidnapping, and it kept getting worse.

We were closing in on Boston; Route 9 was getting ready to become Brookline Avenue again. City neighborhoods and traffic. Martinson started talking. "You know, Dr. Loring is very strange. He used to come in and want to talk about my anxieties, like I really was nuts. And then he'd start saying he had troubles too—that his hospital wasn't making it. But he kept acting like I was his patient." His voice rose indignantly. "I think he's a fairy too."

That amused me somehow. "That's the least of his problems."

Then I saw a black Cadillac, coming in the opposite lane. I tensed, knuckles white on the steering wheel. It came closer. I hunched, waiting. It moved abreast. I caught a glimpse of the driver. An old woman. It cruised serenely past. Damn, I thought.

Martinson had seen it. "What was that?" he croaked.

"Just my own shadow." I wanted to talk now, bury my embarrassment. "How did you get caught up with Lasko in the first place?"

"Look, am I going to be a witness?" he protested.

"About Carib? Yeah, unless you want to be a defendant." Assuming the unlikely, I didn't add, that I still had a job.

Martinson complained to the rear windshield. "It's my damned wife that got me into all this. She didn't need to talk to you. You know," he burst out, "she can't even have kids."

"I guess that makes you the only child of your marriage."

He stared at me. "You don't like me much, do you?"

I eyed him sideways. "Look, you're frightened. I understand that. I'm scared witless. What I can't take is your bitching about Tracy."

His ears perked at "Tracy." "What's my wife to you?" His voice italicized "my wife."

"I met her. I liked her."

"How much did she like you?" he snapped.

"Don't be a fool. She's in love with you, Lord knows why. But we were talking about the Carib deal."

We were in Boston now, heading toward Fenway Park. Martinson brooded for a moment. "What do you want to know?"

"Everything, from the beginning."

He turned back to the rear window. "I was working for Yokama Electric as a manufacturer's rep for the American trade. We lived in Japan. The Yokama thing was my last job." The phrase made it sound like the end of a very long list. "I'd been looking for a big opportunity, something where I could use my talents."

I got a picture from Martinson's eyes, glinting with shortsighted guile. A short-cutter scrambling for the main chance, outsmarting himself. I could see him rambling around Europe from one gamble to the next, until his excuses turned threadbare from overuse. And then Tracy would patch them up again.

He went on. "Part of the job was selling to Lasko Devices. Last June, Mr. Lasko came to Japan and asked for me. I'd never met him but he seemed to know about me. He said that he needed someone to help set up an import company on St. Maarten. I said I was interested. He offered me a two-year contract at seventy-five thousand a year and a hundred thousand bonus. It looked good and"—his voice admitted reluctantly—"it was more money than I'd ever seen."

"How did you end up shown as the founder of Carib?"

Martinson's tone got touchy. "It was part of the deal," he said hurriedly. "Mr. Lasko wanted me to be the paper owner of Carib, so he could buy it from me. He had his people find the warehouse and set up all the paper work. Tax reasons, he said."

"You believed that, naturally?" He didn't answer. "Lasko's corporate records show a sales agreement paying you a million-five. Did you think that was for tax reasons too?"

"Look, he was paying me a lot of money."

"Dr. Loring told me pretty much the same thing."

He digested that for a moment, still turned to the rear. I went on. "You got the money, I take it?"

Silence. I glanced sideways. He was staring down. Lasko's money, and the greed for it, ran through the case like a dirty string. My tone was quiet. "Mr. Martinson, you're not Lasko's bonus baby anymore. Putting him away is your best means of self-defense. You're also party to a laundering scheme which can land you in jail. You got in this mess courtesy of Lasko, with a big assist from yourself. It's up to you to get out."

He slumped silently against the seat. "All right," I said, "let me help you out. This July, Lasko buys Carib from you for a million-five. Carib supposedly deals in chips. But Lasko was already getting chips from Yokama, so why did he need anything in the Caribbean? The company is a shambles, one pug ram-rodding two natives in a corrugated warehouse. You supposedly sold to Lasko in July, but you didn't even sign the papers starting the company at all, but were hired by Lasko to run it. Yet, the corporate records show you as having received one-point-five million. The guy in charge, Kendrick, told me he's never heard of Yokama. But the chips Carib was getting are Yokama chips. Only instead of getting them direct, they're routing them through the Caribbean, which is expensive and just plain stupid from a business standpoint.

"Lasko set up the worthless company, came up with you as the bogus owner, and paid you off. As a laundering scheme, it's beautifully simple. For some reason, Lasko needed money, a lot of it. He wanted to get a million-five out of his own company in a way that looked legitimate. He wanted to do it in a foreign country where we couldn't trace the cash, and where he could take care of any tax complications from the sale. So he set up a dummy company, then bought it. The chips are a cover. But to make it work, you had to get the money."

He was still slumped. "I got the money," he acknowledged finally.

"What did you do with it?"

"Lasko"—Martinson's voice demoted him—"arranged for me to cash the check at a bank in Curaçao. So I did."

"When was that?"

"About the third week of July."

"What did you do with the money?"

"Lasko told me to fly it to Miami."

"Did you do that?"

"Yeah. I put it in a briefcase, flew to Miami Airport, and put it in a locker. Someone else was supposed to pick it up."

The reality of what had happened began to hit me. We were driving toward the fens, the broad grassy field near the ball park. Twilight now. I didn't much notice. The facts formed and marched into place like well-drilled soldiers. I couldn't believe it. But I did. And then the other fact hit me. I had made it big time. I knew enough for Lasko to need me dead.

"Goddamn it," I said to the dark.

Martinson didn't say anything.

THIRTY

I turned then. Martinson's eyes on the rear window
were green slivers of fright.

"See anything?"

"There's a car," he stammered. "I thought I saw
it about fifteen minutes ago."

"What color?"

"Green. Kind of a dull green."

I spotted it in the rearview. I'd seen it too, then
lost it in the city traffic. But it was the same car,
and pretty close to us. Thirty feet, I figured. I
thought I saw two heads in the twilight.

I swerved onto the Fenway and accelerated. In
the failing light the field looked like a miniature
Scottish moor. I knew it pretty well—a mile or so
of marshy grass, waist high, stuck incongruously
between Fenway Park, the Museum of Fine Arts,
and a handful of colleges. No traffic on the two-
lane road. I stomped down harder. We sped past

grey-green fens toward the inner city. The Prudential Center loomed in the distance.

But the Fenway was a mistake. The headlights stuck to us as if welded to our bumper.

"Same car?" I wondered.

Martinson's grip crackled the vinyl. "Yeah."

The speedometer showed eighty-five. I figured the fens would last another minute, at most. Then I heard a rubbery squeal. Two streaks of light stabbed the other lane, then stained the darkness ahead.

"They're passing," Martinson shouted. My left hand on the wheel jumped at his voice. The car did a choppy swerve. Our front beams lit a tree at the side of the road. I lashed the wheel left and we veered back toward the green car, two feet, then one foot apart. The two bumpers scraped. Martinson screamed incoherently. I jerked the wheel right, shielded my face and braked hard. The car pulled to the left, and fishtailed wildly, tires screaming. Then it shimmied down to twenty, in control.

I peered back over the dashboard. The green car was forty feet ahead now. It stopped with sudden violence, skidding at right angles like a sailboat into a night wind. I jammed the gas pedal to pass on the right. The other car straightened, lurched forward, and raced us abreast. A white face leaned out the rear window of the other car, and one arm hung out. The green car inched forward.

Ahead the road bore right. I saw that, and then a sudden streak cracked the windshield. A bullet hole. Martinson screeched and stabbed at his forehead with a fan of bloody fingers. The wheel jerked from my hands, and we shot left toward the green car. It snapped away in a violent reflex and teetered half-off the road. Then it flipped slow-motion in a clumsy somersault. I turned back to a windshield suddenly full of grey-blue grass ahead. Then the car charged into the fens, plowed an angry furrow, and jolted to a stop. I flew weightless into the steering wheel, smashing ribs and collarbone. The seat belt jerked me back and to the side. I doubled over, shaking.

I looked across. Martinson, red dripping from his mouth and bent from the waist, curled like a fetus. The mouth was mashed into the dashboard in an awful parody of a bite. The dashboard was dappled with scattered specks of blood.

I leaned over to grasp him. He flopped heavily back against the seat, now turned toward me. His forehead was bleeding where the bullet had grazed him and his jaw was canted crazily to one side, broken. He didn't move or make noise. I felt his pulse, as I had done with Lehman. But Martinson was alive.

I remembered the other car. I wrenched the door

open, half-falling. Then I righted myself and rolled out.

I heard no one. I crouched by the car, in the dark. It was as silent as a prairie night. Our beams were gone. Scattered out of earshot were distant lights from offices and row houses. The only near brightness was the green car's headlights, piercing the gloom like the hunter's lamps. This car had done a full flip and righted itself precariously over a ditch.

Still no traffic. It seemed that I was the only man on earth, come to visit a dead car. I waited. Then I took a few aching treads toward the green car, half-bent and nauseous. No sound or movement. I edged slowly toward the driver's side, afraid of what I'd see.

What I saw first was the driver. He slumped, mouth mashed into the steering wheel trickling blood, his staring eyes completely blank. His neck had snapped. His arms hung awkwardly, like a large coat on a small hanger.

I looked up at the night. Then I butted my head in the direction of the car and looked again. He had been a stocky man with a red bulbous nose. My head gave a quick little bob, involuntarily, like a hiccup. I looked away.

But there was the second man. I crossed the front of the car while the dead driver inspected me. I saw a gun, then a leg, then him. His face was raw and scraped open beneath the crew cut and he was sprawled on his back, in the awkward attitude of death. His right hand was stretched carelessly toward the gun, as if he had thrown it away.

The man's eyes gave me another once-over. I looked back toward the driver. Once they had surely been cold and efficient. Now they were about ninety bucks worth of lab chemicals, counting inflation. Because I had been lucky. I bent, wincing, and carefully picked up the gun.

The whir of a motor broke in. I squinted down the road. The headlights grew larger, coming from the direction we'd taken. I clicked off the safety on the handgun and stepped out to the road.

The car stopped and a middle-aged man stepped out, wearing black tie and a dinner jacket. A woman was in the car. I put the gun in my pocket and walked up.

The man had glasses and a worried moon-face. He peered out at the cars. "What happened?"

"They tried to run us off the road," I said. "My passenger is badly hurt. What we need is an ambulance and Lieutenant Di Pietro of the Boston police. Homicide."

"What is this?" he asked warily.

"Look, we need help. Please."

He thought about it, too long. The panicky fear hit me that Martinson would die, for no reason, to punish my own arrogance. I moved toward the man. "If you let him die—"

He stiffened. "OK, I'll call when we get to a phone." He made a tardy effort at good fellowship. "Everyone else all right?"

I pointed wearily to the car. "Except for the dead guys."

He stared, appalled. Driving cheerfully to a party, and instead to find this. But he got me to repeat Di Pietro's name, gave some hurried assurances, and drove off.

They got there in about ten minutes, in a fanfare of sirens and flashing lights. A squad car, an ambulance, and two wreckers. What they found was me holding Martinson and sitting by the road, looking like an orphan.

Di Pietro was with two cops. He walked toward me. I pointed silently at the dead men. Di Pietro gave them a quick look. He didn't need a long one.

The ambulance crew bent over Martinson. He was still out. I stood and let them work. Di Pietro drifted back, wearing his impassive mask. "You all right?" he asked, sounding sheepish.

I handed him the gun. "Just shook up and a little bruised."

"How did this start?"

The ambulance crew was still kneeling. I pointed in their direction. "That's Peter Martinson."

Di Pietro's eyes followed mine. "You visited the sanitarium," he said.

"Yeah."

"You know," he went on quietly, "I should have listened."

"I won't argue with you."

His eyes dismissed the subject. "Give me a run-down."

I did that, starting with Loring. Di Pietro folded his arms, asking an occasional question. In five minutes he was caught up.

The driver had been scooped on a stretcher. We watched them cart him to the ambulance. "What about him?" Di Pietro asked.

"I don't know either one of them."

He looked thoughtfully at the ambulance. "Well," he finally said, "we'd better get your statement."

The cops finished cleaning, leaving it just another patch of darkness. Then they took Martinson to the hospital and me to a squad car. The crew-cut man was last. They carried him by on a stretcher, covered with blankets. I didn't look.

THIRTY-ONE

We went to the same dim, green room where I had given the statement on Lehman. Di Pietro leaned in a corner while I sat in a folding chair and went through it again for the police stenographer. This stenographer didn't smile. I wouldn't have either.

Di Pietro stepped out and came back with a report on Martinson. The bullet wound was superficial but he was still unconscious, and they didn't know yet how bad that was, whether there was brain damage, or when he would come out of it. I asked all the questions I could think of. Di Pietro was patient and sympathetic.

The sympathy was for both Martinson and me. "He's no help to you now," Di Pietro summarized in a glum tone. "And they don't know whether he ever will be. What we've got now is your hearsay about what Martinson told you. That might help get an indictment, but it's not admissible in court."

I nodded. "Even if he wakes up, Martinson may

decide after all this that it's better to shut up and take his lumps. I don't know that I could blame him if he did. And Lasko will have succeeded." I felt my hands shaking. "Got a cigarette?"

He stepped out and came back with one from the front desk. "I haven't seen you smoke," he said, handing it to me.

"I haven't in years. This seems like a good night to start."

He nodded. "You were lucky."

"I know." I lit the cigarette. It tasted hot, and the smoke seemed to fog my brain.

Di Pietro went on. "If those two guys hadn't been killed, they would have killed you. But that leaves us without witnesses to work on maybe tracing this thing back to Lasko."

"You know, they match the description of the men Martinson said snatched him off St. Maarten."

He nodded. "We'll try to identify them, see if we can tie them to Lasko some way or another. And we're going to check the shopping center where that car killed Lehman was stolen. Maybe someone saw them there."

"So where does that leave Lasko?"

"I can question him," he paused, scowling, "but I can't hold him."

"When are you going to do that?"

"Now," he said, rising. "He's pretty close—

Beacon Hill. Listen," he added, "let someone run you to the hospital."

I shook my head. "Thanks, but I can't now. Do you have a phone?"

"Yeah." We got up together and left the room. He went out for Lasko. I found the phone and called Tracy Martinson. Her joy that he was alive carried her through the bad news. She took that in and said she would fly there to be with him. I promised for Di Pietro that one of his people would meet her at the airport. She thanked me again. I accepted that with the shamed awareness that my brand of help was less than she deserved. But then, so was Martinson.

I found the coffee machine, went to Di Pietro's office, and sat. I felt displaced, like a man in a strange motel. I finished one cup and killed a second. I bummed another cigarette from the guy at the front desk, a Camel. I looked at it. No filter. He wasn't scared. I looked up. 12:15. I went back for my third cup.

I was standing by the coffee machine when they brought Lasko in. He dwarfed the room and everyone in it. Di Pietro was with him, looking inscrutable. Cops smiled, mumbling in fragments, while Di Pietro talked over the desk. Lasko stared around, marking faces. He saw me then. I leaned casually against the coffee machine, looking as alive as possible.

He blinked and for that moment the fear was in his eyes. Not fear of me. Fear of losing all he'd had—the power and wealth—and going back to Youngstown, or worse. The humiliation opened up before him, and showed in his features. Then they twisted in the terrible intensity of the monomaniac. I felt it then. His drives were basic—pride and anger—and consumed him utterly. It was a hell I never wanted to know.

It vanished from his face as suddenly as it came. His features resumed their mask of controlled calculation, and he gave me a mirthless half-smile that derided the weakness of my position. I was without proof, without Martinson, without connections. It was still only me. The eyes said he could deal with me, one way or the other.

It was a surreal moment. We both knew he had tried to kill me and that I couldn't prove it. And that I was safe only as long as I stood there, inside the police station. Then he turned quickly and followed Di Pietro down a hallway. I watched the retreating backs knowing that Di Pietro would get nowhere with him. Nowhere at all.

I walked slowly to Di Pietro's office and sat, feeling fear and a wrenching frustration. I hadn't gotten Lasko, and he had plenty of help. But there was one thing going for me. No one at the ECC knew about tonight, I figured. That gave me maybe another twelve hours.

I decided to try for a short nap. I scraped the chair back against the wall, leaned against it, and dropped into a deep, achy sleep that felt like shock.

"Want some coffee?" someone was asking.

I flailed at gauzy curtains, trying to escape. My eyes opened then. It was Di Pietro. I looked at the clock. 2:10.

"Did you have to do that?" I asked.

He seemed to smile without changing expression. "I thought you might want to talk."

"Well, if I heard right, I'll take the coffee."

He disappeared. I uncurled and rubbed my eyes. When he came back he was holding two plastic cups and walking with knees slightly bent, like a trained bear. But he didn't spill any, even leaning over the desk.

"Thanks," I said, reaching for mine. "Want your chair back?"

He waved away the offer with heavy amiability, and sat in front of the desk. I looked at him. The watchful stare remained, but the stiffness had gone out of him. I guessed that nearly getting killed had improved my image.

"So what happened?" I asked.

He shook his head. "Nothing. We can't book him. We can't hold him. He said Martinson entered Loring voluntarily and that he was visiting out of concern. Other than that, he didn't say much, and nothing that wasn't shit."

I looked down at my fingers. They were writhing in random patterns. I felt my self-control suddenly slipping. I concentrated on that, and said nothing.

Di Pietro noticed. "Look at the situation, Christopher. We still can't tie him to Lehman. There could be federal kidnapping charges, but only if Martinson wants to talk—if he ever can. The two hoods who tried to kill you are dead, so we can't trace them to Lasko. What we need is some link between Lehman's death, the attempt on Martinson, and you and your investigation—some reason for Lasko to do all this."

I pulled myself together. "So you believe Lasko killed Lehman."

"You made a believer out of me," he answered quietly, "when they tried to kill you."

"So what are you going to do now?"

"For openers, I'm going to give you all the protection you need." The flat voice picked up emphasis. "Right now, you're the only person who can fuck him up. That means that he may kill you if he gets a clear shot."

"So what am I supposed to do?"

"Nothing. Sit tight."

"Look, you said you need a link between Lehman, Martinson, and my investigation. I'm close. One day, two days—if I'm right, and lucky, I can give you that."

"And if you're not lucky, you're dead."

"Lieutenant, tonight, sitting here, I finally had to face all this. If he wants to kill me, he can do it next month, next year, any time he wants. The only way to protect myself is to finish him."

Di Pietro leaned back and closed his eyes in thought. "What would you do?"

"If I don't tell you, then you don't have to lie when someone asks."

His eyes snapped open. "What the hell does that mean?"

So I told him a little about life at the ECC. He shook his head. "And I thought Massachusetts politics stunk."

I smiled. "It does, Lieutenant. It all does. But I guess you can see my problem."

"Who down there will help you?"

"I don't know. But you will."

He eyed his coffee cup as if the answers were hiding in it. "I could hold you here as a material witness."

"That would be no favor to me."

He said nothing. I looked at my watch. 2:30.

"When will all this hit the papers?" I asked.

He craned toward the clock. "It's too late for the mornings. It'll make the first evening edition, about noon tomorrow."

"OK," I said. "Listen, I'd like to take off."

He gave me a hard look. "I'll get someone to run

you to the hotel and put an officer on your door."
It was his answer.

"Thanks." He picked up the phone and called for
a car. I remembered something. "By the way, Lieutenant, that car I rented is wrecked, isn't it?"

"Pretty well. And it's physical evidence. That's a
nice bullet hole."

"Could you call the car rental at the airport?"

"Why?"

"I don't quite feel up to explaining all this."

He almost smiled. "All right."

A cop showed up to drive me. I stood. Di Pietro
raised a cautionary hand. "Look, Christopher, tomorrow Lasko won't be liking you any better than
he did tonight. He won't leave Boston, but he's got
people who work for him. Don't take chances you
don't have to."

I nodded. "Thanks, Lieutenant."

His face was full of misgivings. "Good luck," he
said finally, and waved me out the door.

The next morning I shaved, packed, and checked
the expiration date on my Visa card. I made one
phone call. Then I took a cab to the airport and
caught a plane to Miami.

THIRTY-TWO

The phone call had been to Robinson. He'd picked up the phone and asked how I was, like you'd ask any friend who wasn't there. Fine, I said, knowing then that Martinson and I hadn't hit the morning papers. Then I asked for the number of his Florida friend, the state bank examiner. Could he do anything, Robinson asked. I said it would be easier for me to call. OK—when would I be back? I'd be leaving this morning, I replied. Which was true enough.

They probably wouldn't miss me until this afternoon, when the news broke. And I didn't think I'd been followed to the airport. I tried to be happy with that. But there was a delayed reaction, one that made me sick. I'd nearly been killed, nearly gotten Martinson killed—and accomplished nothing in the process. I hadn't liked that option during Vietnam and didn't like it now. The idea of death was ugly and enormous, like infinity made personal. A flight attendant brought me a doughnut. I couldn't eat it.

But others had died—the two men. I tried to feel something, but it didn't work. I wasn't sorry and never would be.

Eventually I tried my coffee and went over what had happened. I'd turned up where I wasn't expected, broken the carefully placed boundaries. Outside the boundaries, events had a violent, irrational quality. It scared me, badly. Now I was racing to catch up to the answers before anyone caught up with me. That seemed to be the only way out. And no one had paid for Lehman.

I looked for the first time at the faces around me. They chatted and read, on their way to sell things or see things or do whatever fit with the rest of their lives. I envied that. So I decided to imitate them for a while, and asked the flight attendant for the *Wall Street Journal*. I noticed then that she looked like Mary, but without the eyes. Amazing, I thought, the difference that makes.

She brought the *Journal*. It took about a minute to spot the item in the "News in Brief" section on page one:

White House sources indicate that Joseph P. McGuire, tough-minded chief of the ECC's Prosecutions Bureau, is now favored over three other prospects for appointment as a commissioner. The prospective vacancy in the seven-man commission follows the resignation of Commissioner Charles Ludlow, who yesterday announced plans to return to private practice.

It was a minor Washington classic. Dangle the bait for the eager candidate, but remind him that there are others available. And while you're at it, let the press do some digging for you. If it comes out that your boy is a neo-Nazi or was caught last year in Central Park dressed up as Marie Antoinette, you can dump him with a bland denial that he ever crossed your mind. The motive here was pretty clear—to confirm the deal and remind McGuire of the price. Don't push the Lasko case. It was a message he could hardly miss. I folded the *Journal* and picked up my coffee. It was cold.

We reached Miami about 2:30. I walked into the terminal, picked up my bags, and crammed them into an airport locker. Then I found a pay phone and called Ken Parrish, Robinson's friend. Parrish was happy to help. I thanked him and hung up. I looked around. No one near.

The only thing left was to catch a taxi. I stepped through an exit door onto a steaming sidewalk which curved around a small taxi lane. A line of taxis sat by the curb. I waited, staring at the lurid green palm tree which jutted from a patch of grass across the lane. It was clearly thriving. A great place for palms, Miami.

I got edgy. Finally, a cab peeled lazily out of the line and eased up next to me. The cabbie leaned out the door and motioned me to the curb. I got in. My driver had dark hair and a mustache—Cuban, I thought. He turned sideways and spoke to a window. "Where you go, sir?"

"Biscayne Boulevard," I said. "The First Seminole Bank."

The First Seminole Bank was in one of those all-glass towers that would look awful in twenty-five years, if it took that long. I paid the driver, got out, and headed for the door. The glass doors were set back in a small alcove, with a newspaper rack in front of them. I stuck twenty cents in the slot, took a paper, and stopped in the alcove to glance through it. It was the afternoon edition and I had made page two. "Industrialist Queried in Murder Try," the headline read. The first paragraph was a grabber:

William Lasko, Boston industrialist and Presidential friend, was questioned this morning in connection with the attempted murder of an employee and a government lawyer investigating Lasko's affairs.

I read on. It was a wire story. Associated Press, and they had the facts right—what they knew of them. No charges contemplated at this time and no evidence, it concluded. I finished, thinking all hell would break loose. At least they'd spelled my name right. I folded the paper and stepped inside.

The bank was new, with red carpets and formica deposit counters which almost looked like marble. Behind them, tellers idled and chatted with customers. The walls were white and here and there was a picture of a happy-looking Seminole bragging that he got 6¾ percent at the First Seminole Bank. Beyond the counters and carpet stretched a low wooden rail with a swinging door and behind that were the desks of six actual vice-presidents. I picked the nearest one, a smooth looking fellow with perfect grey hair—"Mr. Williams" according to his desk sign. Could he help me, he wondered politely. I showed him my ID card and asked for the president. That chilled him a little. He asked me to wait and headed for a row of offices in the rear.

I fidgeted in my chair. Then Mr. Williams returned and said to follow him. We looped around the six desks and into the office space. At the end was a large office. Mr. Williams steered me in, past a sign reading "Richard Henry, President."

The office held a fine maple desk and conference table, with a couple of seascapes and an ocean blue rug. Two men sat at the table. One was a big man with tortoise shell glasses, and an outsized smile. He rose. "Mr. Paget," he said, "I'm Dick Henry." We shook hands. Henry was built like a running guard, with a rugged face which was all surfaces and angles. From his manner he was the cheerful banker, and I was a big depositor.

The other man remained seated, his face betraying the true extent of my welcome. Henry caught my glance. "This is Larry Carr, our outside counsel," he said hastily. Carr silently extended his hand. He was big, too, except for his mouth, a thin slash which looked more like an incision. But where Henry was bushy-haired and rumpled, Carr was close-clipped and tailored, with constricted, cheerless movements. It made him seem smaller. I turned down coffee, and we all sat.

Henry unknotted his tie and leaned back. "Are you here to deposit money?" he asked, chuckling the practiced chuckle of a second banana on a nighttime talk show.

I glanced at Carr, who was laughing. "I take it Ken Parrish called you," I asked.

"He did, yes," Henry said. "He said you want access to some bank records."

"That's right."

Henry stopped smiling. Carr spoke for the first time, in a clipped, prosecutor's voice. "Do you have a subpoena?"

I looked him over. "You already know the answer to that. You can put me to the trouble of getting one," I bluffed, "but I'm asking for voluntary cooperation."

Carr carefully brushed some imaginary lint from his lapels. "Well," he finally said, "we've got to consider the privacy of our customers."

I looked straight at him, ignoring Henry. "There are some other facts you should know, Mr. Carr. A man named Samuel Green got a $400,000 loan from this bank in July. He used that money to buy Lasko Devices stock, on the orders of William Lasko. Green has a fraud record going back to the fifties—not exactly your prime loan candidate. But Lasko controls 25 per cent of the stock of this bank. So Mr. Henry and his bank," I nodded at Henry, "are neck-deep in stock manipulation."

"We had no idea of any manipulation."

The words had blurted from Henry's red, unhappy face. I turned to him. "Then you've nothing to lose by cooperating."

Carr cut in, less aggressive now. "I'd like to consider your request," he said. "How long will you be in Miami?"

I felt my temple throb. There wasn't time for waiting. I pulled out the newspaper and shoved it under Carr's face. "There's one more thing. Lasko was questioned in Boston last night concerning an attempted murder."

Carr's mouth parted in surprise. He snatched half-glasses from his inside pocket with hasty, scrabbling fingers. Halfway through the article his mouth began moving as he read. He kept staring after he had finished, then slowly raised his head. "He tried to have you killed?" he asked, in a quiet, shocked tone.

"That's right."

Henry blinked at that with real fear, as if I blamed him. The atmosphere had turned visceral and very personal. Which was exactly how I felt about dying.

I had Carr's full attention. "You've got fraud, you've got this"—I pointed at the newspaper—"and you've got a man named Lehman who was killed in Boston two weeks ago." Henry tugged at his tie with sudden violence, like a man hanging himself. "Perhaps you've heard of Lehman, Mr. Henry?"

Carr wheeled on Henry, sudden, sharp eyes asking the question. Henry nodded.

Carr looked warily back to me. "Have I heard it all?" he asked in a voice that clearly hoped so.

"I think Lasko had Lehman killed."

Carr removed his glasses, and looked them over. Then turned back to Henry. "Give him what he wants," he said in a flat voice.

Henry stood then, rubbing his hands and maneuvering his mouth into an awful smile. "What would you like?" he asked me. His forced cheerful tone tried to suggest the conclusion of a tough but mutually pleasing loan negotiation.

I didn't smile back. "What series of numbers would contain two digits—the number 95?"

"Our safe deposit boxes."

"Fine. I'd like the signature card and entry records for number 95."

Henry went for them himself. Carr stared silently out the window. I supposed it was hard to chat with someone who should be dead.

Henry came back a little out of breath and almost throwing the records on the table. I reached for the signature card, glancing at Henry. "This card shows the people who are authorized to enter the box, right?"

"That's correct," he nodded glumly.

I turned it over. Alexander Lehman's boyish face looked up at me.

I pulled over the entry card. On July 24, Lehman had entered safe deposit box number 95. On July 28, he had returned again.

I stared for a moment at Lehman's picture. Then I looked at Henry. "I'll want these records," I said.

He didn't argue.

I left them in the conference room, looking somber, and walked past the vice-presidents and the cheerful Seminoles, out the door.

I took out my slip of paper with the words of Lehman's memo, but I didn't really need it. I had it memorized: "95—Move whole package across the street—J859020. Justice is blind."

There was only one bank across the street. A large sign on an old cement building proclaimed "The Mariner Bank of Miami." I went there.

THIRTY-THREE

The Mariner Bank was old, stodgy, and as reassuring as the U.S. Mint. The president's suite was on the second floor. So I went there and asked for Mr. Glendenning. The starchy receptionist eyed me doubtfully, then dialed. A few minutes later Glendenning's secretary appeared, a chubby, quick-stepping woman with that certain smile which conveys a total absence of warmth. I followed her out.

Glendenning sat behind a Louis the Fourteenth desk in an office filled with antiques. He rose quickly, shook my hand, and asked me to take a chair. I sat, taking quick note of him. He had a sharp badger face and a long straight nose. His clothes were perfect: grey pin-stripe, breast pocket handkerchief and burgundy club tie, very subtle. I could see him shuffling bonds.

"How can we be of service?" he asked curiously. I handed him my card. "I'm with the ECC. I'm working on a case which involves tracing laundered money. I think the money is here."

Glendenning webbed his fingers in a reflective gesture. "What's your basis for that?"

"I have confidential information and what I think is a safe deposit box number. The number should tell whether I'm right."

"Well," he pointed out, "it will show whether someone has a box here, at least. What's the number?"

I pulled the slip out of my shirt pocket. "J859020."

Glendenning's lids dropped. "Did I count six digits?" he asked.

I repeated the number. "Six digits and the letter 'J,' " I added.

"We have those numbers," he said slowly. "On our safe deposit boxes."

"What's your record system?"

Glendenning was a man of precision. "Do you mean how does it work?" he clarified. I nodded, feeling edgy and impatient. "All right. We have a standard signature card for authorized access to the box."

"What I'm getting at is this. I take it that only the people who've signed on the signature card could take anything out?"

He nodded approvingly; I had it right.

"OK," I said. "What I want is the signature card for J859020."

Glendenning's mouth thrust forward, as if nibbling my request. He finally spoke. "I suppose it's best to cooperate. You realize, Mr. Paget, that this bank has no means of knowing the source of anything that's put in the box." His sharp eyes underlined the point.

"I understand that."

Glendenning unraveled his fingers, then stood abruptly. "I'll look over the records, then give them to you. You can use our conference room."

He steered me there, then vanished for the records. The room was deliberately impressive: brass chandeliers and an oversized conference table. The antique bookshelves were graced by leather volumes which I assumed were rare editions. None of that helped. I felt alone and out of place.

I fidgeted for twenty minutes or so, wanting to pace. The records were part of my answer. Finally I went to a window. I was staring absently when Glendenning's secretary burst in. She held the signature card and looked flustered. I took the card.

Robert Catlow's name and picture were on the signature card, with Lehman's. The card showed Lehman's first and only visit: July 28. Catlow had never come.

Glendenning was still in his office. "I want to look in the box," I told him.

"I can't do that," he said. "First, you haven't a subpoena. Second, it takes two keys to open our safe deposit boxes. The bank only has one; the owner has the other."

"What if someone dies and you can't find the key?"

"We have a locksmith drill it."

"I'll make you a deal, Mr. Glendenning. I can be back with a subpoena tomorrow. And if the contents of that box are gone, you've been part of something you wouldn't touch with gloves on. I'll tell you what's in that box. Drill it, and see if I'm right. If I am, then I want your word no one gets in the box."

Glendenning frowned, forehead creased. "All right, Mr. Paget. What do you think is in there?"

"One and a half million dollars," I told him, "in unmarked bills."

He called the locksmith.

I waited in the conference room, hoping I was right. Thirty minutes, then forty-five. I stared at Catlow's signature card, trying to think ahead. There weren't many choices. I needed to move, before Lasko traced me. I needed the memo. And I needed help.

Glendenning opened the door, looking very sober. "It's all there," he said, "in a brown briefcase."

I stuffed the signature card in my breast pocket, and told him to keep the money safe, for evidence. I left without saying good-bye.

THIRTY-FOUR

I couldn't have said how long it took me to get to the airport. I flagged a cab in the kind of daze that follows anesthesia. The cabbie rambled on about sports, politics, and the merits of full frontal nudity. I emitted a few absent grunts and tried to think.

I had the bank records and knew where the money was. But they meant nothing without Lasko's scrawled memo, hidden in my desk. For ten days I hadn't made sense of it. Now the case didn't make sense without it. It was the indispensable link in the chain of proof, tying Carib, Lasko, and Lehman's death in a neat bundle.

And it was my protection—the thing that could end Lasko before he got to me. Lasko would be working overtime, trying to figure how I had found the money. And sooner or later, he'd recall his memo. It wasn't safe, not now, any more than I was. I had to get it out.

"Which airline, sir?" the cabbie was asking.

I woke up. "Oh ... Eastern."

"It's right here."

There was a pay phone in the terminal. I got Mary on the second ring.

"Mary, this is Chris."

"Chris? My God, where have you been?" She sounded intense, almost breathless.

"Miami."

"I've been worrying all day. Have you seen the papers?"

"Don't need to. I was there. Can you pick me up at National? I'm on Eastern, flight 435."

"Yes—sure," she began distractedly. "Please tell me what happened."

"Can't now. Listen, don't come to the gate. Just double-park out front."

"OK, I'll be there," she said, and hung up.

I stood, still holding the phone, hoping that had been the right thing to do. Then I got my bags and ran to the gate, half-glancing over my shoulder. No one following.

I just made the plane.

I sat in tourist, wanting the case to be over, wanting out. The feeling lasted all the way to Washington.

We landed in the dark. Mary was at the gate, leaning on the metal railing. She smiled uncertainly and squeezed my arm. "Chris, are you all right?"

My voice felt as tight as piano wire. "What the hell are you doing here? I said meet me out front."

She stiffened, hurt. "I had to see you."

I took her arm. "Well, let's get moving then. This isn't safe for you."

I pulled her along until she fell in step. We headed toward the main lobby as people rushed around us, bustling to planes. "What happened?" she demanded.

I kept my eyes ahead. "Remember Peter Martinson?"

"Yes, the man on St. Maarten."

"Lasko kidnapped him to Boston, to a place called the Loring Sanitarium."

She turned to me with grave black eyes. "Literally kidnapped?"

"Uh-huh. Last night I got Martinson out. Lasko sent two hoods after us. Tried to run us off the road. But we lucked out. I lost control, and they flipped trying to get out of our way."

She stopped and looked up. Her eyes were big. "My God, Chris," she said. Then she slowly reached up and brushed the hair from my forehead.

We started walking again, with Mary still clutching my arm. "How did you find Martinson?"

"I checked IRS for sanitariums on the dole from Lasko."

Her tone cooled a bit. "Was that another of your little secrets?"

"I'm afraid so."

"When are you going to be honest with me?" she said in a quiet, troubled voice.

"Any day now."

She turned on me, annoyed. "That's not an answer."

I stopped, but didn't reply. We were near the main terminal; the last gate area was to our right. Ahead was a large room with ticket counters to the left, two revolving baggage racks on the right, and automatic double doors straight ahead, leading outside. To the far side of the baggage area was the only other exit: a corridor linking this terminal to others, and enclosing the traffic circle outside in another half-circle. I looked around, but didn't know any of the faces picking up tickets and suitcases or striding away to catch planes. Then I saw what I was looking for.

"What is it?" she was asking, in a quick, tense voice.

It was the mustached man from the sanitarium, Lasko's man, standing by the double doors to the outside. His gaze swept the baggage area to the outside. His gaze swept the baggage area to my right, moving back toward me. I glanced to my side. The gate area was empty. I jerked Mary over past the railing, out of sight of the terminal.

Her annoyance had merged into fear. "Damn it, what did you see?"

"One of Lasko's men is out there. Look, you asked why I didn't trust you. I didn't know who to trust: Feiner's hopeless, you and Woods are political, and McGuire's—well, what he is. Someone told Lasko about Lehman. He's dead and they tried to kill me. I couldn't afford blind faith."

"Chris, what is this all about?"

"Lasko was laundering money to pay someone off. To kill the antitrust case before it ruined him."

"Who was it for?"

It wasn't time for explaining. "We'll talk later," I said. "Right now we've got to get out of here. I've got the facts to nail Lasko for Lehman's murder and Catlow for criminal fraud and looting. I'm giving it all to Woods. Will you help?"

My answer didn't please her, but she nodded, mutely. "All right," I said, "you can start by believing me. There's a man out there who would kill me if he felt he had to. If he sees you with me you could be hurt. Right now you can walk past him and out those front doors. I want you to do that, get your car, and meet me in the traffic circle in front of the United terminal. How long will that take?"

She paused, distracted. "I'm parked away a little. Fifteen minutes."

"All right."

She hesitated. "Just where are we going?"

"My office."

"For what?"

"There's something there I need."

It sounded evasive, and was. Her body tensed. "No way, Chris," she said angrily. "You say this is dangerous. I should at least know why."

I stood there, undecided.

"Do I have to name each time you've lied to me?" she asked.

"Don't bother," I said. "There's a memo hidden in my desk. Lasko wrote it to Lehman. It's the most important piece of evidence I have."

"Why?"

"It's got box numbers in two Miami banks with instructions to transfer the money from the first to the second. It ties Catlow to the money, because the second box is in his name. And it gives Lasko a motive to kill Lehman. I've got the only copy. Is that enough?"

She nodded quickly. "I'll meet you out front."

"Thanks."

She scurried off toward the parking lot. I leaned over the gate railing to see her stride past the man at the door. She hardly rated a glance.

I leaned back out of sight and checked my watch, calculating. They must be covering the airport, hoping I'd turn up. That meant someone else would cover the next terminal too. It didn't leave much margin for error. I waited, managing nothing more than nervous regret that McGuire had put me in this mess, and wondering why he had.

The minutes dragged. I leaned against the rail of the deserted gate area. Strange faces marched by in both directions. Some would give me a vague, curious glance. I watched them, ready to move quickly, or run, I didn't know where.

A big grey-haired man was walking up the corridor toward the terminal, wearing an out-of-season trench coat, too warm for hot weather. He looked at me. My knees tensed. He kept on going. I watched him, turning. He walked into the gate area. A plump woman came forward and gave him a small hug. He kissed her. I looked at my watch. It was time. I started moving.

I turned right through the gate entrance and into the corridor toward the lobby. I went at normal speed looking ahead and to my left, away from the mustached man. The corridor opened up into the terminal. He saw me then. I kept walking, not noting him. He was waiting for me to come to him, hands in his pockets now. I went across the terminal toward him, halfway between the two baggage racks to my right. Then I spun right and started running.

Beyond the space between the racks was the corridor to the next terminal. I squirmed and bumped through the people who milled by the racks, not seeing faces. I got clear of them into the corridor and looked back, still running. The crowd was oozing, parting, making way for the mustached man. I turned ahead, running past shops, dodging bodies. I brushed one against a wall going past as the corridor opened into the second terminal.

This one had two front doors, to the left and right of a long ticket desk. The bald man stood in front of that, watching both doors. He saw me as I burst out of the corridor and veered left for the nearest door.

He was quick, but I was too close. I was three feet from the door when he was four yards from me. He would have had to shoot me. I rushed through the doors into darkness and turned right on the sidewalk.

Mary's car was in front of United, dimly lit by overhead lamps. There were no cars blocking hers. I cut into the circle of slow traffic and drop-offs and weaved through them to her car. Horns blasted. I reached the car and jumped in as she stepped on it. I turned and looked back through the window. Lasko's men were standing amidst the traffic and the wail of angry horns. We sped away.

Mary asked what had happened. I waited until I caught my breath, then told her. Her hands on the wheel were white. "They'll probably check my place first," I finished, "then maybe yours if they got a license number. After that I'm sure they'll think of my office."

We were on the Parkway then, moving toward the Rochambeau Bridge. The Washington Monument punctured the dark, and beyond that, the Jefferson glowed quietly.

"Can we go faster?" I asked.

She glanced over. "I can't believe you hid that memo." Her voice held splinters of anger, mixed with fear.

We were crossing the bridge. The Potomac was black, like a huge ink spill. "Be kind. Remember that you're abusing someone who was nearly the centerpiece at a closed casket funeral."

"It's not funny."

"What isn't?"

She paused. "None of it, I guess, I'm just glad you're still alive."

I turned from the rear window. "Mary, when this is over we'll go up Green Mountain. There's no politics there and no commission."

She tried to smile. We drove silently in the darkness, through the L'Enfant Promenade, past the Capitol, and up to the doors of the ECC. No one behind us.

It was nine o'clock. Only the lobbies were lit and a few random offices. We parked in front. "They'll be looking for us," I said. "You'd better come. It's not safe out here."

"All right."

We got out and went to the door. I opened it for her. We walked into the yellow light. Officer Davis sat at the desk. We showed him our cards. He didn't smile. He never did.

We moved in dim light to the elevators. I pushed the button. One opened. We stepped in and I pressed "Three." The elevator sighed, rose slowly, then rumbled open. The third floor was pitch dark.

We stepped out carefully, Mary holding my arm. "Where are the switches, Chris?"

"I don't know. Nice, isn't it?"

I waved a hand in front of me, as if clearing cobwebs. That didn't work. So I felt our way to the far wall. I groped along it toward my office, scraping my fingertips on cratered blocks.

We turned the corner to the corridor which ran past my office area. A small path of light shone through the area doorway and into the hall. We walked toward it.

My eyes tracked the light. It came from a crack beneath an office door. I froze. They were there, after all.

"Your office?" Mary whispered.

"Uh-huh."

I pushed Mary behind me and edged silently toward the door. I knew who was there.

But then you're never quite as smart as you think you are. I threw open the door.

It was Woods.

THIRTY-FIVE

He stood behind my desk, holding the manila envelope. For an instant, his face froze in surprise. Then it settled into the closed-off pride of a model in a shirt ad. His broken nose lent a hint of violence. The one thing he didn't look was sorry.

"What the hell are you doing?" I blurted stupidly.

He remained silent, giving the room a searching glance. Only the desk was between us. The overhead light cast a sickly yellow tint on the bare walls. The desk touched the wall to my right. But between the desk and left wall was a four-foot space. His eyes gauged it, then turned back toward me.

I felt a sudden wave of anger. "Give me the memo."

He shook his head. My anger was turning into numb disbelief. I had almost outrun them. But all this time I had been a rat in Lasko's maze, with Woods blocking the end. "It was you all along," I said. "Everywhere I went Lasko was ahead of me. And you were the one who kept him there."

He stared at me with contempt. "Nothing justifies the fuck-up you've made, hunting Lasko like a prep school Captain Ahab. You're a fool, with no sense of proportion."

"And you're a low-rent John Dean, Woods, with the ethics of a war criminal."

He answered in a smooth indifferent voice. "Lehman's dead. I didn't want that but there it is. There's only you to say this memo ever existed. And there's no one over me for you to say it to."

The words had a sickening accuracy, and he could make them come true. The indifference was the underside of the wholly adaptable man. At bottom, he didn't give a damn about anything except himself. And he was slick enough to bury the evidence without a trace.

We were both to the side of the desk now. Three feet between us. Woods was framed by the dark window. We watched each other.

"Try to stop me, Paget, and I'll leave you here for Lasko's friends." He pointed behind me to Mary. "Her too, if you care about that."

"No more middlemen, Woods," I answered. "If you want to walk out of here you'll have to kill me yourself. I know it all now. Most important, I know where the money was going."

"I'll bite," he said negligently. "Where?"

"The President."

Woods' eyes froze, but his voice was unnaturally calm. "Just how did you reach that amazing conclusion?"

"It explains everything. You just had to put the facts in order. You start with the antitrust case, which would almost surely ruin Lasko. There's only one man in the government who could kill that case. Lasko's friend, the President.

"The price was one and a half million, with Catlow the perfect middleman. But getting the money was harder. Lasko's first problem was that his company's cash poor. So he used Green to hype the stock offering an extra one-point-eight million, laundered a million-five through Martinson, Carib, and the First Seminole Bank, then assigned Lehman to get the money to Catlow. They probably called it a 'campaign contribution.' "

Woods seemed numbed by my recital—or perhaps he was deciding what role to play next. But the anger seized me now; he had to hear it all. "I could never see why a smart man like Lasko would use men like Green, Lehman, or Martinson. The only answer was that someone big was shaking him down and that the trial was coming soon, too soon for Lasko to plan properly. He had to use what help he could and hope he could slide by, or fix any problems later.

"Lehman was the first problem, and Lasko's men

fixed that. I was the next and you became chief fixer, not out of loyalty to Lasko, but to the President. You thought you had me wired. But none of you knew I had Lehman's memo."

Woods' eyes weighed it all, then seemed to snap to a decision. I tensed, awaiting his move. "You've lost," he said coolly. "The entire government's against you—and without the memo, no one will believe any of this." The words covered his careful slide toward the door. Part of me couldn't believe we were going to fight. But the part that remembered Alex Lehman knew we were. He kept inching. I slid back my right foot, to brace myself.

Woods suddenly dipped his shoulder and shot forward, knocking me against the desk. I bounced off and punched up from the rib cage. It caught him while he was admiring his block. His teeth clicked, then the pain ripped through my forearm. Woods rocked, then caught himself against the wall.

I lunged for the memo. Woods was too quick and too strong. He sidestepped as I stumbled past, off balance. Then his fist crashed into my cheekbone. I staggered, then sprawled face first on my desk, seeing a sudden purple haze. The haze cleared. In front of me was an onyx bookend, a squat hunk of rock. I grabbed it left handed and spun.

What I got was teeth. His hands jerked up to clamp his mouth, as if to hold it together. I cocked the bookend, then hacked at his forehead. I heard

Mary scream. Woods tottered on his heels. I hit him again. He staggered, eyes glazed. Then he slid slowly down the wall. I gaped at him, breathing hard.

I turned. Mary stood in the doorway, staring with shocked eyes. "Are you all right?" she asked in a strangled voice.

"I guess so."

"What should we do?"

I couldn't answer. My face ached and my right hand was a doughy pincushion. I tried to flex it. Woods was sprawled gracelessly on the floor, like the victim of a sudden stroke. His mouth was bloody. I stooped by him, thinking of Lehman and Tracy, McGuire and Lasko—and Mary. Woods didn't care. He was out cold.

I got up. Mary was still staring at Woods. "I can't believe it, Chris."

"Neither can I."

She looked up then and saw it in my face. She froze, irresolute, then turned to run. I caught her and threw her against the wall. She made a little sound, like a hurt cat. Her fingers covered her mouth. I moved toward her.

She shook her head like a mechanical doll. "No. No, Chris. You heard him threaten me too. You can't believe—"

I shook her hard. "Lehman," I demanded. "It was you and Woods."

She stared at my face, mouth working, as if something were stuck in her throat.

"Tell me, before I mash your fucking face into the wall."

Her words escaped in twos and threes. "That night—you said you were going to Boston—to meet Gubner." She paused for breath. "I called Jack after—I got in. He didn't know Gubner either."

"So?"

She hesitated, then spoke quietly. "So Jack called Lasko."

"Go on."

"The case was dangerous—politically—to the White House. I don't know who Jack talked to over there. He never said anything about money—I don't think he knew. Jack's ambitious, if you hadn't noticed."

She had begun to sound more confident. She was still talking, and I hadn't hurt her. My grip tightened. She spoke quickly, as if to stop me. "He said Lasko knew from the name Gubner that Lehman was involved."

It fit. Gubner had said that Lehman's co-workers knew they were friends. "When Woods let me go to St. Maarten, was that because you told him I knew Lane Greenfeld?"

Her eyes dropped. "Greenfeld's been covering Lasko. Jack was afraid you'd leak things if you weren't happy."

"And transferring the case to Justice?"

She spoke to the floor. "Jack's idea. He gave it to Catlow. Catlow sold it to McGuire."

I clamped her shoulders. "Goddamn you."

Her jagged voice jumped. "No one knew Lasko would kill Lehman. I could hardly sleep."

I shook her. "I was there, remember?"

The personal thing was close to the surface. It passed unspoken between her eyes and mine. "Please, Chris," she said evenly. "Let me talk."

I slowly eased my grip. Her mouth worked soundlessly, then started. "I never talked to Lasko or anyone at the White House. I never wanted you hurt. I didn't know, really. I didn't know what I was into—I just tried to help Jack control the case. I couldn't expose him after the Lehman thing. He said we were both in trouble, because I'd known what he was doing. That's the only reason I went on."

"Including tonight, when you called him from the airport?"

"Yes, damn it. Now let me go."

"Did you call anyone besides Woods tonight?"

She shook her head. If that was true, I had time—a little time, maybe, before Lasko's boys showed up. I needed that. I let my hands drop. She straightened and smoothed her hair. She reached deep within and pulled out some poise. I had to admire that, even then. "OK," she said in her own voice. "You want to know about McGuire. He didn't know. Really. That's why he didn't believe Lasko killed Lehman. Of course, he didn't want to."

"What was all that crap about settlement?"

"They dangled a commission seat in front of him. I don't think it was a trade-off. But they made it easy for him to think about all the good he could do if he just let this one go."

It was always "just this one" in this place. Mary went on. "You're very clever, Chris, much more than Woods thought. But you were so hung up on McGuire, you just knew it had to be him. Jack set him up to agree to that settlement. Then Jack played the good guy. You've heard of the 'good guy-bad guy' act, haven't you?"

I couldn't say anything. "You know," she said, "Woods even tried to get McGuire to take you off the case. McGuire wouldn't do it. Jack said he seemed to have some notion that you represented his better side."

I stood there feeling stupid. "All right," I finally said. "You know so much, tell me who started all this."

"What do you mean?"

"Who tipped McGuire on the stock manipulation?"

She smiled slightly. "Ike Feiner."

"Try again."

"I'm serious. We couldn't figure out why Feiner didn't catch it. He did, at least one of his market watch people did. I checked it out. Feiner told the guy that he'd take it to McGuire. He didn't. I suppose that makes him the tipster."

"Why in hell did he do that?"

"My God, Chris. He wanted to be chief enough to poison McGuire's soup. I suppose he thought that the case would either blow up in McGuire's face or that McGuire would get promoted. It was a gamble."

I shook my head. "I'm going to have a tough time accepting that all this happened so that Ike Feiner could be a GS-16."

"I'm sure that wasn't the idea."

"That's the way it turned out." For a moment, I was lost in the last two weeks.

Mary's eyes softened. She spoke quickly, looking at me. "Chris, you think I was with you because of the case. Maybe I used that a little. But I didn't have to come the other night. And I didn't have to stay. I did that because I wanted to."

Two days ago she had been at my place. It seemed longer. I shook my head. "I've had the privilege of hearing one of your little speeches about politics, remember? The President's your man. It's a little tough to buy that you were just helping Woods under pressure, or hanging around me out of sheer adoration. You were just another weapon. If they couldn't kill me, they could catch me at the airport. And if that didn't work, they could use you to pry the memo out of me and give it to Woods. Even after that, you were going to play along."

She nodded her concession. "All right. But that doesn't have anything to do with the other. If I kept you away from Lasko, or got this memo, you would be safe. I cared for you. You were good at things, gentle underneath—and so free. Money does make you free, you know."

"No, I don't know."

"Chris, please let's not lose this too."

It was no good. "I've lost more, and long ago. My martinis will still taste good, and I'll still like the first day of fall. And I mean to live for more of both."

A touch of panic crossed her face. She grabbed my wrists. "Give me the memo, Chris, and I can protect you. There isn't anywhere you can go with this. Not Woods, the White House, or anywhere else."

She was right. I looked over at Woods. Still out. The only glint in his eyes came from the light on the ceiling. But time was running out. I had to do something to stay alive. I turned to Mary and pointed to the chair behind my desk. "Sit over there."

She did that, looking faintly triumphant. "Can we talk this over now?"

I reached for my phone. "First you get to listen to the end of a brilliant career."

Her tone mixed doubt and asperity. "What are you doing?"

"Just sit still." My right hand throbbed as I dialed. It was my last shot.

A man and a woman answered together. I spoke to the man. "Mozart lived to be thirty-five, you idiot. I looked it up."

Greenfeld sounded mildly astonished. "Chris? I thought something had happened to you."

"No. Listen, I'm in a hurry. You still want the Lasko story?"

"Sure."

Mary's fingers gripped both sides of the chair. "I'll meet you tonight," I went on. "But let me run through it, quick, in case I get held up. That may help protect me. Got a pencil?"

"Yup. Go."

"OK. Lasko's company is cash poor. Lasko drove up his stock price to get extra money out of an offering. Your source is the testimony of Sam Green. Lasko took the one-point-five million and laundered it through a dummy corporation on St. Maarten, run by a Peter Martinson—"

"He was the guy with you yesterday, right?"

"Uh-huh. Martinson passed the money through a bank in Curaçao and then Alec Lehman passed it through on July 28 to a vault at the Mariner Bank in Miami. I've got a memo from Lasko and bank records. The box was in the names of Lehman and Robert Catlow."

"Jesus. Why? A payoff?"

"I figure they were going to make a 'contribution' to the President. The timing fits with your source's story that the antitrust case almost settled. But our investigation held settlement up, so the money didn't move from the second bank and I can't prove it. Can you print this?"

I heard him exhale. "All except the bit about the President. It's probably true, but the money never got there. You've got documentation or sources for everything else."

"Good enough. Put me down as an additional source."

"Are you sure?"

"Yup. Fame is the best way to keep me breathing. Listen, what do you see happening to Lasko and Catlow?"

"When we print this? The President will be forced to drop them, and Justice will have to prosecute on manipulation and embezzlement. And the antitrust case against Lasko will go to trial."

I looked over at Woods. Still out. "There's more. Two weeks ago Lehman's lawyer called me to set up a meeting." Mary leaned forward waiting to hear her name. "Jack Woods called Lasko to tip him off. Lasko had Lehman killed before he gave me the memo. A Boston cop, Lieutenant Di Pietro, is working on it now. This—and publicity—should light a fire under him. And that's my way out."

I could imagine Greenfeld scribbling furiously.

"This is incredible," he finally said. "Can you document the part about Woods?"

"Maybe."

"That's the one weak part."

"I'll work on that. Anyhow, I went out to Lehman's place and found the memo from Lasko with the deposit box numbers on it. I hid it in my desk." Mary tensed, as if holding her breath. I went on. "Woods found out about it and tried to jimmy my desk. He's currently stretched out on my floor, where he fell after I hit him with an onyx bookend."

"Goddamn, Chris." He paused, mind racing. "What about McGuire?"

The courtship of McGuire was a link to the White House. But McGuire would never be a commissioner now.

"Chris, you still there?"

"McGuire's not involved."

"Certain?"

"Yeah, I'm certain. Listen, can you get this in the morning paper?"

"The later edition, if we move."

"Fine. How long will it take you to get to my office?"

"Ten minutes."

"Sure?"

"Yeah."

"OK. Meet me in front. By the way, was that Lynette who answered?"

"Yeah. She's back."

"Amazing," I said, and hung up.

Mary stared at me in stark disbelief. "Why didn't you tell him about me?" she finally asked.

"I have reasons."

Her face relaxed. I looked at my watch. 9:35. Greenfeld was due in nine minutes. I dialed again and got lucky. Di Pietro was in his office. He sounded surprised. "Did you get anything?"

"Lehman was handling the laundered money. I've got a memo from Lasko giving Lehman instructions and deposit box numbers. That's what he was going to tell me. I've also got records from banks. Is that enough to indict Lasko for Lehman's murder?"

"It's what we need. Martinson came to this morning and gave a statement—everything he told you. And mug shots of the two guys who tried to kill you were identified by a carry-out boy at the shopping center, the one where they stole the car to run down Lehman. I'll pick Lasko up tonight. Just lie low and you may be all right."

"Great." I checked my watch. 9:39. Greenfeld was due in five minutes. "I'll send you this stuff."

"Thanks, Christopher. You've done a nice job."

"Thanks for everything, Lieutenant." The phone clicked off.

I grabbed a notepad from my desk. "Check out Feiner," I scrawled. "Market watch had Lasko stock pattern." I initialled it CKP and stuck it in an envelope. I wrote "Attention—Joseph P. McGuire" on the envelope and put it in my pocket.

The time had done Mary some good. A smile flirted at the corners of her mouth. "You're going to take care of everyone tonight, aren't you?"

"That's right."

Woods moaned, but didn't move. Mary glanced at him dispassionately. "You know, he was right. You can't do to him what you've done to Lasko and Catlow."

I shrugged. Her eyes were imploring now. "Chris," she said urgently, "there has to be some way to make this better."

I didn't answer. Instead I looked at my watch. 9:43. Greenfeld should be out front in one minute. I picked up the phone and placed my last call.

An operator answered. "Police Emergency."

"Yes. I'd like to report an incident. The address is the ECC Building on D Street, Northwest, third floor, 327. I've just caught a man trying to burglarize my desk. I knocked him unconscious, possible concussion. I'll need a couple of officers and maybe an ambulance."

Mary bolted upright. The operator repeated the address. "We'll have someone there within three minutes," she said.

"Thank you."

I put down the phone. Mary lunged for the door, half-tripping over Woods. I caught her by the wrist. She wriggled, then stopped. I pulled her to me. "OK, Mary, the cops will be here in about two minutes. I have to leave. I'm giving you a choice—stay or go."

She stared at me furiously. "I want to leave."

I forced myself to be very calm. "Choice one is to stay and tell the cops the truth. That Woods said he called Lasko about Lehman, that you called Woods tonight, and that after that he broke into my desk—"

"I didn't know he was going to do that," she interjected.

"And along with that you do your Miss Innocence routine and try to wriggle out. Tell them you stayed as an act of civic virtue. If you can pull that off, I won't stop you."

Her eyes were black pools. "And if I leave?"

"Then I give your name to Greenfeld and you become as famous as Lizzie Borden."

She clutched my shirt. "Do you know what that would do?"

"I figure disbarment at the very least. You've got about a minute to decide."

She dropped her hand. "I'll stay, damn you."

"Good. Tell the cops I'll be by in the morning."

Woods was moaning and the blood had dried on his mouth. The memo still lay by his hand. I picked it up and turned to leave.

"You're a bastard, Chris." She said it in a clear, quiet voice.

I turned back. She was watching me, with a funny expectant look. "Greenfeld will be calling the police at exactly midnight to check your statement on Woods, for his article. If you change your story or tell the cops where I am, you'll be reading about yourself tomorrow morning."

Her mouth parted. I'd never seen her prettier. "It could have been worse, Mary," I said quietly. "It could have been a lot worse." I turned and walked out.

I glanced back at the room as I rounded the corner. Mary was staring down at Woods. The yellow light was surrounded by darkness. The room looked like a cell. I turned and felt my way to the back stairwell.

There was a mail slot in the wall. I stuck McGuire's note in, then looked down the stairs. They were lit. I took them. It wasn't enough, I thought, not after all of this. But Lasko would pay for Lehman, and Woods and Catlow would be ruined. The President wasn't getting rich, this time, and Martinson was safe, for Tracy's sake. And I was still alive. All I had to do was get to the *Post*.

I reached the main floor and pushed the door. It opened into a corridor, around the corner from the elevators. I stepped out and turned the corner. Then I loped past the elevators into the front lobby, holding the memo. Officer Davis was nowhere in sight.

Two men burst through the doors. Uniformed

police. They ran toward me. "Where are the elevators?" one asked.

I pointed behind me. "Back there."

"Thanks." They rushed past.

"Sure thing," I muttered.

I got to the glass doors, then glanced back. The two cops stepped into the elevator. I watched the doors close behind them. Woods might turn around and screw her. But then that wasn't my problem. I turned away.

A car squealed to an abrupt stop in front of the building. It wasn't Greenfeld's car. I looked around. The reception room was off the lobby to the right. It was dark, and the door was open. Two men jumped out of the car. I scrambled into the room and leaned up against the wall. My forehead was dewed with light sweat.

The two men opened the front doors and stood in the lobby, staring. I peered out of the darkness. Lasko's men from the airport. Oh Jesus, I thought. Then they ran toward the stairs, heading for my office. Their footsteps faded. I grinned weakly in the dark. That, I thought, was going to be a nice party. I walked softly out of the dark room, peering back over my shoulder. They were gone.

I looked through the glass. Greenfeld's Alfa was double-parked in front.

I opened the door and left.

Be sure to read these other novels
by Richard North Patterson

- **DEGREE OF GUILT**
- **PRIVATE SCREENING**
- **ESCAPE THE NIGHT**
- **THE OUTSIDE MAN**

Please turn the page for the compelling first chapter of some of these
novels.

DEGREE OF GUILT

CHAPTER ONE

The woman froze in the hallway, staring at the num-
bered doorplate.

For a moment, she felt uncertain that this was the
same suite she had left perhaps a minute before. Then
she turned the knob slowly, wincing at its metallic
click.

The door cracked ajar, a pallid sliver of light coming from inside. She paused, looking over her shoulder, less from fear of being seen than the desire to
stay suspended in time, outside the room.

Time. She glanced at her gold wristwatch. When
had it happened? she wondered. No way of telling
now. Thirty minutes, she decided arbitrarily. Thirty
minutes, and she had not decided what to do. Her
mind was sluggish, numb with disbelief. She felt
drugged.

Her fingertips were damp, she realized. With every
thought, her choices seemed to narrow. She fought
the impulse to stop thinking, to run. It took all her
will to do nothing.

The chime of an elevator rang.

She flinched. Quickly, she tried to remember arriv-
ing in the elevator, how far it was down the hallway.
Afraid to turn, unable to recall the corridor right behind her.

She straightened, squaring her shoulders, and
pushed open the door.

The rectangle of light from within captured her like
a photograph, a slender woman with long black hair,

standing motionless in the door frame. The elevator opened. A second chime penetrated her shock.

She stepped inside and shut the door behind her.

Closing, it sounded heavy. Final, she corrected herself. It sounded final.

She turned to face the room.

Her eyes sought out details. Drawn blinds. Her black leather purse on the floor. The gold neck of an empty champagne bottle, above the rim of a silver ice bucket on a glass coffee table. The two crystal glasses. The heavy oil painting of San Francisco Bay she had remarked on, slightingly, when she first entered. Her panty hose on the carpet, ripped in one leg.

She touched her throat, feeling for scratches. She had broken a nail; it was that, oddly, which made her remember her own fragility.

Finally, she looked at him.

There was blood on the carpet now, beneath his chest. His pants were pulled below his knees.

A sudden jumble of images: Legs splayed at crazy angles. Blue argyle socks. A curly shock of red hair. Thin craggy face, turned to chalk. Eyes open as if to stare at the black handgun, lying near his head where she had left it.

For an instant, she was paralyzed.

She breathed in deeply, once, and exhaled. Then she took three steps, standing over him, and stared down at his bare buttocks.

The wave of revulsion hit her again, rose to her throat. She felt sure she would vomit; some cold, distant part of her brain wondered how that would look to them. Perhaps they would see her fear, see how afraid he had made her. Then the hatred ran through her again, hard and deep and raw.

She shut her eyes, remembering. What he had done. What he had wanted to do.

When they opened again, she felt stronger, more ready. More like the woman who had come here. More like the woman she had always been.

The nausea had passed. She sat beside him on the carpet.

There was no hole in his back, she saw; the bullet had not gone through. The flabby skin of his buttocks was turning gray. She could hardly see the scratches she had left there.

In her new resolve, she tried to summon a clinical dispassion. Perhaps forty minutes before, she realized, his heart had stopped pumping blood. The great man, bottom in the air, pale as a fish. It was almost comic.

The smile, small and involuntary, hurt her bruised mouth. The dark mirth vanished.

The rest of her life, she resolved, would not be about him. She would not let him do that to her. She would leave this day behind her.

Starting now.

She looked down at her watch. Too much time had passed. She must think quickly.

She stood with a kind of awkward dignity, preparing herself.

Walking carefully around the dead man, she knelt again on the other side, to pick up her panty hose. She left the gun where it was.

She held the hose dangling in one hand, reflecting. Then she hitched up her skirt, examining her legs. The scratch on her left thigh traced the tear in her panty hose.

They would ask to see her legs, she was certain.

Long, slender from the twenty years of exercise since college—running in the morning, gyms at night. Twenty years of willpower: like everything else in her life, her body was as nearly perfect as she could make it. But today, it had seemed, not perfect enough.

Struggling into the hose, she realized that her shoes were still under the coffee table.

What mattered? she wondered. It was hard to know.

She walked to the coffee table, staring down at the tape recorder.

Small and black, it stood upright near the glasses. Through its plastic window she saw that the tape had played until it stopped. And, with it, the woman's voice. Low and smoky, damning in a monotone a man whom she had never met and yet had believed in. Until now.

It was a moment before she realized that her fists had clenched. Another before she could move again.

As if in her sleep, she straightened her dress, put on her shoes. Looking around the suite, she saw that the bedroom door was shut. Strange, she thought, that he had not shown it to her.

She looked back toward the room.

The desk drawer was still open. She walked across the room, past the body, and closed it.

As she turned, the mirror above the couch caught her face.

It stopped her. With an odd detachment, she realized that the cameras would magnify the bruise beneath her eye.

She found nothing else. Neither the years since Washington, nor the past hour, had changed her much. No matter what he had said or done, or could not do.

She studied her reflection.

A face that photographed well, filmed well. A strong face, high cheekbones, clear brown eyes. It had always helped her, whether or not she had wanted that kind of help. She did not know whether it could help her now.

Turning, she took one final look at him, then at the room around her. To remember. Simply to remember. It would be a long day, she knew, a long night without sleep. Perhaps many nights until she slept. But she would need to remember, not forget.

Briefly, she thought again of the boy, and was ready.

The telephone was on an end table, next to the couch. She picked it up, standing stiffly, listening to the dial tone. Then her gaze caught the tape recorder.

They would record her, she knew. Listen to her words over and over. Listen to her tone of voice.

She swallowed once, clearing her throat. Her mouth tasted bitter.

Willfully, she stabbed the numbers.

The dial tone broke, became a ringing on the other end. She listened, steeling herself for the answering voice. But the man's brusque tone startled her. How foolish, she thought, to have wished for a woman.

"San Francisco Emergency," the male voice snapped again.

She found herself staring at the man on the floor, fixated on the black gun by his head. A foreign object, she thought. Foreign in her life. Foreign in her hand.

"There's been an accident," she said simply.

Teresa Peralta glanced at her watch. It was close to five, and he still had not sprung the trap.

The deposition had been going for seven hours. It was like watching a cat-and-mouse game where the cat had his eye on a second mouse; what lent the game its fascination was the smugness of the second mouse, who sat watching the cat toy with the first mouse, secure in his delusion that the cat had not seen him.

"Perhaps I can refresh you memory," Christopher Paget said pleasantly, and handed the first mouse a document. "Can you identify Defendant's Exhibit 13?"

This particular cat wore a navy double-breasted pinstripe of soft Italian wool. With that came a silk floral tie; a white cotton shirt; square gold cuff links. As with other things about Christopher Paget, Terri wondered whether the careful dress was a form of camouflage, meant to deflect attention from who he really was.

They sat in a large conference room with a view of San Francisco Bay. Two lawyers on each side of the table, a witness and a court reporter. Terri was next to Paget, watching. The document—which seemed to have transfixed the witness—was his last.

"Please take your time," Paget suggested calmly.

Time, Terri thought again. Through the window, dusk was falling across the bay; lights were beginning to glimmer from the city and, across the gray swath of water, from Marin County. Five o'clock; the day-care center would close at six. It was on the other side of the Bay Bridge, for Richie's convenience, near where they lived because Richie liked Berkeley better than the city. Next to her was a message, brought in at four-thirty. Richie was having dinner with some "business associates," to work on his new software "deal"; Terri must pick up Elena.

Forget it for a moment, she told herself. Learn something. Watch him do this.

Her metaphor, she decided, was better than she had thought. Paget had a cat's patience, a cat's still blue eyes. And there was a look of fineness to him, the result of great self-discipline and much exercise. The copper hair, ridged nose, and clean angles of his face seemed little different from the classic photograph, taken fifteen years before.

Christopher Paget had been famous so young, she knew, that some saw his career since then as an afterthought; the picture had been on the cover of *Time*, when he was twenty-nine.

She had found it in the library, as she was about to interview for a job as his associate. It was a well-known cover: a young lawyer testifying before Congress, the portrait of idealism and risk. Curiosity had led her from one article to another, relearning things she had heard about but had been too young to remember clearly.

The case had involved William Lasko, a close friend and financial supporter of the President. Paget was an investigator for the Economic Crimes Commission, assigned to check out Lasko's stock transactions. A key witness—one of Lasko's employees—had died in a hit-and-run "accident," leaving behind one ambiguous memo and the suspicion in Paget that someone within the ECC was betraying his inquiry.

Slowly, Paget had begun to uncover corruption within the ECC, which, he came to suspect, reached all the way to the White House. Then a second witness was kidnapped. When Paget persisted, someone had tried to kill him, just before he pieced together the meaning of Lasko's transactions.

The transactions, it turned out, were meant to funnel one and one-half million dollars to the President's campaign. And the man who had been leaking information about the investigation to Lasko was the chairman of Paget's agency. A man named Jack Woods.

It was never clear, Terri had found, whether Paget had entirely uncovered the corruption within the ECC itself. But he had taken the story to the Washington *Post* and then to Congress. A second witness had come forward—a young woman lawyer who was Wood's chief assistant. The results were prison sentences for Woods and Lasko, and political ruin for the President.

Christopher Paget was the first twenty-nine-year-old, a columnist wrote sourly, to bring down a President without using sex. The columnist seemed slightly nettled; Paget refused all requests for interviews.

As far as Terri could tell, he had never spoken of the Lasko case again.

The strain must have been enormous; everyone wanted a piece of him. The young woman witness, Terri knew, had become a television journalist. But Paget seemed to want no part of it. And, much more than the woman, he had earned the undying enmity of partisans of the President, who felt that he had tampered with the scales of history. He had left Washington and returned to California for good.

He had started his own firm, turned down requests to enter politics, made a specialty of white-collar crime. Within the office, Paget's time in Washington was treated like some private trauma, which people were too tactful to mention. In six months, she had learned almost nothing about him except that he was very good at his job.

"Mr. Gepfer?" he asked politely.

Across the table, the witness was staring at several pages of handwritten figures, seemingly unable to move or speak. He *looked* like a mouse, Terri decided: thin, sharp face, sandy hair combed to cover a bald spot, small eyes that shifted between avarice and fear. Had he not been so dishonest, and the moment so sublime, she would have felt sorry for him.

"I don't recall this document," opposing counsel broke in. "I'd like to know what this is and where you got it."

It was with Starr that Terri's conceit of cats and mice broke down. He had a basilisk face, slicked-back gray hair, and an air of deliberate shrewdness; it had not surprised her to learn from the skinny associate who sat next to Starr that he treated his staff like serfs.

Ignoring him, Paget turned to the court reporter, a young woman who sat watching from the end of the table, fingers poised over her machine. "In Mr. Starr's excitement," he said, "the witness may have forgotten the question. Perhaps you should read it back."

Starr leaned across the table. Terri scrutinized him, trying to figure out how much he understood. Not quite enough, she concluded; he looked like a man who was prepared for a setback but not for a disaster.

"Oh, go ahead."

"Thank you." Paget's tone held the barest trace of irony. He nodded to the reporter.

"Can you identify Defendant's Exhibit 13?" the reporter read out.

Almost inaudibly, Gepfer answered, "Yes."

Paget took up the questioning. "And is that document in your handwriting?"

"Yes"

"Could you read the heading at the top center, please."

Gepfer's eyes shut. "Liberal Accounting Adjustments," he said in a monotone.

"How did you come to call it that?"

"David Frank suggested it."

"When he was still chairman of Lyon Industries?"

"Yes."

"Did you also get the figures under that heading from Mr. Frank?"

Starr watched the questioning without changing expression. What Terri noticed was how intent he was.

"He set the direction," Gepfer answered miserably. "I came up with the numbers for him."

"And what do these numbers represent?"

"The amount of additional income Lyon needed to show a profit in fiscal 1991."

"Additional, or imaginary?"

Gepfer frowned, as if pondering a complex thought. "We didn't make the money," he finally answered, "if that's what you meant."

"But the figures on the document," Paget said, "became the figures on Lyon's financial statements, correct?"

"Correct."

"And were used to raise $53 million in the public offering?"

"Yes."

"Mr. Frank sold stock in that offering, correct?"

"Yes."

"And made several million dollars."

"Yes."

"And you also sold stock in the offering?"

"Yes."

"And made roughly $670,000."

"Yes," Gepfer said again.

Paget had him in a rhythm now. "Whose idea was it to change the books?"

Gepfer's voice turned accusatory. "Mr. Frank's."

"And you just went along."

"Yes."

"Did my client, Steve Rudin, know about this?"

336

"Objection," Starr cut in. "Calls for speculation."

Paget's eyes widened. "Really, Mr. Starr, I'm proving your entire case. I'd think you'd be more grateful. . . ."

"Come off it. Frank killed himself. How can this man know who Frank talked to?"

Paget looked at him a moment. Not for the first time, Terri had the sense that nothing surprised him; that something had taught him not to show what he felt; that he expected very little from anyone. "You mean you haven't asked him?" he asked Starr softly. "You're prosecuting this case against my client, this man's cooperating with you, and you haven't asked him yet?"

Starr leaned back. "I'm not the witness here," he retorted. "I'm not telling you what I've asked or haven't asked. That's work product."

"I'll try another question," Paget said agreeably, turning to the witness. "Before today, when was the last time you saw this document?"

Starr's face said everything; too late, he saw where this was about to go. Could hear the next five questions before they were ever asked.

"July," the witness said. For Gepfer, Terri knew, the worst had already happened; the questions were now worse for someone else.

Paget sat back, looking at both Starr and the witness. "At that time, did you give this document to anyone?"

"Yes."

Paget had stopped looking at Gepfer now. When he asked the next question, his gaze was fixed on Starr.

"And who was that?"

"Objection!" Starr stood up. "That's work product."

The court reporter's head had begun moving back and forth, following the voices.

Paget turned to Gepfer. "You may answer."

"Press on," Starr snapped, "or we're walking out."

"That hardly seems reasonable." Paget had yet to raise his voice. "Let me suggest this, Mr. Starr. Why don't we call a magistrate and get a ruling by telephone."

"Fine." Starr spoke with more assurance. "But the courts close at five—there's no one there to give us a ruling. I'm busy the next few weeks. Maybe sometime in February."

Terri suppressed a smile.

"Curiously," Paget said to Starr, "I anticipated this problem and called Magistrate Riordan's office this morning. He'll be available until six."

Starr stared at him. Paget pointed toward a telephone table. "The telephone is over there," he said. "Just dial nine for an outside line. I believe Ms. Peralta's written the number down for you, if you haven't yet committed it to memory. . . ."

"This is abuse. You're trying to invade the tactical decisions of opposing counsel. That's the classic definition of work product."

"Hardly. In fact, I'm fascinated to know how the identity of the nameless person with whom Mr. Gepfer shared this document could be *anyone's* work product. Really, Mr. Starr, it seems you have but two choices. The first is to call Magistrate Riordan and present an argument that, quite likely, is without precedent in the annals of Western jurisprudence. That's the option I favor, if only for the sheer interest of listening to it.

"The second and more mundane choice is to take a ten-minute break and see if we can resolve this matter without compelling Mr. Gepfer to answer any more questions."

Starr was impassive. Finally, he waved Gepfer and the court reporter from the room.

"If you have something to say to me," Starr said at length, "I'll give you ten minutes."

Terri could not help but admire the gall that made a trip to the abattoir sound like a concession to good manners.

"Ten minutes," Paget responded, "is all I'm giving you to drop this lawsuit."

338

"What kind of crap—"

Paget reached beneath the table, pulling a typed agreement from his briefcase. "This is a stipulation of settlement. It recites that you have become aware that your charges against Steve Rudin are mistaken; that Mr. Gepfer has confirmed the error; that you are dismissing this lawsuit; and that your firm is paying Mr. Rudin $250,000 to compensate him for his time and expenses."

"I won't sign that."

"For at least six months," Paget went on, "you've had this document. Which means that you've known for at least six months that my client was innocent of fraud."

"You can't hold me responsible for what Gepfer says now."

Paget looked at his watch. "Why don't we save eight minutes and ask Gepfer what you knew?"

"That man's admitted falsifying documents. Now you want him to give false testimony. Whatever he says, no one will believe it."

"Won't they? Frank was bankrupt when he killed himself. That leaves only two defendants with money. Gepfer has less than a million; but my client is *very* wealthy *and* covered by insurance. So you make a deal with Gepfer: if he doesn't give anyone else the document and doesn't tell anyone what really happened, you let him keep the money he stole and try to extract a settlement from my client by tying him up in an endless lawsuit you know to be a fraud."

Starr folded his arms. "You can never prove that."

"Care to find out? Because if the case against Steve Rudin goes one question longer, you'll find out more than that. Whether we can prove it. Whether we can win a suit for malicious prosecution. Whether the legal press will enjoy watching us try. Whether the Bar Association will let you keep your license. Whether every judge in this district will start looking at you like some evolutionary cul-de-sac. And the only person who will enjoy that more than I is Steve Rudin—

the man you charged with fraud." Standing, Paget looked at his watch again. "You have five minutes, it seems."

Terri followed him to his office.

It was sparsely furnished: bright modern prints; two plants; a glass table; a single picture of a dark-haired boy. Paget collected art, she knew; one of the prints was a Miró. She had no idea who the boy was.

Paget stood staring out the window.

"Will they go for it?" Terri asked.

"Yes." He answered without turning. "Starr is driven by sheer self-interest."

"I can hardly believe he knew."

"Oh, he knew. Always expect people to be what they've been in the past. That way, they don't surprise or disappoint you." Paget shoved his hands in his pockets, sounding suddenly weary. "Being surprised is a sin, professionally. But it's the disappointment that can be so soul-wearing."

The remark was uncharacteristic; it was almost, Terri thought, as if he were talking to himself.

"How *did* you get the document?" she asked.

"I promised not to say." He turned, smiling faintly. "But Starr really should treat his employees better."

There was a knock on the door. Starr's associate came in, holding the settlement papers. He paused, glancing at Terri. She wondered if the associate, who seemed a little too interested in her, realized that she was married. It wasn't as though he *knew* her at all, and lately it was harder to believe that men could find her attractive. What could you say about a nose that she thought was a little too sharp, crescent eyes a little too small for her liking, straight brown hair that she shared with fifty million other Hispanic women in the Western Hemisphere alone? You could say what Richie said in that ambiguous tone of voice—that she looked smart.

"He signed them," Starr's associate said, and handed the papers to Terri.

"Thank you," Paget answered civilly. The associate looked at him, then at Terri, and left.

Terri felt a rush of triumph, although the triumph was not hers. Without really thinking, she said, "I thought maybe the watch trick was overdoing it a bit. At least on top of handing him the agreement."

He shrugged. "Apparently not."

"Did you ever do that before?"

He regarded her a moment. "Once. Years ago."

"Did it work?"

"After a fashion."

There was distance in his tone, perhaps preoccupation. Feeling awkward, she looked at her watch.

"I have to run. A kid emergency."

"I have somewhere to go too. We'll call Steve Rudin in the morning."

The telephone rang. Distractedly, Paget answered it. Terri paused in the doorway, thinking it might be something about the case. But what kept her there, forgetful of herself and time, was the stillness that came over him.

"Where are you?" Paget finally asked.

He listened for another moment.

"Don't talk to anyone," he said. "I'll be right down."

Paget sounded quite calm. Only when he put the telephone down, with almost exaggerated care, did she notice he was pale.

She looked at him quizzically.

Paget seemed surprised to see her. Then he said simply, "Mark Ransom's been killed."

It startled her. She did not know why someone would be calling him or how he was connected to the famous writer. Finally, she asked, "Who was that?"

He paused a moment. "Mary Carelli."

"The TV interviewer?"

The description seemed to surprise him. Suddenly it came to her: the woman in Washington, the second witness against Lasko. Then, as if correcting her, Christopher Paget replied, "My son Carlo's mother."

341

PRIVATE SCREENING

PROLOGUE

THE KIDNAPPING

April 7

From a distance, the players could have been anyone; two figures flailing soundlessly at an invisible ball.

The court was a green rectangle in a crevice of the Napa Valley. For half a mile the terrain swept downhill toward them. A sequence of gullies and rises covered with low green brush, it resembled a sea of heather which swelled to pine-covered ridges miles beyond the court. At odd intervals, oaks cast late-afternoon shadows from the west. Between them, two men with semi-automatic weapons crept toward the tiny figures in white.

They loped, bent to the brush for cover, traversing the gullies and rises in a deadly zigzag forward. As minutes passed, the eye would lose them, find them, lose them again: with each rise they reappeared, but smaller, closer to the court. The only constant was the players, heedless as children.

The men disappeared in a wrinkle thirty feet from courtside. There was a last few seconds' peace. Charging to the net, one player raised his arms in a comic gesture of victory.

The two gunmen burst onto the court.

The players stopped; their masked invaders faced them, a pantomime of indecision.

Suddenly a white van appeared at courtside. Hooded and armed, its driver moved toward the four waiting figures. Without hurry, the new protagonist raised his curiously-shaped weapon, and then announced to those who watched him, "I am Phoenix. . . ."

Tony Lord turned up his television, uncertain of what he was seeing.

Deep yet slurred, the taped voice was like a record played too slowly. "For the next eight days, through Satellite News International, you will participate in all I do. . . ."

The picture changed abruptly.

In close-up, Lord recognized the two players as Colby and Alexis Parnell.

He stared at them in disbelief. Instinctively, Parnell moved to shelter his wife from the camera; the gesture was touching and pathetic, a moment from a Chaplin film.

The new angle was that of Phoenix.

"Three days ago, I captured Stacy Tarrant's personal manager, John Damone. Tonight, as you can see, I've taken Alexis Parnell. Tomorrow, I will broadcast my first demand to Stacy Tarrant and Colby Parnell by satellite, for them to answer as you watch on Satellite News International. . . ."

The two armed men moved toward Alexis. Turning to the camera, Parnell mouthed across the tennis net, "Take *me*."

"On television, you will see whether this wealthy newspaper magnate and famous rock star care for the people closest to them as much as for their privilege. And then you will join me as their jurors. . . ."

Lips closing, Parnell watched one gunman bind Alexis's hands as the other held his weapon to her temple. She looked stunned yet perfect, a well-coiffed mannequin; Lord could feel her shock.

"My intentions are unprecedented: a trial for social justice viewed by millions, with Colby Parnell and Stacy Tarrant as defendants, and the lives of those they love at stake.

"No one will stop this electronic trial before its verdict, or rescue my hostages. No one can find the place where I have taken them or track my frequency to its source. No one should try: this place is not only protected by armed guards but by dynamite set to detonate

343

on intrusion, and my pulse is monitored by an electro-cardiograph wired to plastic explosives. If my heart stops beating, it will trigger an explosion within fifteen seconds, blowing Damone and Alexis Parnell to pieces. Their lives depend on me alone, and *you. . . ."*

Astonished, Lord watched the two hooded men push Alexis toward the van.

"John Damone will die unless Stacy Tarrant can persuade you to pledge five million dollars, through a unique and public act of selflessness which I will disclose on my first broadcast, tomorrow night. . . ."

The van's rear door opened. Stumbling, Alexis fell beside it, scraping her knee on gravel. Reflexively, she tried to touch the scrape, then remembered that her hands were bound.

"As for Alexis Parnell, in the days that follow you will judge her husband's televised compliance with my demands. Then, on the seventh day of her captivity, you will cast an advisory vote through SNI as to whether she will live or die. . . ."

As the lens moved in, Alexis looked up at it.

"And on the final day you will witness her release or execution—live."

Silver-blonde mane glinting in the sun, Alexis Parnell stared from Lord's television. When the picture froze, there were tears in her eyes. Beneath her face appeared the caption "Courtesy of SNI."

"Mother of God," Lord murmured involuntarily, and then Alexis vanished.

The weekend anchorwoman began speaking in her actress's crisp staccato:

"The shocking film you've just witnessed was found with Colby Parnell early this morning after the terrorists left him, bound but unharmed, in the pasture of a Sonoma County farm. With it was an audiotape in which the so-called Phoenix threatened to execute Parnell's wife, Alexis, if he did not ensure its broadcast over SNI. The terrorists further claimed to be holding John Damone, manager of singer Stacy Tarrant, who was taken late last week from his Los Angeles home.

344

And now the communications magnate and the feminist superstar of rock must wait with millions of others for the broadcasts which 'Phoenix' claims are coming.

"What makes this even more extraordinary is that the Parnells and Stacy Tarrant have suffered prior tragedy. The Parnells' son, Robert, vanished from their Tahoe cabin in a 1968 kidnapping, while Tarrant's close relationship with presidential aspirant James Kilcannon ended in his assassination here last June by Vietnam veteran Harry Carson. . . ."

Her words became the narrative for a clip of Stacy Tarrant. It was a file film, Lord saw at once, taken as she'd left the courthouse. Face drawn as he remembered, she entered the limousine without speaking or looking at anyone.

"Miss Tarrant has not appeared in public since testifying at Carson's highly controversial trial. . . ."

Lord's telephone rang. Hitting the off button, he went quickly to the kitchen and answered.

The downstairs guard sounded harried. "There's a camera crew in the lobby, Mr. Lord—something about 'Phoenix.'"

It took Lord a moment to react. "Put them on."

"Tony? Tom Isaka, Headline News."

"If I'd known you were coming, Tom, I'd have invited you."

"We went by your wife's—she said you'd just left off your son."

Lord could feel Marcia's bitter triumph in passing on what she had come to hate. "Ex-wife. Frankly, I don't like people knowing where I live."

"Why so rigid?"

Lord considered hanging up. "Because I got sick of Tarrant and Kilcannon's admirers calling to say what they'd do to my son *before* they dumped his body in the bay. Look, I just saw your newscast—there's nothing I can add to *that*."

"But UPI quotes the president as saying that defenses like your Carson case encourage 'this unprecedented act

345

of terror.' Considering that Parnell, Damone, *and* Stacy Tarrant all figure in your career—"

"Tell me," Lord cut in, "can this mutant really broadcast?"

"With smarts, and equipment like they used for Carson's trial. The Damone, *and* Stacy Tarrant all figure in your career—"

"He'll threaten to kill both hostages if they don't. And you'll run their film clips, I imagine."

"It's news, Tony."

"Not with my help. Enjoy." Lord hung up.

For a time, his thoughts drove him to the window, staring out at stucco houses colored the pink and white of Portofino; the slim masts of boats in harbor; the azure bay specked with sails and flashes of sunlight through the Golden Gate. But this beauty seemed unreal, a deception.

Turning, Lord saw Christopher's toys still scattered through the apartment. Distractedly, he began to pick up metal cars.

This televised extortion of celebrities—an eight-day race against a public execution to ensure that millions watched—could transmute terrorism by succeeding. And the mind which conceived it had secured the perfect victims: Stacy and Parnell must feel they'd awakened from a recurring nightmare, to find it real.

Putting Christopher's cars away, Lord wandered to the bathroom.

Two razors lay on the sink. Only one had blades. During the Carson trial, when Lord had still been married to Marcia, Christopher had shaved with him to give them time together. It had become a ritual: Christopher had stood next to him in solemn imitation, pushing lather around his face with a bladeless razor. But now he was too old for such pretending, Christopher had announced this weekend—he was a baseball player.

Lord put one razor in a drawer, and closed it.

That left Christopher's cot, and the second mitt which Lord had bought him.

Putting the cot away, Lord contemplated the mitt.

Since the divorce, it had been Lord's superstition that to put away Christopher's last toy was to put away Christopher. He left the mitt where it was.

Fuck *her*, he thought.

When the phone rang again, he was walking toward his television.

This time it was Cass, demanding, "Have you seen that film? UPI keeps calling. . . ."

"I've seen it." Lord realized that in her three years as legal assistant and friend, this was only the second time he had heard Cass shaken. "I hope this lunatic won't kill them. . . ."

"You *do* know what the president said."

"Yes. Has he brought on the usual death threats?"

"No—not that."

"What is it?"

He heard her exhale. "Stacy Tarrant left her number with the service."

Lord looked out the window. Finally, he answered, "It's a joke, Cass."

"I called information. She's not listed, naturally, but it's a Malibu exchange. That's where she's been holed up since you and Harry drove her into exile, as *People* magazine would have it."

Lord was silent.

"Tony? Let me give you the number, just in case."

Lord wrote it down. "Anything else?"

"Only one." Her tone was flat. "Larry Parris called from Hollywood. He says you'd better sell film rights to the Carson case before 'Phoenix' makes him passé. He's quite concerned that what with your divorce, Harry's been 'bad luck' for you, moneywise."

"Tell him luck is a talent."

"He also thinks he can get Jaclyn Smith as Stacy Tarrant."

Lord now remembered Stacy as he had asked his final question at the trial. "She doesn't look like Tarrant."

"Nobody looks like Tarrant."

"Then maybe he should try Jodie Foster."

She spoke more gently. "Feeling lousy, aren't you?"

Lord could hear her concern. "You're a nice person, Cassie. I love you, in my funny way."

"Ah, honey, if only you weren't a boy. . . ." She waited a moment. "I can't help feeling sorry for her, now."

Through the window, dusk fell like pink powder on a gray-blue bay. Closer, in the attic of a brown Victorian, Lord saw the sudden glow of someone switching on a television; he imagined this repeating in homes across the country. Finally, he said, "And I can't sell those film rights."

"I know."

Cass rang off.

Disconnecting the telephone, Lord walked to the living room and turned on SNI.

They were running the other film of Stacy, as he had known they would.

Preparing for the trial, Lord had studied it perhaps twenty times. But cross-examination, when he had forced her to watch with him, was the last time he had seen it. Kilcannon lay wounded on the stage; as the lens closed in, Stacy bent her face to his. Her lips moved, and then Kilcannon's. She looked up, beseeching help, into the eye of the camera.

With Carson's life at stake, Lord had asked her if his act seemed rational. But neither of them, he understood now, had truly known the answer.

Once more, SNI began to run the kidnapping.

Lord returned to the kitchen. The terrorist's words pursued him like the voice of a fun-house monster: "I am Phoenix. . . ."

It troubled Lord that he was already used to the name.

"John Damone will die unless Stacy Tarrant can persuade you to pledge five million dollars, through a unique and public act of selflessness which I will disclose on my first live broadcast, tomorrow night. . . ."

At that moment, Lord was certain that the hostages would not be rescued.

Reconnecting the phone, he dialed the number Cass had given him.

"Hello." A woman, answering on the second ring.

"Stacy?"

"Yes?"

"This is Tony Lord."

Silence. "I wasn't sure you'd call."

Lord recognized the voice now, smoky and a little low. It was so bizarre that, in his discomfort, he almost laughed. "It really *is* you."

"It's really me."

Her tone was cool. "About Damone," he said. "I'm sorry."

"I suppose you are." That was meaningless, and meant to be. "I want to see you."

Lord paused. "Are you sure it's really me you want?"

She ignored that. "He's televising tomorrow night. Can you come?"

The tape of Phoenix echoed from Lord's living room: "And on the final day you will witness her release or execution—live. . . ."

"I'll come," Lord answered. "You knew that."

ESCAPE THE NIGHT

CHAPTER ONE

Alicia Carey cried out.

Snakes writhed on the bare walls of the labor room. The thin white gown became a straitjacket. The nurse holding the fetoscope was a withered hag.

She had been hallucinating for five hours.

She had lost dominion over her body. The scopolamine warping her senses left her numb. In lucid moments she recalled dimly the wetness of her water breaking and Charles rushing her into the cool dark. She remembered hating him more clearly than she remembered his face.

That had been twenty-six hours ago. Their driver had sped them to an emergency entrance framed by sickly cracks of light. Its doors slammed behind her. An attendant wheeled her alone to a narrow bed. The nurse shaving her pubic hair frowned at her slim hips. The doctor stabbed her with Nembutal.

Except for nausea that shot was the last thing she truly felt or perceived. The i.v. piercing her arm went unnoticed. The overhead light became the sun. She vomited.

Her makeup had run and her ash-blond hair was lank with sweat. Her legs thrashed beneath the hospital gown. Her mouth tasted bitter.

Only her eyes hadn't changed.

Since the moment of her debut, Alicia's eyes had excited and disturbed, their charged bright greenness promising intensity past reason to that man who could touch it. When Charles Carey first entered her, they had filled with tears. Carey felt as if he had lost his soul.

He sat in the waiting room with an ashtray stuffed with cigarette butts and a New York *Times* folded in his lap. He had shaved and changed into a windbreaker and slacks, but fatigue took the edge off his vitality. Dr. Schoenberg approached him with hesitance. This was unusual: few people had ever felt sorry for Charles Carey.

Charles rose. He seemed younger than thirty-two, a blade-slim man with an auburn shock of hair and a tactile gaze that grasped Schoenberg's pity and shot back a split second's resentment. Since childhood, Carey had hated sympathy for the fear it made him feel.

Charles Carey had seldom been afraid. He had made first-string back at Harvard by playing on an injured knee. Later, in the Air Corps, he had learned to fly and shot down twelve German planes. He took chances others would not take. When anti-aircraft fire tore through his fighter, he crash-landed in the English Channel. A cutter found Charles Carey treading water, one arm crooking the neck of the skinny tail gunner who had passed out from the cold. They gave him the Air Force Cross. The doe-eyed nurse who treated him took him home.

In bed, they laughed over his luck. Half facetiously, she asked whether he'd run for governor of New York if he managed to survive the war. Carey turned quiet, and said that he had something else to do.

Charles Carey became the only man to successfully defy his father.

In 1907, John Peter Carey had quit eighth grade to scuttle coal at Van Dreelen & Sons and take their books to the bindery in a horse-drawn wagon. When America entered World War I he was twenty-four and half the sales force had disappeared. John went to the sales manager. Thinking to discourage him, the man asked that Carey call on the firm's most recalcitrant

351

customer. John Carey returned with a massive order. Later he took the man's job.

John Carey rose within Van Dreelen & Sons, marrying a Van Dreelen daughter and ignoring their own two sons. When there were no more Van Dreelen sons, he renamed the firm Van Dreelen & Carey and turned it into a predator. Publishing rivals called him "Black Jack," less for his saturnine looks than for the authors he stole. He fished with Hemingway for marlin, loaned Fitzgerald money, drank all night with Faulkner. By 1942 John Carey's books ruled the bestsellers lists, their taloned eagle—a symbol of his own invention—staring past his shoulder from the cover of *Time* magazine, unprecedented for a publisher. "Which one is the eagle?" an assistant joked, then fretted for a week. His editors slaved in rabbit warrens, their doors left open on John Carey's order. From behind the Louis XIV desk that graced his own oak-paneled office, John Carey issued still more edicts, their reason less important than that they be obeyed. Part of this hunger for respect became dandyism, culminating in the iron rule that all male employees wear hats. Its darker side was a stifling paternalism: John Carey backed his staff until they opposed him. Those few who did were terminated.

In 1945, Charles Carey reported to his father's firm, without a hat.

The receptionist glanced up, startled. Within twenty minutes Charles sat in his father's office amidst the sweet, familiar pungency of thin cigars, ordered hand-rolled from Havana. John Carey leaned forward across his desk, barrel chest straining his three-piece suit, his anger—etched like scars running from his nostrils to the corner of his mouth and then to the square of his jaw—leaping from his black hawk's eyes. "Buy a hat," John Carey snapped. "Today. Otherwise you'll not set foot in this firm again."

Charles listened with the watchful stillness he had assumed in his father's presence since boyhood. "I've killed people," he answered. "And saved others. I didn't do those things to wear a hat."

John Carey stared through the smoke. "You think the war made you different. It didn't."

"Not the war. You." Charles's eyes riveted his father's. "I've watched you ever since Phillip and I were small and you were peddling books. You'd come in at the train station with that big trunk, trailing orders and neglect like some god that appeared and disappeared at will. Phillip never got over it. He still believes in God. *I* don't. You're just a man." Charles finished, in a soft voice, "I'm as smart as you, perhaps smarter. But if you fire me now, we'll never know."

John Carey brooded for a day, then he rescinded his rule. It was the cost of learning about his own son.

Their edgy truce lasted, day by day, for seven years. Where John Carey was shrewd, Charles had taste. His dash and nerve balanced his father's toughness. He signed young writers his father could not reach—men who had returned from the war to write of things Charles knew in his bones and marrow. John Carey learned the advantage of appearing to tolerate a son: it lent him a humanizing flaw. But Charles was useful in one other way.

His brother Phillip joined the firm in 1947. As if to counter Charles's perversity, the younger Carey willed himself into an avatar of his father, affecting dark suits and an entrepreneurial flair. As a child, Phillip had clung to his mother. In his twenties he chose to become John Carey—and to inherit his firm. Charles was his only rival; for five years John Carey teased them with his choice. He knew of Phillip's need, and that Charles's indifference was feigned.

Phillip festered, became fearful of mistakes. The defiant Charles prospered under pressure. He found new authors, made money for the firm. He grew in reputation. His friends were writers, athletes, actors and intellectuals. He took part in Democratic politics, was good copy for Leonard Lyons. Women responded to his zest. He had a bright, fantastic smile that ban-

353

ished the wariness from his face and made them wait for it again. For a while he was seen with Audrey Hepburn, displaying the same gallant detachment that had enabled him to enjoy other women until they wanted more and, without remorse or backward glances, he would play out the end game, and gently disengage. "I'm not the tragic lover type," he once remarked.

Then he met Allie Fairvoort . . .

"How is she now?" he demanded of Schoenberg.

The obstetrician shifted on the balls of his feet. "It's a difficult labor. She either can't help, or doesn't want to."

Carey felt hot. Acrid smoke rose from the ashtray to mingle with the smell of floor wax. The waiting room—worn green rug, cheap coffee table with tattered magazines—reminded him of a bad motel. Its foreignness chafed his nerves. "Is there some way I can be with her?"

Schoenberg turned away, shaking his head. Carey gripped his shoulder. "You see, she doesn't want this baby . . ."

What Allie Fairvoort wanted was a perfect union with a man.

It was as if that single ambition sprang from all the others she'd never needed. Her family was wealthy and secure. She had learned to ski in St. Moritz and breezed through Wellesley without trying. She wrote poetry and burned it in tides of elation and despair. In college she had acted, living in some psychic twilight between her own life and the roles she played. But she had no desire to become more polished, and would not learn. She wanted neither career nor children. She attracted men, teasing and discarding them, and took no lovers. She was waiting to be consumed.

One cool spring evening, at a glittering East Side party, she saw Charles Carey, and learned his name.

He was standing near three other men, sipping a straight-up martini as they listened to a dark and pretty guest from Mississippi lecture on the Southern woman. "We're not like the others," she was saying. "We find our strength in submissiveness."

The three men, older than Charles, nodded and smiled. Charles watched her gravely, head slightly tilted, saying nothing. Taking in the cut-glass features and cobalt-blue eyes, Allie realized with a rush that he was more attractive than any man she'd known. But she was captured by his stillness: it was the stillness of someone in perfect control of his own thoughts.

"So," the young guest began, challenging her listeners, "how would you define the Southern woman?"

The bearded man furthest to the left gave a gallant smile and said, "Dazzling." Her head bobbed down the line as the next man announced, "Mysterious," with an air of drama, the third leaning forward to purr, "Desirable," as if hoping to top the others. Allie Fairvoort thought they were fools.

The woman turned to Charles Carey. He seemed to breathe in, as if considering whether to speak. Softly he answered, "Angry and repressed."

Ten minutes later, the woman left with him.

That night Allie twisted in her bed, hating the dark-haired woman, imagining her cries as Carey's body moved on hers, his mouth seeking her nipple . . .

Two months later, lying naked under Charles Carey, Allie cried out for him to kiss her breast.

She had planned it with care. Avoiding Charles, she quietly tracked him through a mutual friend, learned that he seemed driven by things he would not reveal, tested his nerves on polo and sports cars and Black Jack Carey, dated women who were shimmering and impermanent. Quickly, she declined the offer to arrange a meeting. Instead, with the delicacy of a finely wrought drama of which she was the protagonist, Allie crept into Charles Carey's mind. A glancing smile at a party, a chance meeting at the theater, the merest hint of interest, enough for a first evening out, then another. She was planning to surprise him, just as she was planning how he would feel inside her the first time they made love.

Sensing these things, Carey still did not grasp them. He was used to women of a blithe sophistication that never surprised him, whatever form it took. Trained to coolness, he was moved by Allie's buried passion without being sure of what it meant. Instead, he began feeling that they were linked in a subtle exchange as elaborate as a minuet, and as silent. He accorded his actions new weight: quick to sleep with women, he made no move with Allie, and received no invitation. Only once did she teasingly touch the subject: in a taxicab on the way to the Stork Club she suddenly asked, "Did you ever sleep with that silly girl from Mississippi?"

Charles leaned back, curious. "I make a point of never saying. Some of the women I've known are still speaking to me."

Allie smiled in the dark. "I wonder if *I* will," she replied, and then was silent.

They spoke nothing more of this. Public people, they dated in public—at the ballet, opera or theater—their thoughts remaining private. They were a striking couple: Charles's look of energy without waste, Allie with the provocative air of a woman who would say what she pleased, with quicksilver movements and eyes that changed like a cat's in the light. They laughed often. He was amused by her elaborate sympathies for people she hardly knew—derelicts or writers without money—and by the way she took Manhattan personally, as if its charms and defects were meant for her. "You're laughing at me," she challenged him early on.

They had been strolling past the Pulitzer Fountain after brunch at the Plaza—Charles in a pin-stripe suit cut crisp as a knife, Allie's hair bright as champagne in sunlight as it rippled in the fresh breeze—when she abruptly knelt in front of a stranger's poodle, ruffling its ears and cooing in a happy lilt that seemed their own language. Charles and the man passed bemused smiles across the rapt pair until Allie rose and caught Charles's look in the corner of her eye. "You *are* laughing," she insisted. "The others never have."

"They're too scared. Beautiful women do that."

She smiled at the compliment. "And you're not frightened?"

He appraised her with that same sideways tilt of the head she had first seen directed at the dark-haired woman. Without smiling he had answered, "Perhaps when I know you better."

The night it happened they had gone to *A Streetcar Named Desire* and then on to the upstairs bar at Sardi's, drinking cognac and talking about everything and nothing. Carey felt her tension: her gestures were broader, and her smile, too quick to flash and vanish, seemed wired to her nerve ends. On the way to her apartment Allie unexpectedly asked him in. Once there, she moved to the sofa without speaking and sat looking up at him.

He went to her. She kissed him avidly, pulling him down until they lay pressed against each other, then pushed him away. He stood by instinct, watching mutely as she raised her dress above her fine long legs, to show him. She quivered as he undressed.

Had Charles Carey known her fantasies, he would have said that no man could ever be that shining, and left. Unseeing, he tried to match them, then loved her for the tears in her eyes, not knowing feeling from imagination.

Allie Carey felt only sweat and revulsion as they put her on the delivery table and pushed her feet and ankles through metal stirrups bolted to its end, straddling her legs. Schoenberg and the anesthesiologist sat on metal stools by her head, next to a machine with tubes and a black rubber mask. To Allie they were dwarfs who had stolen her sense of her own body.

"I have to take the baby," Schoenberg said. "Put her all the way under."

Her neck twisted as the anesthesiologist pushed the mask to her nose and mouth and turned on the ether. A nurse checked the oxygen on the baby warmer and took a pack of glistening steel instruments from a bare shelf. The forceps fell clattering to the floor. As Allie passed out she could smell the faint freshness of ozone, before it rains.

It was raining when Phillip Carey reached the hospital, perfect as a male model and trailing the faintest whiff of cologne. He fished in his pocket and produced a box of English Oval cigarettes. Charles took one, snapped his lighter, had one deep drag and asked, "How's the patriarch?"

Phillip's smile was thin. "He said he's both too young and too old for this sort of thing. 'I'll wait until they produce something,' I think were his exact words."

"Ever the family man." Charles glanced at the *Times*, saw WEST BERLIN BORDER HOMES SEALED BY EAST GERMAN POLICE without interest or comprehension. "I wonder how much emotion he expended on our mother."

"He outlived her." Phillip shrugged. He inspected the waiting room with distaste. "Don't let you do this with much grace, do they?"

Charles looked up with a glimmer of amusement. Phillip had grown a clipped mustache to go with his tailored clothes and pearl cufflinks. His natural movements were willowy: Charles could see the military strut of Black Jack Carey in the way he held them in, discerned a tension running parallel to his own. "Childbirth is the great leveler," Charles answered. "Another Bolshevik plot for your friend Englehardt from HUAC: 'I have here a list of five hundred babies . . .'"

"We'll never agree on that, will we?"

"Politics, or babies?"

"Either one, I expect." Phillip carefully placed his hat on the table and sat across from Charles. "How's Allie taking to her new role? She's not generally noted for supporting parts."

Charles paled slightly: by now anger changed only the color of his face, not its expression. Knowing that Phillip used his conceit of Allie as actress because it touched a nerve, he remained silent: to respond would be to acknowledge the unspoken war which now embraced even childbirth, but which only John Carey could end, by dying. Instead, finishing the cigarette, Charles watched the sinuous twist of smoke as it vanished, thinking of Allie's almost sensual relation to poetry, and how her moods—bright or melancholy—vibrated with the music she had heard. Pregnancy had cracked her like a glass.

Slowly, Schoenberg sliced her open: her hips were narrow and a Caesarean section too risky. But there was more blood than usual, and it took him a moment to see the head.

He opened his forceps, slid them through the incision, and clamped. His forehead glistened. Slowly, he pulled the baby from its mother. Its hair was matted with blood and its skin was blue from drugs and lack of air. The nurse cleaned mucus from its nose and mouth with quick jabs of a bulb syringe. Schoenberg spanked it.

Its head lolled. Schoenberg slapped it again. The baby neither cried nor moved nor breathed. Quickly Schoenberg cut its cord and rushed it to the baby warmer, clapping an oxygen mask on its face. "Damned Nembutal," he muttered.

The baby's leg moved. Slowly, its skin grew flushed. It squalled, then curled on its side, scarcely more conscious than its mother.

When Allie awoke several hours later she lay rigid, refusing to hold the baby or look into its face. They took it to the nursery.

* * *

359

Staring through the glass, Charles saw Allie Fairvoort in the blondness of its hair.

He glanced up, caught Phillip Carey's reflection as he looked down at the baby. For an instant, Charles read fear and vulnerability, felt their father pass between them like a feather in a vacuum, leaving no trace. Blindly, the baby reached toward its uncle with a tiny fist: Phillip's face softened.

"Ah," he said quietly. "The son and heir."

A nurse appeared, riffling a sheaf of forms. "Is one of you the father?"

Charles nodded. "I am."

"The mother won't give us a name."

Charles turned, hands in his pockets, watching his son as if wondering what its life might hold. Then he turned back again, facing his brother for a long, cool moment before he looked at the nurse. "John Peter Carey," he told her softly. "The second."

SILENT WITNESS

Richard North Patterson

'Patterson is one of the best in the business' *Time*

Two brutal murders. Two dead high school students. Two families bereaved. Two men suspected of killing their lovers . . .

Twenty-eight years separate the crimes that link Tony Lord and Sam Robb.

In 1967 Tony Lord is suspected of killing his girlfriend Alison, but the case never comes to trial, and tony has never officially cleared his name in a case that is still open.

In 1995, Tony is a successful San Francisco attorney and receives a desperate call from Sam's wife: Sam has been accused of the murder of one of his students. Reluctantly, but inevitably, Tony agrees to defend his boyhood friend.

At once, Tony is plunged into the unfinished business of his past. And in the merciless arena of the murder trial, he must face not only his fear that Sam is a killer, but also the dark, buried truths that surround Alison's death all those years earlier . . .

'Destined for celebrity status alongside Scott Turow and John Grisham'
Los Angeles Times

'Patterson has his finger on the pulse of contemporary America'
Cosmopolitan

OTHER BESTSELLING TITLES AVAILABLE